# LINEAR TACTICAL: OAK CREEK
# HERO'S PRIZE

USA *TODAY* BESTSELLING AUTHOR
## JANIE CROUCH

Copyright © 2024 by Calamittie Jane Publishing

All rights reserved.

No part of this book may be reproduced in any form or by any electronic or mechanical means, including information storage and retrieval systems, without written permission from the author, except for the use of brief quotations in a book review.

This a work of fiction. Names, characters, places, and incidents are the product of the author's imagination or are used fictitiously, and any resemblance to actual persons, living or dead, business establishments, events or locals is entirely coincidental.

Cover created by Deranged Doctor Designs.

A Calamittie Jane Publishing Book

HERO'S PRIZE

*Dedicated my Aunt Sherri...*
*Spending time with you is always one of my very favorite things to do.*
*Thankful to call you family, blessed to call you my friend.*

# CHAPTER ONE

"Listen, damn you. You're going to do what I say, or I will literally destroy you."

Ella O'Conner didn't tend toward violence, but today was an exception. She was running on her twenty-five-thousandth night of no sleep and couldn't get the scent of fondant and modeling chocolate out of her nose.

"Oh shit, Elly-Belly is cursing to herself. That is not a good sign."

Ella grimaced at the childhood nickname, even though her friend Lilah Collingwood didn't mean it with even one iota of malice.

Lilah had had a crappy nickname too. But *Lilah-Crylah* had been used a grand total of twice by Jonathan McMahon in second grade before Lilah popped him in the nose and put an end to that.

Ella wasn't a pop-someone-in-the-nose type of person. In second grade or now. But the modeling chocolate on the table in front of her might truly send her into a life of violence if it didn't start cooperating.

"You okay over there, Ella?"

Ella set down the carving tool and got up off the stool at her workstation, stretching her shoulders and neck. She smiled over at

Becky Mackay, who had been her best friend since before either of them could walk.

"I just want these to be perfect, you know? Sugar and Spice are such a huge part of the bride's life. They're even in the wedding, for crying out loud."

She glanced back down at the mini-Aussiedoodle and yellow lab dressed as a bride and groom she'd been trying to create out of a mixture of modeling chocolate and fondant icing. She wanted the cake topper to be absolutely perfect for her friend Eva.

Ella wiped the back of her hand across her forehead, studying her not-quite-right creations. "I shouldn't have left this to the last minute. And now you guys are bogged down with me."

Lilah let out a snort from where she was making delicate flowers out of icing to go on one of the tiers of the cake. It was amazing that a woman known all over the world for her fighting prowess could also be good with work so delicate. Not only that, seemed to really enjoy doing it.

"You didn't leave it to the last minute," Lilah said. "You didn't expect the last week to be taken up with every past, present, and future resident of Oak Creek wanting you to supply them with Fancy Pants sweets while they were here."

That was true. When Ella had agreed to make Eva Dempsey and Theo Lindstrom's wedding cake, groom's cake, and treat baskets for all the families coming into town for the wedding, she hadn't expected to also have a mad rush at her bakery every single day.

Great for business, not so great for Ella having any time to sleep.

"And we don't mind helping." Becky shot Ella a gentle smile. "It's kind of nice to be away from all the madness for a little bit."

Eva and Theo's wedding was in two days. The ceremony was being held on the Linear Tactical property since Theo ran the survival and defense training center and Eva worked there full time as a vet, taking care of the therapy animals Linear had incorporated in the last few years.

The reception would be about an hour away in the glory of Wyoming's Teton mountains. Since so many people were coming in from out of town, they'd decided to make it a weekend extravaganza, full of parties and fun and…stunts.

*Stunts.*

No, Ella wasn't going to think about that, lest it derail her entire day.

"Are you sure Eva doesn't need you two for anything today?" Ella sat down on the stool again and turned back to the chocolate dogs. "Isn't a bride supposed to be surrounded by her bridesmaids every waking moment two days before her wedding?"

Becky was arranging different treats into small white boxes that would be going up to the Tetons tomorrow. "You know Eva—she doesn't want a big production. And after so many years of being separated from her parents, I think she's really wanting to spend time with them right now."

Lilah cracked her knuckles, and Ella and Becky shot looks at each other. They both knew the action meant their friend was envisioning using her fists on someone—in this case, the man who'd kept Eva separated from her parents all those years.

"Her bastard ex is in jail, Lilah," Ella said. "Don't ruin your beautiful flowers over him."

Lilah took a steadying breath. "Five minutes alone with him. That's all I would need."

They'd all like five minutes alone with the man who'd spent years gaslighting and emotionally abusing their friend, making her a shadow of the woman she'd once been. Ella might not be able to fight as well as Lilah, but she could get a few good blows in.

"Let's not think about that," Becky said. "Let's think about how much Eva and Theo love each other and how she has been absolutely glowing the past few months."

Lilah went back to her flowers. "And how fucking fantastic Eva is for choosing amazing bridesmaid dresses instead of ones we'll never wear again and that make us look frumpy."

Ella smiled at that. Eva had asked her to be a bridesmaid also, but Ella had been more enthused about providing all the sweets for the wedding. Fancy Pants wasn't just her business; it was her passion.

Plus, unlike Lilah and Becky, almost every dress looked frumpy on Ella.

She'd long since accepted that *frumpy* was just sort of who she was. Plain. A little overweight. No need to cry about it.

But no need to announce the frumpy either by standing in front of all their family and friends—and *him*—with a stunning bride and two gorgeous bridesmaids.

"You all will look amazing." Ella had no doubt of it.

"At least Eva is giving us the choice of whether to be bridesmaids or not." Lilah shot a pointed look at Becky. "Unlike your weddings. Both of them."

Becky grinned, glowing just as much as Eva had been lately. She hadn't had wedding attendants at either of her weddings to Derek Bollinger—not the one in Vegas years ago no one had known about or the one that had happened at the July Fourth picnic last year.

"Yeah, but there were fireworks at my wedding." Becky winked at them.

"How is Derek doing?" Ella asked.

"We take it a day at a time." Becky shrugged. "PTSD can be pretty damned insidious, but for the most part, my sexy hubby is kicking ass. Speaking of needing to kick some ass, did you hear about last night at the Eagle's Nest?"

Lilah muttered a curse under her breath. "That's half the reason I'm hiding in here tonight."

Ella's eyes grew wide. "What? What happened? I've been stuck in here and missing all the gossip."

Lilah let out an exaggerated sigh. "Evidently, our fathers and uncles were reenacting some Cowboy boogie dance they once did."

"Oh dear Lord. Not *The Cowboy Git Up*." Ella shook her head. "Please say it wasn't so. Were Electric Smurfs involved?"

"Yep and yep, unfortunately," Becky replied.

All three women groaned. The blue alcoholic drinks were legendary in Oak Creek back from when their parents had basically run the town. Maybe legendary wasn't the word—*infamous* was more like it.

"And there was footage involved." Lilah shook her head without looking up from the flower she was completing. "You know that means we're going to be required to watch it. My father was a Navy SEAL, for God's sake. I cannot believe he was involved with this. Sigh. Where's the self-respect?"

Gabe Collingwood—codename *Angel*—was a giant of a man and obviously a warrior even now in his sixties. He had always seemed a little scary to Ella growing up, although he'd never been anything but gentle and kind to her.

Seeing him do some sort of line dance to a song from decades ago about being a cowboy? Ella couldn't wrap her mind around it.

Becky shook her head. "Oh, my dad too. And the wives were all there cheering them on—my mother apparently was one of the rowdiest ones."

This story just kept getting better. "She was?" Ella couldn't imagine quiet Dr. Anne ever being rowdy.

"Right? I expect that from my mother-in-law. Charlie Bollinger prides herself on still being boisterous, even now. But Mom? For shame." Becky shook her head.

"Who else was in on it?" Listening to this was actually helping Ella relax, and the modeling was coming much easier.

"Everybody, it sounds like," Becky said. "Even Uncle Dorian and Aunt Ray."

"And Uncle Boy and Aunt Girl Riley," Lilah put in.

Ella's head flew up before she could stop herself. She found Lilah looking at her with one eyebrow raised.

Ella cleared her throat then deliberately looked back down at the modeling chocolate in front of her. "Of course they're here. They love Eva and Theo too."

"And because Colton is one of the groomsmen."

Ella didn't look up this time, but there was no point in trying to hide what everyone in the room—*hell, everyone in Oak Creek*—

already knew: Ella O'Conner had a big, fat, honking crush on Colton Harrison. Had for years.

But she wasn't going to admit it outright either. What was the point since nothing was ever going to come of it?

Colton Harrison, like his father, was an extreme sport superstar. He had millions of followers who watched with bated breath every time he broadcast one of his jaw-dropping stunts.

Snowboarding, BASE jumping, Jet Skiing, motocross, abseiling, skydiving.

Why focus on just one when you were pretty damned amazing at all of them? Especially when you could have the most charming grin and a wink for the camera while you were doing it.

Ella couldn't think about that sexy grin right now. Not if she wanted to be able to finish everything on her literal and figurative plate.

"Of course Colton is one of the groomsmen." She hoped she sounded as light and breezy as she did in her mind. "He and Theo have been friends their whole lives."

"Have you talked to Colton since he got into town?" Becky asked gently.

"Nah." *Light and breezy. Light and breezy.* "Too much going on in here."

That much was true, at least.

"You need to ask him out, for fuck's sake." Lilah had never been, nor ever would be, as gentle as Becky. "For fuck's sake. *Literally,* for fuck's sake."

She laughed at her own unintentional pun.

"Lilah," Becky chided softly, but Ella could hear the smile in her voice.

"What?" Lilah stepped back from her finished flower before starting another. "Hell, we've both been contributing to that digital scrapbook for as long as I can remember."

Ella grimaced at the mention of that thing. Her friends had started the shared file in Ella's name years ago where they could all place digital clippings about anything Colton Harrison. She hadn't opened it in years; although she got a notification every time one of her friends placed something in it, which was pretty regularly. That thing was massive now.

"Yeah, but that scrapbook is mostly a joke," Becky said.

"You know what's not a joke? The fact that Colton is who Elly-Belly wants. How is she ever going to get him if she doesn't let him know that?"

As if. As if that was all it would take—for Ella to just shimmy up to Colton, bat her eyelashes, and lead him to her bed. And they would live happily ever after.

This wasn't the first time her friends had encouraged her to ask him out. Ella needed to nip this in the bud before it became a full lecture about *taking what she wanted*, complete with inappropriate sound effects from Lilah.

"This isn't the right time to tell him." *Light and breezy.* "I've got my hands full with the desserts, and he's got that snowboard stunt on Sunday."

That was part of the reason for the unusual second reception in the mountains.

Lilah shook her head. "Yeah, I can't believe he's got that stunt scheduled for the same weekend as the wedding."

Ella didn't know all the details, but she knew it involved a helicopter and a particularly treacherous pass that would be live-broadcast for Colton's gabillion followers. Social media had been buzzing about it for weeks.

Which Ella knew because she was a pathetic regular on the fan sites.

"In Colton's defense..." She tried to stop herself but couldn't. "The stunt had been planned before the wedding details were solidified. It's not like he's trying to grab the attention from one of his best friends."

Ella grimaced as Becky and Lilah shot each other a glance. She was just making it worse by defending him. Reinforcing her patheticity. Which wasn't a word, but close enough.

Lilah was about to launch into another tirade about why Ella should let Colton know she was interested, but Ella didn't have time for it, so she cut her friend off.

"I tell you what, next time he's in town and there's no wedding or huge stunt planned, I'll talk to him. Scout's honor."

And she would. She wouldn't ask him out, but she would talk to him. Hell, they'd known each other most of their lives, so of course she would talk to him if the situation arose. A friendly hello. Catching up. They did it basically every time they saw each other.

But more than that wasn't ever going to happen.

# CHAPTER TWO

"I'M THINKING a frontside 720 out of the helo. Really grip them from the beginning, you know?"

Colton Harrison stood near the top of Grand Teton, the highest of one of the most majestic sets of mountains in the United States. Hell, the whole world. He looked around, turning slowly, taking it all in.

"You know, do the flip late, so it looks like you're about to crash headfirst straight into the mountain before the stunt even starts. We'll have both the A-camera and B-camera pointed on you at that point—do live cuts back and forth to make it more dramatic."

Colton was only vaguely listening to the head of his PR team, Tony Salaun, as the man continued to talk about how the snowboarding stunt on Sunday could be made as epic as possible.

They'd already gone over all these details before. Multiple times. With a stunt of this magnitude, they tried to prepare for every possible outcome. What Colton did for a living was dangerous—many of his stunts being life-threatening.

But he was never reckless.

Tony walked away, dictating points into his headset while jotting down more info in his paper notepad. Normally, he was surgically attached to his electronic notebook, but it was too cold up here for the computer tablet to work.

"That dude is a little intense."

Colton chuckled as his friend Thomas "Bear" Bollinger walked over to stand next to him.

"Tony and his public relations team are the best at what they do." That was why Colton had hired Tony around a year ago. The guy was young and hungry and determined to make a name for himself. Ten years ago, Colton had been in the exact same mind-set and had had the exact same hunger. So, he hadn't minded giving Tony a chance.

But yeah, the guy was intense. Wanted to make sure every shot was planned perfectly so Colton could get as much publicity mileage out of it as possible.

"You don't seem very enthused about your guy being a PR rock star."

Colton shrugged. Bear had been one of his best friends since the time they could walk. The two of them—along with Colton's twin, Tucker—had been getting into trouble together their whole lives.

Colton didn't keep secrets from Bear.

"I don't know, man. I'm just feeling a little off."

"About the stunt? Do we need to put a hold on it?"

Colton spun slowly to look at the stunning view available in three hundred and sixty degrees around him. A low fog had moved in, so they were actually above the clouds, giving the whole place a sort of surreal feel.

"No, it's not the stunt. Everything is shaping up perfect for Sunday. Weather is supposed to be clear and brisk. And I've got the best pilot in the country handling the most dangerous part."

Bear grinned. "Derek would be both stoked and mortified that you called him that."

"Regardless of whether your brother can take a compliment, it's still true." Colton pointed up to where he'd be starting the stunt on Sunday. "Hovering the helicopter near that ridge will be one of the most dangerous parts of the day."

Bear's brother, Derek Bollinger, was an exceptionally accomplished airplane and helicopter pilot. He worked for Teton Helitack team, performing all sorts of insane maneuvers while fighting fires and rescuing lost or injured civilians.

There was no one Colton would trust more to get him to the top of this mountain, able to hold the helicopter steady so low to the ridge, while Colton jumped out on his snowboard.

"Sure," Bear chuckled. "You speeding down that mountain at Mach 1 isn't dangerous at all."

Colton cracked a grin. "Not even a little bit."

Despite the joke, Colton still felt off. Not because of this stunt. Or...not *just* this stunt.

He'd been feeling off for the past couple of months.

Bear cleared his throat. "Want to talk about it? Whatever *it* is."

Damn it. For being a mechanic, Bear Bollinger was way too damned observant.

Colton let out a huge sigh. "Well, Doctor, let me think. Really, all my problems started when I was a baby and my mother dropped me on my head. I don't think she ever really loved me. She—"

Bear laughed and slapped him on the back, which he could hardly feel through their thick jackets. It was fucking cold up here. "All right, asshole, I get it. You don't want to talk about whatever is bugging you. Although I wouldn't be surprised if Aunt Girl had dropped you on your head on purpose."

Colton smiled at his mother's nickname like he always did. Since his parents both had the same first name, they'd been called Boy Riley and Girl Riley when they'd first gotten together. Then, once all the Linear Tactical gang had started having kids, they'd become Uncle Boy and Aunt Girl to all Colton's friends.

No matter what anyone wanted to call Girl Riley Harrison, Colton had the greatest mother in the world. The fact that she fought multiple sclerosis every day just made her more amazing.

Everyone assumed it was Colton's dad, a world-class extreme sport athlete himself, who had influenced Colton's career. But the truth was, it was watching his mother not take any day for granted that had influenced him just as much.

"I don't know, man. I'm just off," he told Bear quietly, knowing his friend was listening even though he wasn't looking. "I've felt that way for a while now."

"Yeah? What does it mean?"

*Retirement.*

Colton didn't want to say the word out loud, as if he was afraid speaking it into the universe might make it true or some such shit.

Because honestly, he wasn't sure how he felt about retirement.

He looked over at Tony, still jotting down notes and talking to himself at the same time. There was a whole team of people who'd have to find new jobs if Colton decided he didn't want to do stunts full time anymore. He was their business.

Plus, what perfectly healthy male retired at thirty-two years old?

"I can't seem to find the exhilaration anymore." He turned back to Bear. "I used to wake up thinking about all the things I could do, all the challenges I couldn't wait to conquer. But now, the thrill doesn't seem to be there anymore."

"Do you think it's gone permanently or temporarily?"

"Who knows?"

Tony chose that moment to turn toward them, giving them a huge grin and a thumbs-up. Colton managed a smile and waved in return.

Bear crouched down to touch a little of the snow at their feet. "Well, you've certainly got a lot of fans who are going to be disappointed if you decide to pack it in. Think of the ladies. They'd be devastated." He thumped his chest slowly. "Hell, think of your poor wingman."

Colton had to chuckle at Bear's theatrics. Yeah, they'd wing-manned for each other all over the world. Bear would come out to support a stunt or just hang out, and between the two of them, they rarely encountered a lady they couldn't convince to give one of them a chance. At this point, they practically had it down to a science.

"I think my poor wingman would do just fine on his own."

Hell, Bear Bollinger would never have a problem with the ladies whether Colton was with him or not. Colton might have some fame Bear didn't have, but Bear was 6'2" of muscle that came from real-life physical work, not hours in a gym.

The guy was the epitome of tall, dark, and handsome.

Bear raised an eyebrow. "Ladies just not doing it for you anymore?"

Colton shrugged. "You know how it is… It's always fun in the moment."

"It's the *after* that feels like shit."

Colton shrugged again. "There doesn't seem to be any connection. And not just with women. I feel like I've got no connection with anyone or anywhere. I just bolt from place to place and pretty face."

Bear stood back up and nodded solemnly. "You should really think about getting that embroidered on a pillow. Especially since it rhymes."

Colton flipped his friend off, but he didn't take any actual offense. "I think I just want the chance to slow down. Not constantly be on the go. *Connect* to something."

"Why don't you come stay in Oak Creek for a while? You know I've been working on that camp for siblings of terminally ill kids coming up in a few weeks. I could use all the help I can get."

"How's that going?"

"Damned near perfectly. We're going to have our first set of campers this spring for ten days."

"Tell me more." Colton felt like shit. His schedule had been so hectic, he didn't even know much about Bear's passion project. "I don't think I'd be a good candidate for taking kids camping."

Bear chuckled. "It's not that type of camping. I mean, yeah, there will be a little bit of wilderness survival training that will include some camping, but it's more about giving these kids a chance to get out from the shadow of terminal illness."

He couldn't imagine that sort of toll. "It's an amazing idea."

Bear shrugged. "They deserve a chance to just have fun and be kids, and I'm glad we can give it to them. I've got different people from around Oak Creek offering their unique expertise."

"Like you with mechanical stuff?"

"Yep. Then Lincoln is doing some basic computer skills. Ella is teaching cooking. Dr. Annie is doing a brief CPR class. Some of the guys are doing wilderness training."

He loved to hear the excitement in his friend's voice. "Sounds like a solid group. You know I'll help out any way I can."

"I'm sure we'll be fine. But if you need a break, whether you help out with the camp or not, Oak Creek is always an option. It is home, after all." Bear turned to him with a grin. "Plus, I know for a fact there are people who would be more than happy to show you how good life in the slower lane can be."

"Dude, are you hitting on me?"

"I'd have to get in line."

Colton's eyebrows squished together. "What does that mean? Are you talking about someone specific?"

Bear tilted his head to the side. "You really don't know?"

"Know what? I don't even know what the fuck we're talking about right now—I'm assuming it's not your teen camp. Please enlighten me."

His friend just grinned like the cat who'd eaten the canary. "Nah. You'll eventually figure it out. You always were pretty stupid."

"Don't make me pound you into the ground so that your own brother has to fly you straight to the hospital when he comes back here to pick us up in a few minutes."

Bear's grin didn't falter in the slightest. "All I'm saying is that you've got people who know you and love you in Oak Creek. Don't discount it as a possibility if you're looking for somewhere to lay low for a while."

Colton decided to let it go. Despite his easygoing manner, if Bear didn't want to share info, nobody could get it out of him.

"I would never discount Oak Creek. Like you said, it's home. So, when I get ready to pack it up in a few years, I'm sure that's where I'll be heading."

A few years. That sounded so goddamn long.

Further conversation was interrupted by the sound of the helicopter coming back in to pick them up. Without a word, Colton and Bear began making their way up to the flat horizontal ledge that would act as Derek's landing point. Tony was heading that way quickly too.

Derek made holding the helo steady look easy as they got in—a testament to his skill as a pilot.

"Everything looking the way you expected?" Derek eased the helicopter back into the air and away from the mountain. The fog was dissipating, giving them an absolutely breathtaking view of the Tetons.

"Yep, we're set. This stunt is going to be epic."

"Hell yeah, it is," Tony chimed in.

Colton was only halfway listening as his PR team leader launched into all the shots they'd plan to get. The live feed would be pretty basic, but Tony was also thinking about an edited version later that would draw in even more viewers.

And that summed it all up in a nutshell, didn't it?

More.

Always more.

Always *faster. Higher. Farther.*

He could hear the thrill in Tony's voice as he talked about it. Damn, Colton missed the excitement that used to permeate his mind at the thought of it all.

It seemed nowhere to be found anymore.

He glanced out the open door of the helicopter. In two days, he'd be speeding down this mountain in a way no one had ever managed to before.

The cold, the wind, the speed… It would chase out everything he was feeling now, only leaving room for the *thrill*.

Retirement would be nowhere near his mind then.

# CHAPTER
# THREE

Ten hours after the minister—aka, Kendrick "Blaze" Foster, who'd gotten himself ordained through multiple channels on the Internet just to be sure—pronounced them husband and wife, Theo and Eva were still beaming at each other.

Everyone could almost tangibly feel the protectiveness Theo felt toward Eva. And from what Colton had heard about her ex, Theo had every reason to feel that way. Eva seemed to bask in it, as happy to relax into Theo's protection as he was to provide it. It was like the two were connected—an invisible string joining them, causing them to orbit around each other.

Colton wasn't one to wax poetic—he'd always been much better with action than words—but he could appreciate the bond between the newly married couple.

He'd seen that bond his whole life between his mother and father. Yeah, they'd sometimes fought passionately, but that tie between them had never once been severed.

Colton leaned his elbow against the cocktail table and watched the bride and groom as they danced—laughing and chatting with the people around them, but their eyes constantly remeeting each other's.

*That* connection was what he wanted. Not the empty, hollow

interlude of a hundred different nights with a hundred different women.

Not that he'd ever really lived that way, despite the trappings his wealth and fame afforded him. But even a hundred nights with a dozen different women didn't hold much appeal.

He wanted something *real*.

"You're not dancing?" Lincoln Bollinger, his and Bear's cousin, came over to stand with Colton at the cocktail table. "Theo and Eva specifically chose this location so that everyone could dance the night away."

The wedding had been in Oak Creek this afternoon, followed by a small reception just for the bride and groom's family. Then the party had moved here to Jackson, at the base of the Tetons.

"Just taking a break. Not as young as I used to be. Do you dance, Linc?"

He couldn't recall if he'd ever seen the other man on the dance floor. Although surely if he'd seen Lincoln Bollinger, prodigious savant, out cutting a rug, Colton would remember.

Lincoln tilted his head, watching everyone on the dance floor, as if he were solving a complex equation.

*Complex equation* was pretty much how Lincoln saw everything.

"Their movements and steps are in time to the music. Music, at its rhythmic core, is a series of mathematical formulas. Given that, yes, I can dance."

Colton had no doubt that was true. Hell, he could see Linc's eyes moving and knew the other man's giant brain was calculating speed, trajectory, angles of the dancers out on the floor...not unlike what Colton did when he was researching and performing a stunt.

"You going to go out there and put your academic knowledge of the physics of dancing to use, Linc?"

"No."

Colton slapped the other man good-naturedly on the back. "Afraid your calculations will be wrong?"

Lincoln scoffed. "Of course not. But I'm also aware that dancing and my inside voice may not meld together well."

*Inside voice.* It was the term the Bollinger brothers had created for Lincoln as kids when their cousin sometimes didn't realize that what he was saying was coming across as jarring or offensive.

Even as a child, Lincoln had been a genius with most anything to do with facts, data, or computers. But with people…not so much. So, telling Lincoln to use his inside voice had become code for letting him know that other people were finding his words or actions unsettling.

"I'm sure you'd do fine, man. Your other cousins are out there. They'll stomp on your toes if you get out of hand."

"They could just tell me. They wouldn't need to apply contact force to my foot."

Colton looked over at Lincoln with one eyebrow raised. "Didn't mean it literally, Linc."

The man nodded, not offended, taking in the data. "Right. Missed that cue. I'll consider the dancing. Why aren't you out there? You're normally in the center of the crowd."

Colton rubbed the back of his neck. He wasn't exactly sure why he wasn't out there. It wasn't tomorrow's snowboarding stunt that had him over here like a wallflower. Everything was ready. He, his dad, and Tony had gone over all of it again this morning before the wedding. Every detail was accounted for.

And all his friends were out there on the dance floor. Everyone was having fun. It was usually what Colton enjoyed most.

The wedding had been wonderful. The delight on his parents' faces as they saw all their closest Linear Tactical friends—some who had moved away from Oak Creek years ago—had been a joy to see.

But perhaps the most meaningful element of the wedding for everyone had been seeing Dorian Lindstrom stand up next to his son as Theo's best man. The emotion in Dorian's eyes as he'd looked at his son, his wife, his daughters…everyone had been caught up in it.

Dorian and Ray Lindstrom weren't here for this reception. They still had enemies that would hunt them down if they discovered

Ray was alive. So, they kept to areas where they could control entrance and exit options.

Even at the wedding itself, some of the former Linear and Zodiac Tactical team members hadn't attended, offering instead to provide security outside with Oak Creek's sheriff, Callum Webb. Having people Dorian and Ray could trust watching their backs had enabled them to enjoy their son's wedding.

And that, in turn, had made it more special for everyone. The Lindstrom family had been through enough over the years. They deserved this one day of peace and joy, and they had gotten it.

So...

Great wedding? Check.

Stunt ready? Check.

Here with friends he knew and loved? Check.

Fantastic food and free-flowing alcohol where all he had to do was make it upstairs when he was ready to end the evening? Check.

Not that he was drinking heavily the night before a stunt. It wasn't scheduled until tomorrow afternoon, but he was not going to be recovering from a fucking hangover as he faced one of the biggest challenges of his life.

But still, Lincoln had asked an understandable question. Why was Colton not participating in the festivities?

He looked over at Lincoln and shook his head. "Yeah, normally I love to be in the center of the action—whether that's a party or otherwise. Honestly, I'm not sure what my issue is."

"Oh." Lincoln nodded solemnly. "I thought it was because Ella is managing the desserts rather than dancing."

"Ella?" Colton glanced around to get a look at her sweet face. Had he even seen her today? She hadn't been one of the bridesmaids, but he knew she was here.

"Ella O'Conner."

"Yeah, I know who you're talking about, Linc. I've known Ella since we were in diapers. What about her?"

"I just thought maybe you were waiting for her to go out and dance before you went out on the floor."

"Why do you say that?" Colton forced himself to be patient. Lincoln wasn't being a tease—the man only dealt in strict logic, not conversational nuances.

"Because she's had a huge crush on you for years."

He couldn't have been more surprised if Lincoln had reached over and slapped him. *"What?"*

Ella had never done or said anything that would suggest even a hint of being interested. Lincoln had to be mistaken.

"Yes." Lincoln straightened his tie, still looking out at the dance floor, still calculating movements, his words almost secondary. "Evidently, a 'giant-ass' one, according to Lilah. I heard her tell Becky that the best thing that could happen to Ella would be to get into your pants."

*"What?"* he repeated, almost double-checking that his jaw hadn't hit the floor.

Lincoln turned to him, nodding solemnly once again. "Just so you know, Lilah's statement doesn't mean Ella would want to literally fit inside your pants with you. It's a euphemism for sex."

Jesus Christ. "Yeah, I caught that. Thanks."

He tried to wrap his head around the fact that sweet Ella O'Conner had a crush on him. For *a long time*?

He played their interactions over the years in his mind. He got to Oak Creek as often as he could and always loved seeing everyone there—including Ella. She was witty and kind, authentic and fun.

A good friend. Someone he enjoyed talking to. But only in the furthest recesses of his mind had he let himself even think about the possibility of more than that. Despite his attraction, he hadn't wanted to jeopardize any camaraderie he had with Ella.

And hadn't thought she was interested at all.

How had he not known about this crush? Because he certainly would've acted on it if he'd known. Wouldn't have been able to stop himself.

Even now, he had to shift and try to low-key adjust himself as he got turned on at the thought. He would've made a move on Ella years ago if he'd known she was interested.

"So, you're waiting for her?" Lincoln asked. "That's who you're waiting on to go dance and enjoy yourself?"

"No." Colton was still trying to spot Ella. "I had no idea she thought of me that way."

Lincoln muttered a curse. "I shouldn't have said anything, should I? My damned lack of inside voice."

Ella chose that moment to come out of some sort of back room next to a member of the hotel staff who was carrying a tray of delicious-looking treats. Her gaze didn't stop floating from serving table to serving table as she took in everything around her.

She said something to another staff member, smiling gently. The other woman rushed off to do Ella's bidding. Ella walked with purpose to a second table where the wedding cake had been before the bride and groom cut it.

She looked the way she always did: efficient, friendly, and... *adorable*.

Her brown hair was pulled back into a chic ponytail, and her blue dress and short heels allowed her to move freely as she worked.

And those curves... Colton's fingers itched to run along her skin —to get her out of that functional yet appropriate attire. Now that he'd started thinking about her that way, he wasn't sure he was ever going to be able to stop.

As if she could feel his thoughts, Ella glanced up at him and their eyes met. He watched as those green eyes widened, then her face turned a bright red, before she looked away.

Hell, if that wasn't proof that Lincoln was correct.

"She *does* have a crush on me." He couldn't keep the wonder out of his voice.

The other man nearly sagged in relief. "Okay, good. So, I didn't say anything wrong?"

"The opposite, Linc. You said something very, very right."

And there was no way in hell Colton wasn't going to act on it.

# CHAPTER
# FOUR

THERE HAD BEEN no disasters with the wedding or the reception.

No bad-guy kinds, no kinds where anybody had to draw a weapon, no near-drowning kinds—all of which had happened at past weddings with people from Oak Creek.

But Ella was most happy about there being no dessert-related disasters.

Honestly, she would've been okay with someone having to draw a weapon—she knew for a fact Lilah was wearing a .38 Special strapped to her thigh, and had no doubt some of her other friends were armed as well—as long as no treats were harmed in the process of defending the world against threats and tyranny.

"You know Eva's going to come kick your ass if you don't leave stuff alone and go have fun."

Ella didn't have to turn around to know it was Lilah behind her.

"I know. I know." Although the bride didn't have a violent bone in her body. "I just want to rearrange how these are displayed then I'll be done."

Theo and Eva had insisted over an hour ago that Ella's job was finished, that she'd gone above and beyond what they'd expected. That they just wanted her to enjoy herself.

And Ella was enjoying herself. Keeping busy and making sure everything flowed nicely and tasted wonderful kept her happy.

Even if she had no idea why every time she'd looked up for the past hour, she'd found Colton Harrison's eyes on her.

"We're all already mad that you missed the bouquet toss."

Ella laughed. "I'm not. I thought it was hilarious that you caught it." Lilah was the least likely person on earth to be the next one married.

Actually, that wasn't true. Ella most definitely claimed that honor since Lilah generally had men fawning all over her.

Ella finished arranging the last display plate and held up her hands. There, that was it. That was all she was going to do. The reception was winding down, maybe an hour left, but Ella knew she could make her escape early. She'd chat with everyone for a few minutes before sneaking out and heading up to her hotel room.

"You know that none of us wanted to catch that bouquet out of anything more than competition. There's only one person who'd want it—*you*." The beautiful bunch of flowers landed on the table next to the plates Ella was working on. "You should've joined us for the catch, Elly-Belly. I would've made sure you got it."

Ella picked up the blooms, stargazer lilies mixed with jasmine and gardenias, and touched them softly, but she still didn't turn around to face her friend. "I know you would've. But I didn't want the bouquet. If I had ended up with it, everybody would've been staring at me, and we both know what they would've been thinking. It would've been awkward for both me and..." She trailed off.

She hadn't wanted anyone looking at her, and she especially hadn't wanted their glances to have made their way over to Colton. Her one saving grace was that Colton didn't know about her crush, even if everyone else from Oak Creek did. Her catching the bouquet and a hundred people turning in his direction probably would've been a tip-off.

Even though she was done, she started rearranging plates again with one hand, holding the bouquet in the other. She should just stick with what she knew: food. Food, she understood. Food didn't require flirtations or batting eyelashes. Food was understandable. She would stick with food and not worry about Colton Harrison.

And if she had the extra pounds to show for it, then so be it.

Or maybe Lilah could start training her like how she'd worked with Becky. It was different—Becky had needed to learn self-defense to protect herself—but maybe Ella could work out with Lilah a couple times a week. That would be pretty painful, but it would at least help with the extra pounds.

She stopped moving the plates around. Lilah was right. Eva and Theo would come over here and fuss at her if she didn't stop. She didn't want them to even be thinking about her at all on their special day.

"Do you think you could start training me? Or maybe we could start working out together sometime?" she said to Lilah without looking at her.

"I'm always down for a workout."

Ella froze. *That wasn't Lilah.* That wasn't a female voice at all.

It was the one person who Lilah would make herself scarce for so Ella could talk to him privately, damn her hide.

She spun around, hoping her ears were deceiving her through the music, but knowing they weren't. Sure enough, all that filled her vision were deep brown eyes, a granite jaw, and a smile made for sin.

"Hey, Colton." It was all she could manage to get out.

"You've been over here by the desserts all night."

Oh God, did he think she'd been over here *eating* the whole night? She could feel heat creeping up into her face.

"I was…uh…in charge of the desserts this week." She forced the brightest smile she could, bringing her hands up to punctuate the words. "The cakes and the cupcakes and the gift baskets. It's because of Fancy Pants. My bakery. Eva asked if I would provide sweets for them."

Holy hell, was she really swinging the bouquet in her hand around in the air to make her point? She looked like a damned lunatic. The flowers caught him on the chest, and he took a slight step backward, eyebrow raised.

Grimacing, she set the flowers down on the table beside her before she accosted him further. "Yeah. So, I wasn't just sitting over here eating."

Yep, definitely sounded like a lunatic.

"Everybody's been raving about how good your...*treats* are. I decided tonight I had to try them for myself."

Ella froze, feeling like some sort of prey that had caught scent of a predator, but wasn't sure. Colton's smile hadn't changed, his eyes were still as deep and clear as they always were, but his words...

Was she crazy, or did it seem like he was *flirting* with her?

She caught a glimpse of Lilah over Colton's shoulder, now standing next to Becky. They were both watching and nodding enthusiastically, gesturing with their hands for Ella to get closer to Colton.

She ignored them. Colton wasn't flirting with her. Of course he wasn't. He was being friendly. It was what Colton Harrison did—was a huge part of his charm. It was why he had literally millions of fans.

When he talked about trying her *treats* for himself, it was not a euphemism for something else. No matter what obnoxious gestures Lilah was now making.

Ella deliberately turned away from her friends and shot a friendly smile at Colton. "I hope you liked whatever you tried."

He nodded. "Very much so. I hope to try more soon."

Damn it, there it was again. That hint of flirtation. "High praise, indeed."

He tilted his head to the side. "You headed out to the dance floor now?"

She ignored how his voice affected her. No need to announce that she sometimes listened to his audio clips at night while she was lying in bed just so she could hear his voice.

*Patheticity.* Definitely needed to be a word.

"No, I think I'm going to head up to my hotel suite. It's been a long week." She didn't want to sound like she was complaining. "A good week, but a long one."

Although she didn't really want to leave. Not with Colton being close by and them having a sort of *moment* where he was flirting with her, at least in her mind.

How often had she imagined this? She wanted to stay here and talk to him, to enjoy being close enough to smell the subtle scent of his cologne and appreciate how good he looked in a suit.

Colton Harrison wasn't spotted in a suit very often. Any number of survival or adventure outfits? Yes. Fitted T-shirts that showed off his well-developed chest and shoulders? Absolutely. But she didn't think she'd ever seen him in a suit.

It did not disappoint. Perfectly fitted but not snug, it spoke to another, more sophisticated, side of Colton. A very appealing side. As if all sides of him weren't appealing.

But staying here talking to Colton wasn't going to do anything but lead to more stares and whispers. It was only Becky and Lilah watching them now, but it wouldn't stay that way.

Plus, he was just being friendly. Ella knew better than to let her imagination run away with it.

"It's good to see you, Colton." She forced the words out when he didn't say anything. "I hope you're doing well. Good luck with the stunt tomorrow. I'll see you next time you're in Oak Creek."

"Thank you." He picked up a plate with a miniature cupcake, studying it intensely. "Can I ask you something before you go?"

The way he was examining the baked good, she prepped herself for an ingredient question. Did he have a food allergy she didn't know about? "Sure."

His eyes left the cupcake and met hers, and her breath hitched as his face morphed into a slow, sexy grin.

"I'm wondering if you'd like any company up in your hotel suite?"

# CHAPTER
# FIVE

"I'm wondering *if you'd like any company up in your hotel suite?*"

Thirty minutes later, Ella stood in her room, staring at herself in the mirror, wearing the resort bathrobe, Colton's words playing on repeat in her mind.

What the actual heck was she doing?

She had already tried on the only three outfits she'd brought with her and discarded them all as useless.

After all, she'd only planned to be here in the Teton mountains for thirty-six hours. She'd thought jeans and a sweatshirt for working earlier to get the desserts set up, her dress for the reception itself, and then some casual clothes for hanging out tomorrow while watching Colton's stunt would be plenty.

But she'd brought absolutely nothing that would make her more confident about going to Colton Harrison's hotel suite. Of course, she could've brought the entire contents of her closet at home and probably would still be here in front of this mirror in the robe.

Why had she agreed to go see him?

She'd been caught off guard by his oh-so-casual request for company. Had just stood there and stared at him—waiting for the punch line—until things had gotten pretty awkward.

"No worries. If you don't want company, it's no problem." He'd given her a friendly nod then turned to walk away.

There hadn't been a punch line. The request for company had been a genuine offer. It had been an offer she'd dreamed about for years, and instead of taking him up on it, she'd been standing there like an idiot, not saying anything.

She'd reached out and grabbed his arm. "No. I mean, yes, I'd like company."

His smile had seemed so authentic. She hadn't been able to see anything but that smile.

But still, she'd brought up the fact that her hotel room was in shambles, thinking maybe he would take the out. Instead, he'd shrugged and told her his room number and said they could meet there instead.

She looked at herself in the mirror again.

What the heck was she doing?

What the heck was Colton doing?

In what alternate universe did he ask her to come spend time with him in his hotel suite? He could have his choice of women to spend the evening with. Although the wedding reception had been private, the rest of the hotel was packed full of Colton's fans here to witness his snowboarding stunt live tomorrow.

Ella had seen them herself. And a lot of them were young, thin blondes.

She looked at herself in the mirror again, phone in her hand to text him and bow out. She could say she was tired. She could say someone needed her. She could say there was a dessert emergency.

*No. Stop being a coward. Just go. You will never forgive yourself if you don't.*

She changed out of the robe and back into her jeans and sweatshirt. It wasn't sexy, but hell, that was what she'd been wearing most of the time Colton had ever seen her anyway.

Besides, maybe she was misreading all this anyway. Maybe he just wanted the company of a friend. Maybe he was a little nervous about tomorrow's stunt and wanted a friendly ear.

Maybe it was better that she didn't have any sort of sexy outfit to put on if he was just looking for someone to hang out with. The more she thought about that, the more it made sense. Yeah. Colton was looking for a buddy. That made all sorts of sense. Some sort of sexy outfit would just mortify them both.

They'd known each other their whole lives. He needed a friend, maybe some snacks. Ella could help on both counts. Hell, she was the queen of snacks.

Jeans, sweatshirt, snacks, buddy.

Feeling much more confident now that she'd solved the puzzle—although maybe just a little sad—she loaded up a tray with some treats that hadn't made it to the wedding and headed out toward his room. Her steps got a little heavy the farther down the hall she went, but she forced herself to keep going. Forced herself to knock when she arrived, not run back in the other direction.

Colton's smile was still just as big as he opened the door. "There you are. I was beginning to think you were going to stand me up."

She laughed, the sound awkward to her own ears, but he didn't seem to notice. "No, it just took me a little bit to get situated."

He held the door open, and she walked inside. He was still wearing his dress pants and shirt from the wedding, although the jacket and tie were gone. His sleeves rolled up to show a hint of his strong forearms were almost her undoing.

He took the tray and two gift bags out of her hands as she passed and put them on the counter of the room's kitchenette. "What's all this?"

She laughed nervously again. "I thought you might be hungry. The Linear guys, including your brother, are always trying to get me to bring them any extra food. So, I thought you might want the same…"

But now that she was thinking about it, that was probably stupid. Colton was a world-class athlete. As far as she knew, he didn't even eat sugar.

If that was the case, he didn't mention it. "I will definitely take these off your hands, although, honestly, my team will probably get to it before I can. It's ruthless around here when it comes to good food."

She looked around his hotel suite. It was definitely one of the bigger ones, with a separate bedroom, living room, and kitchen.

The entire living room area and a big part of the kitchen were covered in papers and pictures and even drawings of what was obviously Colton's upcoming stunt. Ella walked over to study them, a little mesmerized by all the various information.

"I have a stunt tomorrow."

She glanced over her shoulder at him. "I know. I think everyone knows."

"I didn't mean for it to be the same weekend as Theo and Eva's wedding. Fortunately, neither of them was upset about it. At least, I hope they were telling the truth about that."

She stepped closer to a large whiteboard that had pictures drawn in different boxes. "They would have told you if it bothered them. Theo loves you like a brother, but there's nothing he wouldn't do to make Eva happy."

Colton nodded. "Good. That's the way it should be."

She studied the images again. "This is all for your stunt tomorrow? Even these pictures? It looks like a comic book."

"That's the storyboard that my PR team came up with. The shots they want to get."

She stiffened slightly when she realized he had gotten a lot closer.

Like...*a lot*. He was right behind her.

Not that she wanted him to move away. She just wasn't sure what to do. What would it be like if she could just relax and lean back against his chest?

"Do you do this prep work for all your stunts?" she managed to get out.

"Maybe not to this degree—this snowboard run has a lot of moving parts. But yes, we always map out as much as possible beforehand."

She kept expecting him to move farther away as he spoke—hell, she could smell the woodsy scent of his cologne—but he didn't.

"I didn't realize so much planning went into it."

"Most people don't. But now, what I do is a business in a lot of ways. I don't necessarily think of it like that, but believe me, my public relations manager, Tony, and his team sure do."

One of his strong arms came up as he pointed to one of the boxes in the storyboard. "This is the big money shot."

She was staring at the drawing of the helicopter and what was obviously Colton leaping out of it, but she was so distracted by the muscles of his bicep straining against the sleeve of his shirt that she could barely focus on what he was saying.

"Money shot?" The words squeaked out.

"Yeah. Viewers want to be excited, so we play that up as much as possible. Me coming out of the helicopter is pretty dynamic, so that's one place we're really focusing on."

He brought up his other arm, and he pointed at a second picture a little farther down on the storyboard. She was now, in essence, trapped in his arms. "And here. Flips, spins, fancy footwork stuff… always seems to get pulses pounding."

Her pulse was pounding without any of those things. She had no idea what to do. She could almost hear Lilah telling her to take a chance, to make the first move, to turn around and plant a kiss on him.

But her feet felt glued to the floor.

"Are you ever scared during your stunts?"

"If you're not scared at least a little bit, then you're not taking it seriously enough. So yeah, I'm always cautious."

"I've watched all of your stunts, and sometimes I'm terrified for you."

"You watch my stunts?"

Should she not have admitted that? Did it make her sound more pathetic than she already felt? "I—"

"I like the thought of you watching me."

Was it her imagination, or had his voice just gotten deeper? And why were his arms still up with his hands on the whiteboard?

It was like they were embracing without actually embracing. Close, but no actual cigar.

"Why did you bring those desserts with you here to my room, Ella?"

She hadn't been expecting that question. She shifted, thinking he would move his arm so she could put some distance between them, but those arms stayed firm on either side of her.

Unless she wanted to turn around and be face-to-face, then she didn't have many options but to stay put.

"I had them in my room." Her voice came out like a little squeak, so she cleared her throat. "I thought you might be hungry."

"Did you bring them because you thought that was why I asked you to come here?"

She wanted to lie, but she couldn't. "Yes," she whispered.

"And if I told you I was hoping for something sweet, but what you brought wasn't it, what would you say?"

He wanted something different? She racked her brain for an inventory of what she still had in her room. "Was there something specific you'd wanted? I don't have a lot of inventory left here at the resort, but I—"

Before she could finish the sentence, Colton grabbed her elbow gently and spun her around so she was facing him.

"Oh, there is definitely something sweet that I want, but it's not food."

"It's not?" She was standing there, his arms still caging her in on either side, still almost-embracing. But then he took a slight step back—more along the lines of what she was expecting.

"Look." He ran a hand through his dark hair. "This is a little new for me."

She raised an eyebrow. "Having a girl in your hotel room is new to you?"

"Having *you* in my hotel room is new to me. And no, I did not ask you here because of your baking abilities. But also, I don't want you to think that I expect anything from you." He ran his hand through his hair again. "I'm sure it's easy to believe that I'm with a different girl every night, but I'm not. And even if I were, I wouldn't want you to think that I would lump you in with them."

Was it just her, or did he truly sound nervous? Nervous about *her*.

He let out a sigh. "All I'm trying to say is that I'm fine with whatever happens here tonight. If it's just talking, that's fine—"

Ella kissed him.

Somewhere, Lilah was probably doing backflips in excitement. Then all thoughts of Lilah flew from her mind. This felt right. Her lips on Colton's felt oh-so *right*.

But then she realized he wasn't kissing her back. Her gut knotted. Oh no. She *had* misread the situation just like she'd been afraid of.

She stepped back, dread pooling in her belly. "I'm sorry, Colton. I didn't let you finish what you were saying, did I? This wasn't what you—"

This time, it was Colton who used a kiss to stop the conversation. He slid one of his hands into her hair, while he wrapped his other arm around her hips and pulled her tightly against him.

"Oh, this is very definitely what I want," he said against her lips. "I just realized you taste like butterscotch."

"Butterscotch?" She loved the flavor and had had a piece of candy before she left the room in an attempt to calm her nerves. "Is that bad?"

"No. It's my favorite."

# CHAPTER
## SIX

Most adults probably fantasized about the actual act of sex, but somehow for Ella, when she'd thought about Colton, her daydreams had always centered around kissing.

She'd had fantasies about what was happening right now for years—an embarrassing number of hours thinking about his mouth on hers. The reality didn't disappoint, especially now that Colton had taken over.

The kiss started as gentle, searching—his lips exploring hers, learning them like how he'd obviously learned the mountain he'd be snowboarding down tomorrow. All she could do was melt into him. This was definitely better than what her imagination had come up with.

She slid her hands up his chest to wrap around his neck and pull him closer. Wanting more. But he was taking his time, sipping from her lips with slow, deliberate motions.

Warmth flushed through her body as he used his hand in her hair to hold her just how he wanted. A little moan escaped her as his lips moved along her jaw and down to the side of her neck.

"Be careful, Butterscotch. That sound is going to get you carried over to my bed pretty damned quick."

There was nothing more she'd like than to be in his bed, but she had to laugh at that. "I'm too heavy to be carr—"

"Hush." The sentence was cut off and the laugh disappeared as he shifted, and she found herself swept up in his arms. "Or, on second thought, don't hush… Make that sexy little moan again."

She was still self-conscious, but he didn't seem to be having any trouble carrying her, so she didn't argue. Then *couldn't* argue when his lips took hers again. A few moments later, he lowered her onto the bed and covered her body with his.

And yeah, that moan escaped her once again when his lips found her throat with gentle nips.

Was this moving fast? Yes. But she didn't have any desire to stop it. It was so much better than what she had imagined in her head.

This was *Colton*.

He slid his hand down the outside of her thigh, hitching her leg up so that he was more fully pressed against her. This time, they both moaned.

She pushed away the insecurities that wanted to grow inside her mind. The ones that could visualize the location of every roll of fat and inch of flabby skin anywhere on her body. The ones that said her nose was too crooked and her eyelids too droopy.

The ones that could run through every supermodel Colton had dated over the past few years. None of them looked like her. Ella was never ever going to be mistaken for a supermodel.

"Hey." He lifted his head, and all she could see were those chocolate-brown eyes. "You still with me? Do we need to slow down? That's more than okay."

"I'm still with you. I don't need to slow down."

"Thank God."

He uttered the words like a prayer, causing her to relax. He *wanted* to be here—that much was obvious by the hard length of him pressing against her.

And she wanted to be here just as much. She refused to let her insecurities ruin this.

His lips found hers again, and Ella let herself sink into it. The way his tongue teased and dueled with hers? The way he nipped at her bottom lip then soothed the gentle pain with his tongue? She could keep kissing him all night.

But she wanted more than that. If she only got one night with Colton, she wanted more than just kissing. So when he eased back so he could sit her up and slip her sweatshirt over her head, a few seconds later, she had no thoughts of stopping him.

Especially when he was staring at her breasts like he couldn't wait to devour them once her bra quickly followed suit.

She arched into him, a breathless sigh falling from her lips as his mouth found one nipple and began to play with it, sucking, nipping gently, and teasing. She threaded her fingers into his hair, keeping him pressed against her.

"Fucking beautiful," he muttered.

She knew those were just words said in the heat of passion and she shouldn't take much stock in them, but she didn't care. She was panting by the time his lips left her breasts and made their way down her stomach. He pulled off her shoes and socks then unbuttoned her jeans and eased them down her hips along with her underwear.

Insecurity crept back in when she realized she was totally naked while he was nearly fully clothed. "Off," she demanded as she tugged at the front of his dress shirt. She wanted to feel his naked chest against hers.

"Yes, ma'am." His arms moved away from her as he reached to shrug off his dress shirt and toss it on the floor, before kissing her again. Both of them hissed out a breath at the feel of skin on skin.

He met her eyes. "Are you sure?"

"Absolutely. Are you?"

His laugh was deep and sexy as he grabbed her hand and pressed it against him through his dress pants. "More than sure."

She nodded, smiling as she helped strip him of his pants and boxer briefs.

This was really happening.

"I need to get protection."

"Um, I'm on birth control, if you're comfortable with that." She could feel her face burning. She wasn't used to having this type of talk and wasn't sure if she was making things awkward.

But his gaze turned almost primal. "If you're okay with that. I always use a condom since…"

He trailed off, and she didn't want to think too hard about what the rest of that sentence would be.

Since he slept with three different women a night?

Since he had so many supermodels throwing themselves at him?

"Oh." She wasn't sure what else to say.

He grimaced. "I just mean, I'm clean. It's part of my quarterly check-in with my physician. And there's nothing I'd love more, since I trust you, to not have to leave this bed to go find a condom. To just feel you."

"That sounds perfect to me."

She loved the smile that crept over his face before he laid her back against the bed and kissed gently over her cheeks and eyes.

She ran her hands up his shoulders as he moved his lips down her jaw to find her neck once more. He shifted his weight to the side so he could slide his hand down her body and in between her legs.

This time, Ella's moan was closer to a hiss. It had been so long, and even then, it hadn't been Colton.

Those brown eyes met hers. "So wet. So delicious."

She couldn't manage to force words out, could only feel and enjoy as his fingers teased her closer and closer to the edge. It wasn't long before her hips were rocking up toward him—a silent appeal for more.

"I want you inside me." She hardly recognized her own voice, but she loved the shudder that shot through him at the words.

He moved so he was fully on top of her, hiking one of her legs up over his hip. Slowly, eyes on hers, he slid inside.

It was the single most intimate moment of her life—her gaze held captive by his as he filled her inch by inch. There was no way to escape him, not that she had any interest in doing so.

He held still for a moment, eyes still on hers, once he was

completely seated—giving her time to adjust. Making sure she was still okay.

"More," she whispered.

That slow grin spread over his face once again, before he reached a hand into the bend of her knee and hooked her leg up higher, opening her wider, his body now pinning hers completely to the bed.

And he began to move. Slow thrusts at first, giving them both the chance to bask in the connection. Then faster, harder.

All Ella could do was hold on. There was no escaping the tiny bolts of pleasure ricocheting through her body. Not that she wanted to. She wanted it to last forever.

But then she saw him grimace.

She gripped his shoulders, a black hole growing in the pit of her stomach. "What? What's wrong? Do you want to stop?"

"Are you kidding? No." He slowed his thrusts. "I'm trying to figure out how to not make this embarrassingly short. I can't seem to find any control around you, Butterscotch."

She felt like her smile would split her whole face. She loved every single thing about that statement. The thought that she could make him lose control?

"Then don't worry about control. Let's both just feel."

That was all the permission he needed, evidently. With a growl, he wrapped both her legs around his hips and began to move in earnest, angling himself in a way that made her gasp.

It didn't take long as pleasure washed over her, and her orgasm almost caught her off guard. Her head fell back as she called out his name.

Colton's thrusts never stopped, as he hooked one arm under her leg and lifted it toward his shoulder. The position opened her more fully and left her almost helpless to whatever he wanted to do.

The pleasure gave her no respite, building up again, crashing over her as he found his own release with another sexy growl.

It took them long minutes to catch their breaths and get their hearts beating at some sort of normal rate again. She trailed her fingers up and down his back, relishing the feel of his collapsed weight on her and his face buried in her neck.

She could lie here forever.

But when he moved away, she knew she had to let him go, despite wanting to keep this connection between them. He got up out of bed and walked to the bathroom, leaving her wondering what she should do.

What was proper protocol? Did he expect her to get dressed and go? Was this it? Sex was done, and now Colton was done with her?

But a few seconds later, he came back out of the bathroom, washcloth in hand. She could hardly take her eyes from his naked body as he walked toward her.

"I just wanted to get us cleaned up." She sighed as he sat down next to her and gently ran the washcloth between her legs. "And if you'll give me an hour to nap, I'd like to show you that I'm capable of going longer than forty-five seconds."

Her eyes flew up to his as a giggle escaped her. It had been much longer than forty-five seconds, but the fact that he wanted another go thrilled the deepest feminine parts of her.

She winked at him. "Yeah, but it was a pretty great three-quarters of a minute."

He threw back his head and laughed. "Oh, you're in for it, Butterscotch. Just you wait. Power nap, then you're all mine."

He threw the washcloth back into the bathroom then got into the bed, pulling her close to his side.

Definitely better than her fantasies.

They were both nodding off when Colton muttered, "Man, I owe Lincoln a drink. That's for damn sure."

She chuckled but had no idea what he was talking about. "Why is that?"

"He's why you're here." Colton's yawn was huge. "Thank God Lincoln is Lincoln and he doesn't have much of a filter."

She could feel Colton's body relaxing, drifting toward sleep. Hers was doing the same. She let out her own yawn.

"Oh yeah?"

"Yeah." It took so long for him to respond, she thought they'd both fallen asleep. His words were almost mumbled. "But damn, I'm glad he told me about your crush."

Her eyes blinked open. Had she just heard him right? "What?"

Colton gripped her hip, then rubbed little circles with his fingers. "I'm glad you have a crush on me. Made my day to hear it."

Ice pooled in Ella's veins.

*What?* Lincoln had told Colton she had a crush on him? That's why he'd invited her here?

She froze, having no idea what to say. She felt like mortification would consume her from the inside out and burn every other part of her to ash. What was she supposed to say?

Colton's soft snore saved her from having to say anything at all and galvanized her into action. She couldn't stay here. Couldn't go for round two after a nap, knowing he'd only brought her here because she'd been served up as *a sure thing*.

Or worse. She couldn't bear the thought of that.

She eased out of his grip and slid off the bed, silently finding her clothes. She took them into the living room area to put them on, wanting to make sure not to wake him. She could not bear facing Colton right now.

She didn't even put on her shoes. She had to get out of there.

She made it out the door, shutting it silently behind her. She closed her eyes as she leaned back against it and took a breath.

God, she'd made such an ass of herself. To actually think that Colton had magically felt some attraction to her after all these years and invited her up?

That was not what had just happened. She knew what had just happened but didn't even want to allow herself to think of the phrase. At least not until she got back to her own room and could fall apart.

"I'm telling you, Colton's suite is right down here. I paid a bellboy *a lot* to find out."

Ella's eyes flew back open at the conversation. Two women—

young, slender, blonde...definitely Colton's normal type—were walking down the hallway and almost to her.

"Money well worth it if we can casually run into him, right?" the other woman responded.

"Yeah. I mean, we might have to camp out in this hallway to make it seem like a casual encounter, but..."

"So worth it," they both said at the same time, giggling.

Ella pushed away from the door, but they were too close and could obviously see that she'd just come from the room they knew was Colton's.

"Oh." Both of them stared, eyes flicking from the shoes she held in her hands to what she was sure was her mussed hair and makeup.

Ella didn't say anything, just walked past them, glad when they stepped out of the way.

It was silent for a moment, but then she heard snickering and whispers. Most of it she couldn't make out because she was trying her best to get down the hallway as quickly as possible.

But one phrase was definitely clear. The one she hadn't been allowing herself to think at all. The one that encapsulated the whole night with Colton.

*Pity fuck.*

# CHAPTER SEVEN

"You look like shit."

Colton took the cup of coffee from Tony's hand as his PR manager walked into the suite.

"Thanks." The words came out through gritted teeth.

It was all Colton could do to be polite when the only thing he wanted to do was put his fist through the wall. They were two hours until wheels up for the stunt. Tony and his team had already been in and out of the suite a dozen times, running around handling last-minute PR stuff.

That was normal—almost part of Colton's process. The more everyone buzzed around him before a stunt, the calmer and more focused he became. He preferred the chaos.

Tony had already warned Colton that it was pretty much a mob of fans down in the lobby area and not to go down there unless he wanted to take time to talk to them.

He didn't. He didn't want to talk to anybody.

He shouldn't feel betrayed that he'd woken up to find Ella gone after their lovemaking. He'd had plenty of casual encounters with women over the years. Sometimes when the sex was over, it was just...*over*. With a hug and a kiss, Colton was gone. No promises asked; none given.

Hell, he made it a normal practice of going to women's places rather than having them come to his, for multiple reasons. He wanted them to feel safer and more comfortable. But also, because he wanted to have as much control over egress as possible—easier for him to leave than to make someone else go.

He always tried to be respectful of women, even his casual rendezvous. Just because he wouldn't be having a relationship with someone didn't mean that person didn't deserve consideration.

And hell, more than once, he'd left an encounter with a woman very clear that he hadn't been much more than a trophy for her. Something she could brag about to her friends.

He had not even considered that would be the case with Ella. Maybe Lincoln had been wrong and she didn't have a crush on him at all. Maybe she'd just wanted to have this notch in her belt.

What was truly surprising was how disappointing that was.

He'd been telling the God's honest truth when he said he was perfectly fine just talking last night. Hell, he would've been more delighted spending a night talking and laughing with Ella than all sorts of sexual gymnastics with a stranger whose name he wouldn't remember in a couple weeks' time anyway.

He hadn't expected sex, but he certainly hadn't been disappointed when things had gone that way.

Who was he kidding? His mind had been damned near blown by the chemistry between them. He'd definitely planned for a round two. And maybe a three, four, and five.

Only to reach for her after he'd woken up to find their encounter obviously hadn't meant anything to her at all.

He had to stop himself from crushing the coffee cup in his hand.

Tony walked back over to him after talking to a few members of the team. "Hell, Colton, we're going to have to put some fucking makeup on you. Nobody wants to see their favorite action hero looking like he's just coming off a three-day bender."

Colton rolled his eyes. "Pretty sure I'm wearing a helmet, so I don't think we have to worry about that."

But Tony was right. He did look like shit.

He didn't care.

Tony was wise enough not to argue the point and returned to his team. Colton didn't get testy very often, but when he did, his crew knew to give him some space.

Colton nearly growled when there was another knock on the door. There were too many fucking people in here already. Tony shot him a wary look and answered it.

"Enter at your own risk," Colton heard Tony mutter.

Bear just chuckled and walked directly over to Colton. "You look like shit."

"So everyone keeps telling me."

Bear's grin didn't falter. "What's the matter, asshole. Nervous?"

Colton took a sip of coffee, forcing it down even though it was lukewarm. He poured the rest into the sink. "Can I ask you a question?"

"As long as it has nothing to do with the trajectory of that mountain you're about to go down. I know nothing about that."

"What do you know about Ella O'Conner?"

Bear blinked like he couldn't quite understand the question. "The woman we've both known since we were in diapers? What do you think I know about her that you don't?"

"I don't know. I just..." He scrubbed a hand down his face. What info was he trying to get from Bear, exactly? He didn't want to explain what happened with Ella.

"I saw you talking to her last night. Good for you."

"Does she...*talk* with a lot of guys, do you know?"

"Pretty sure Ella is particularly interested in *talking* to just you." Bear's eyes narrowed. "Did something happen?"

*Yeah, I finally felt like I really connected to a woman, with bonus points because she's someone I've known for years. We had ridiculously fabulous sex, but then she snuck out while I was sleeping, and now, I'm pissed.*

"Lincoln mentioned she had a crush on me."

Bear raised an eyebrow. "You weren't aware?"

"Were you?"

"I think the whole town of Oak Creek has been aware of it for some time."

Colton shook his head. "Well, the whole town of Oak Creek may have been mistaken."

"What makes you say that? Something did happen last night, didn't it?"

This definitely wasn't the time to get into it. Maybe in a decade or two. "No. She just let me know in no uncertain terms that she wasn't interested in anything real with me. Let's just leave it at that."

For a moment, Bear looked like he was going to argue the point, then he glanced around before leaning back against the kitchen counter and crossing his arms over his chest.

"So, is this stunt of yours still going down in a couple hours?"

Colton nodded. "Of course. Why wouldn't it?"

"I'm no expert at stunts, but I am your best friend. Either get your head in the game, or call this thing quits and reschedule. What you're doing today is too dangerous to be thinking about a woman. Even someone as amazing as Ella—for good or bad reasons."

"I'm fine." And even if he wasn't, he wouldn't let the situation affect what he was doing today.

Bear took the slightest step closer. "You may be fine, but look around you—your entire team is feeding off your energy, and not in a good way. This stunt is dangerous for you, but it's also dangerous for them. You need to be the leader they need right now."

The words were soft enough that nobody else could hear them, but Colton knew his friend spoke the truth. Shit. "Yeah, you're right. I'll pull it together."

"Good, because I just talked to my brother, and he says that conditions are damn near perfect out there for the stunt today. He can't wait."

Colton pushed off from the kitchenette counter. "You hear that, everyone? Our helo pilot says that it's looking right as rain out there. Or snow, as is the case. Who's ready to give everyone the show of a lifetime?"

Cheers erupted throughout the suite, and the tension was broken. Bear had been right—Colton had been bringing the team way down, and he hadn't even realized it.

He looked over at his friend. "Anybody ever tell you you're pretty fucking smart?"

Bear blew a kiss at him. "Every damn day."

Colton actually had already talked to Derek twice this morning and knew about the weather conditions. Yes, he was upset about what had happened with Ella, but he wasn't so far up his own ass that he was willing to risk his life over it. He was still taking the stunt seriously. And it was now time to give it his undivided attention.

Disappointment that the first woman he'd felt a real connection with in a long time didn't feel the same would have to wait. No more thoughts about her soft curves or those sexy-as-fuck sighs she'd made.

Now was time for the stunt only.

The weather was perfect. All equipment had already been double-checked. The team was ready and itching to get going.

All that was left to do now was to go out there and do what Colton Harrison did best:

Cheat death.

## CHAPTER
# EIGHT

"ETA ninety seconds."

Derek's voice filled Colton's head through the comms unit inside his snowboarding helmet. He gave a brisk nod to the primary cameraman who would be shooting footage from inside the helicopter as Colton jumped. The other footage would be made up from the two cameras strapped to Colton's body and various other camera crews strategically stationed down the mountain.

"You good, Colt?" Tony asked. He wasn't with them in the helicopter, but only because he hadn't figured out how to clone himself. He desperately wanted to be here but was needed in control central to be able to live edit the footage coming through.

"I'm ready."

And he was. His mind was clear and focused. The talk with Bear had helped, then an even bigger source of support had shown up: his dad.

His parents came to a lot of his stunts, but he'd expected them to stay in Oak Creek this time, visiting their friends. When he'd gotten to the resort's helo pad and found his dad there, he had felt nothing short of immense relief.

If there was anyone in the world who understood what was

going through Colton's mind right now, it was Riley Harrison, a former extreme sport athlete himself.

"I checked with Derek about payload, and he said we were within acceptable limits with me on board, but I'm good either way," Riley had said after hugging Colton. "Just wanted to be here for support and deliver the hug your mother sent."

Colton had immediately dragged his dad onto the helicopter. As long as it didn't put them over the weight limit—hell, even if he'd had to get rid of some of his crew or gear, he would've done it to have Riley on board with him.

He looked at his father now and found him staring back, doing a last-minute mental safety check all the way down Colton's body for any noticeable concerns.

"I'm ready, Dad."

Riley cracked a smile. "Never crossed my mind that you weren't."

"Thirty seconds," Derek said. "Everybody prep."

"Roger that." Colton buckled his boots into the snowboard and tightened the strap of his helmet. He knew it would only be a second before—

Yep, his dad reached over, gave the strap another tug before placing a hand on either side of Colton's head and shaking them to make sure the helmet was situated as snugly as possible.

Riley had been doing that since he'd put Colton's first helmet on him when he was two and taught him how to do a wheelie on a skateboard.

Colton put his gloved hands over Riley's. "Thanks, Dad."

Riley winked then thumped the top of his helmet—also a tradition. "Glad to be here. I'll have the best vantage point."

Once Colton was on his way down the mountain, the helicopter would be catching some of the most amazing aerial shots.

"I'm in place, Derek."

"Okay, let's do this," the pilot responded.

"Don't forget—720 out of the helicopter," Tony said. "Let's give them a show they'll never forget."

Dad rolled his eyes, but Colton just grinned. He wouldn't miss a chance to do a double front flip even if there were no cameras anywhere around.

"Okay, we're coming up on the mark," Derek said. "Get ready."

Holding the copter steady at this altitude wouldn't be easy. Riley thumped him on the head again and then got out of the way. Colton slid the rest of the way to the open side area of the helicopter.

Tony had all the camera operators give a final check, but Colton wasn't listening. He was completely focused on what was in front of him. The jump, then the route he'd take down the mountain, that included some almost sheer cliffs, which would once again allow for acrobatics.

The first cliff was the most dangerous. After that, Colton would just add maneuvers to make it look as thrilling as possible. In fifteen minutes, it would all be over but the celebrating.

The helicopter arrived about twenty feet over the decreed jumping point, and Derek eased it into a hover. "In place. On your mark, Colton."

Colton didn't hesitate. "Three, two, one... *Go.*"

He was falling.

He didn't have much skin exposed, but he could still hear the wind. He used his core strength to flip himself around then do it again as the earth hurtled nearer—making it look like he was going to crash headfirst right out of the gate. Tony definitely had his 720.

The landing was critical—and probably the most dangerous part of the stunt. When Colton handled it with no problem, he heard the cheering over the comms, but he stayed focused on the snow in front of him.

They'd gone over the route so many times, it was basically tattooed on his brain. Not having to focus on the path allowed him to be able to perform all sorts of cuts and ollies and corked spins.

Allowed him to be free and do what he did best: tackle the challenge in front of him.

"Looking great, Colt," Tony said. "Got that big cliff coming up."

Colton didn't respond, knowing Tony wouldn't expect him to.

This was the second-most dangerous part of the stunt—and the most thrilling. He curled himself a little lower so he could pick up speed.

The plan was a backside rodeo 540. It would be tight, but just like the leap out of the helicopter, it would provide quite the money shot.

He launched himself over the side of the cliff, grabbing the back of the board and flipping and twisting himself around at the same time. Keeping his focus on the horizon so he was sure to know which end was up, he curled in as he finished his twist, then let his body do what it knew how to do.

As almost always, his body didn't disappoint him. Colton landed smoothly on the snow where it began to angle out from the mountain.

He'd cleared the cliff.

Once again, cheers roared in his ears.

"All right, you're home free now," Tony said. "Just have fun and give everybody a show."

Colton grinned and cut to the left, using as many opportunities to jump and flip as he could find, loving the feel of the wind in his face.

How could he leave this? This feeling right here was one of the greatest in the world.

He was enjoying his minor stunts, almost on autopilot, when he felt the slope fracture under him like broken glass. It only took a split second for every survival instinct he had to snap into place as he realized what was happening.

*Avalanche.*

Damn it, they'd placed explosives farther up the mountain a couple weeks ago to trigger their own mini avalanche to keep this from happening during the stunt at the spot where it would be most likely.

It shouldn't have been necessary this far down the mountain.

Colton's instinct was to try to outrun it, but he knew that

wouldn't work for long. Avalanches could move at speeds up to two hundred miles per hour.

"Shit, Colton, you've got a fucking avalanche!" Tony's panicked voice squeaked in his ears.

*Yeah, already aware.* "Roger."

Tony was screaming other stuff at people, but Colton tried to block it out. He needed to focus on what he was doing.

Suddenly, there was blessed silence over the comms unit. Colton didn't know why, and he didn't care. Nobody could help him right now. He was on his own.

"Son, listen, it's right behind you." Dad. He'd switched to a private channel. "It's going to take you under. You've trained for this. Swim. Air pocket. Stay alive. You have the beacon. We'll come for you—"

His dad's voice was cut off as snow slammed into Colton, knocking him forward off the snowboard. Immediately, he used his arms in a swimming motion to try to remain toward the top of the tidal wave of snow.

The sheer force of Mother Nature's power was humbling. He could do nothing to get out of it. All he could do was try to stay alive until it slowed.

The few seconds it took felt like an eternity, but finally, the deafening momentum eased just slightly. Using all his strength, Colton flipped himself over onto his back. He wanted to be faceup for what he knew was coming next.

The snow was going to bury him.

The thousands of pounds of snow slowed further, but that meant it would pile, trapping him. Sure enough, a moment later, a blanket of icy white poured over him, like freezing concrete.

White. The entire world was white.

The snow's movement was almost stopping. This was it. He had to create an air pocket for himself as he came to a halt. It was going to make the difference between suffocating and maybe being able to stay alive long enough for rescuers to get to him.

The roar of the moving snow lowered as it halted. Colton

couldn't see anything but white all around him. He thrust up an arm and expanded his chest to create as much airspace as possible. As he came to a complete stop, he angled his head around to try to make even more space between him and the deadly frozen white.

And then he couldn't move. Not even one inch of his body. There was absolutely nothing he could do.

*Don't panic. Stay calm.*

That was part of the avalanche survival training—hyperventilating was just going to cause you to use up oxygen more quickly. But staying calm was much fucking easier said in a ski classroom than done when your body temperature was plummeting, you couldn't move, and you knew the oxygen was extremely limited.

He could still see the light coming through the cracks in the snow, but only for a few seconds. It got darker as the snow filled in even the tiniest crevice.

And then there was only blackness—the whiteness gone. It was one hundred percent dark.

He had no idea if he was buried six inches or ten feet under the snow. Ultimately, it didn't matter; either one would kill him if rescuers didn't get to him in time.

Colton was completely entombed.

# CHAPTER
# NINE

ELLA HEFTED the last of her boxes onto the luggage cart and eased it out her hotel room door. She had no idea why she was doing it herself. She could've paid someone to do all this—brought an assistant from Oak Creek or even given the bellboys here at the resort a large tip to load it for her.

It wasn't like her family didn't have the money. Ella and her sister Jess had grown up with money. Their dad, Cade Conner, had been a huge music superstar when they were young. Some of Ella's earliest memories were of her family sitting on a giant hotel bed together, eating room service breakfast—she and Jess laughing their heads off at something their dad said, their mom's quiet smile and gentle eyes taking it all in.

They'd spent a lot of Ella's youth traveling around with Cade Conner's tours. Luxury had been part of that. But her parents had also taught her to value money and never take it for granted. Taught her that the hard work she did herself would always mean more than what she paid others to do.

Loading up boxes after a catering event probably hadn't been the hard work they'd meant, but Ella still didn't mind doing it herself.

Plus, it gave her an excuse not to talk to anyone or sit and gawk over Colton's stunt like everyone else would be doing. She'd already heard the commotion in the lobby as she'd supervised the pack-up of the kitchen items. Everyone had been there for hours, waiting for the start of the stunt.

Which should be about right now. Ella didn't have to check her watch to know. Colton was probably in that helicopter heading up the mountain right at this second.

She wasn't going to watch. She knew all her friends from Oak Creek were in the lobby too—probably with a prime viewing location on some large screen. But she didn't want to talk to them. Didn't want them all studying her a little too closely like they did whenever she was watching anything Colton.

And she definitely couldn't take a chance on running into those two women she'd met outside Colton's door last night. Couldn't risk word spreading that she'd been in the suite with him at that hour of the night.

Her phone buzzed in her pocket, but she ignored it, taking the elevator down to the hotel's service entrance, where her van was parked. When she got out of the elevator, her phone was buzzing again. This time, she glanced at it, but she stuffed it back into her pocket when she saw it was Lilah.

No doubt, her friend was wondering where Ella was and why she wasn't watching Colton's stunt with bated breath, as always. Lilah would just have to wonder because Ella definitely wasn't going to explain what happened.

"What the hell are you doing?"

Ella was loading the last of the boxes into the van, thinking she was going to make a clean getaway, when Lilah's voice boomed out behind her.

"Don't start with me, Lilah."

Lilah rushed over to her and pulled her into a bear hug. "Are you okay? It's going to be okay. It has to be."

Ella blinked multiple times at her friend's embrace. Lilah was not typically a hugger. She must've found out about what had happened between her and Colton. Ella didn't know how, but that didn't really matter anyway.

"Yeah, I'm a little embarrassed by how it all went down, and no, I don't want to talk about that, although I'm sure you have an opinion." She pulled away and hoisted the last box into the back of the van. "It happened, it probably won't happen again, and—"

"Oh my God. You don't know, do you?"

Ella spun toward her friend, noticing for the first time how pinched and pale Lilah looked. Her heart began racing in her chest. "What? What's going on?"

"There's been an accident."

Ice formed in Ella's veins. "Who? Mom? Dad? Jess?"

"Colton."

If possible, her heart seized even more. "But he's out on the snowboarding stunt right now."

"There was an avalanche a few minutes ago. I started calling you immediately as soon as it happened."

"*Avalanche?*" Ella whispered the word like she had no idea what it meant, but she did. They all did. They lived surrounded by the Grand Tetons. Avalanches happened all the time, but not usually while people were barreling down the mountain at top speed doing tricks.

She felt like all the oxygen had been sucked from the planet. "Is Colton… Is he…?"

She couldn't bring herself to say the word.

Lilah squeezed her arm, then held out her phone where she was watching the footage. "We don't have any news yet. Let's get to the TV so we can see better."

They sprinted to the lobby, only to find Colton's fans glued to every television available in the large room as well as the ones in all the restaurants and bars. Most people were watching silently, but some were crying and holding each other.

It was impossible to get near a screen with the crowds. Ella wanted to tear a path through the people, scream at them to get out of the way.

But what good would that do? Being closer to the TV wasn't going to get her closer to Colton.

Lilah grabbed her arm. "Manager's office. There's a private television. Becky is already in there."

Ella ran in that direction, not caring how it looked. Lilah was right behind her, phone to her ear.

As soon as Ella opened the office door, she found herself engulfed in Becky's embrace. Ella couldn't look at her or return the embrace. All she could do was stare at the screen attached to the wall, praying she'd see Colton's grinning face at any moment, laughing about how he'd cheated death. Instead, it was an overhead shot from local news of the damage the avalanche had done as tons of snow had slid down the mountain.

*Extreme sports superstar Colton Harrison taken out by avalanche.*

The words rolled in repeat on the bottom of the screen as a reporter talked to someone Ella didn't recognize.

"How did reporters get here so fast?"

Becky shook her head. "They were already here to cover the event. They just pivoted their story."

"What do we know?" Ella's voice sounded weak and croaky to her own ears, eyes still glued to the screen.

"Colton was more than halfway down the mountain, past all the most dangerous parts of the stunt, when the avalanche hit like ten or fifteen minutes ago," Becky explained. "He stayed in front of it for a little bit, then…"

Then he went under.

"Was it ten or fifteen minutes ago?" Ella whispered.

Becky blinked at the question. "Honestly, I'm not sure the exact time. Why?"

"The first thirty minutes with an avalanche are the most important." Ella forced the words out. She knew this from research she'd done about some of Colton's other stunts. "After thirty minutes, life expectancy…"

She didn't finish. She didn't have to. The reporter on the screen was talking about the same thing, statistics popping up. Survival probability plummeted from ninety-two percent at fifteen minutes to nearly zero after thirty minutes.

Every minute they didn't find Colton literally brought him closer to death. So, whether the avalanche was ten or fifteen minutes ago made a huge difference.

"He was wearing a beacon," Lilah said. "They'll get to him."

A beacon meant they weren't looking for a needle in a haystack, but it didn't necessarily mean they'd get to him in time. Not to mention the injuries he could've sustained during the avalanche itself. The sliding snow looked deceptively smooth when watching it from a distance. But in reality, the force was enough to take down buildings.

Lilah's phone rang, causing them all to jump. "Bear. Talk to us. I've got Becky and Ella here with me." She put the call on speaker so they could all hear.

"I'm on the comms system with Derek and trying to relay info to you guys and Aunt Girl as we get it, so bear with me. The helo has the beacon signal, and they are over Colton's location."

"What do we know?" Lilah asked. "How many minutes has he been under?"

"Seventeen," Bear said, his usually jovial voice more somber than Ella had ever heard it.

Seventeen minutes. Ella looked down at her watch and marked the time.

"Derek is in the helicopter with Uncle Boy and one of the camera operators. Derek is getting them as low to the beacon as he can. They don't have a lot of equipment, but they're going to be Colton's best chance."

Because no other rescuers would be able to get to him in time.

"Derek and Uncle Boy Riley know what they're doing," Becky said, wrapping her arm around Ella.

Becky had every confidence in her husband's piloting abilities, and honestly, Ella did too. And Boy Riley—Colton's dad—had more experience with stunts and rescues than the majority of the people on the planet.

But everybody in the room knew the odds were not in Colton's favor right now.

"There's no place to land close enough to get to Colton in time," Bear said. "And... Shit. Hold."

Bear's voice cut off.

They all looked up at the screen as they waited for Bear to come back to the report. The news had switched to footage of people all over the resort, both inside and outside, watching their screens. Some were crying; some were praying.

"That's so damned fake. What do they care? They don't even know Colton." Ella knew her rage at Colton's fans was misplaced, but she couldn't stop it. "I found two of his little fan club members outside his door in the middle of the night last night. They'd paid hotel staff to tell them what room Colton was in. But they didn't know him. They don't really care about him."

Becky's arm tightened around her shoulders. "It's going to be okay, Ella."

"You don't know that." Ella glanced at her watch. Colton had now been entombed nearly twenty minutes. "He's running out of time."

"Holy shit." Bear's voice came back on the line. "Derek couldn't land the bird, so Uncle Boy Riley jumped while Derek hovered as low as he could. He's in the snow, digging with a fucking helmet. Sorry, I had to tell Aunt Girl first."

No one could blame Bear for giving Colton's mother an update before them.

"Can they tell how deep in the snow Colton is?" Lilah asked.

"Derek said the beacon was reporting four to six feet."

Ella shuddered at the thought that Colton was currently six feet under. It felt way too ominous.

"Nobody will fight as hard for him as his dad," Becky said. "We'd all do whatever we could, but Phoenix won't stop, no matter what."

*Phoenix.* Boy Riley's nickname back when he did these same sorts of stunts as his son. They needed Phoenix's son to rise from the ashes now.

A tear fell from Ella's eyes. She couldn't help it. Why had she snuck out while Colton was sleeping? Why hadn't she used every second possible with him?

Becky noticed. "Ella, Colton is going to be okay. He's cool under pressure, and he has the beacon. Those are two huge factors in his favor."

Ella checked her watch again. He'd been under for twenty-one minutes. Time was running out.

"He was talking about you this morning, El," Bear said.

Ella knew Bear was trying to distract her from the potential tragedy at hand, but she felt her face flush red anyway.

"Very interesting. Especially since Elly-Belly just let slip that she saw two no-good skanks outside Colton's room last night in the middle of the night." Lilah raised one eyebrow. "Question is, what were you doing at Colton's room in the middle of the night?"

*Damn it.*

"This is not the time to discuss this." If possible, Ella's face turned even more red.

"Oh, if I know Colton Harrison, even now, his ears are burning inside that snow, and he's fighting harder to get out because a pretty woman is talking about him," Bear said. "Hell, he'll probably meet his dad halfway."

Ella laughed, but a couple seconds into it, it turned into a sob. Immediately, Becky's and Lilah's arms were around her.

"He's going to be okay, Ella," Becky said again.

"He has to be." Ella couldn't think about a world without Colton in it.

"I just got word—Riley's got him!" Bear yelled. "Derek said he's pulling Colton out of the snow right now. The rest of the rescue team will be there soon to get him down the mountain, but it looks like Riley got him out of the snow!"

A grin broke out on Ella's face. They'd found him. They'd found

Colton in time. She hugged her friends, and this time as she cried, it was tears of relief.

"Oh shit." The single horrified phrase from Bear destroyed their joy instantly.

"What, Bear?" Lilah demanded. "What?"

"Riley has started CPR. Colton isn't breathing."

# CHAPTER
# TEN

They were on their way to the hospital. Lilah was driving, cool under pressure, her tactical expertise with vehicles coming into play as she flew around any car in their way.

Becky was in the back seat with Ella, holding her hand. "They got him breathing. That's the most important thing."

Riley Harrison had single-handedly performed CPR on his son there in the snow until the rescue team had arrived on snowmobiles sixteen minutes later, gotten him a little farther down the mountain to where a medevac could land then get him to the hospital.

They hadn't received any update beyond the fact that Colton was breathing on his own.

"Um, I beg to differ." Lilah's eyes didn't shift from the road in front of her. "I believe the most important thing is Ella spilling about what happened between her and Colton last night."

Ella gritted her teeth. "Focus on driving."

"Oh, don't think I can't handle both at the same time. Spill, sister."

"You don't have to talk about it if you don't want to." Becky was much more diplomatic. "But you know we'd love to hear about it. And maybe it will help us get our minds off this until we get to the hospital."

The hospital they'd taken Colton to was about thirty minutes away by car. They'd gotten him to it much quicker in the medical helicopter.

Ella wasn't sure she really wanted to talk about what had happened with Colton last night, even if it was appropriate. But on the other hand, *all* she wanted to do was talk about him. As if talking about him would ensure he was okay.

But she definitely was not going to tell them the whole story.

"It's really nothing. We started talking at the wedding" —*because Colton got word that I had a crush on him and was feeling sorry for me*— "and decided to meet up last night."

"I knew it!" Lilah tapped her hand excitedly on the steering wheel. "I knew you guys did the down and dirty."

"Maybe we just talked, ever think of that, Lilah?" Ella rolled her eyes. "Maybe Colton just needed a friend."

Ella's stomach churned at the thought that maybe that was the truth. Maybe he hadn't really been looking for sex at all. Had she done something to instigate their physical start? She thought he had instigated it, but now, she wasn't entirely sure.

"If you guys just talked, that's fine too." Becky's voice was gentle as always. "He is your friend, after all."

"That's bullshit," Lilah scoffed. "I mean, sure, they can talk, but I saw the way Colton was looking at Ella. He wanted more than to just talk."

"It's not what you think, Lilah." Ella shook her head.

"What I think is that you guys bumped uglies. Is that true?"

"Jesus, Li," Becky muttered under her breath with a laugh. "How about a little tact?"

"Fine. What I think is that Ella and Colton made beautiful, passionate, worshipful love to each other last night. Better?"

"Really? There's no middle ground between bumping uglies and worshipful?" Becky asked.

"I don't care what you want to call it, Elly-Belly basically has already admitted two separate times to being in Colton's room in the middle of the night. As much as I'm sure they enjoy each other's conversational rhythm, I'm still pretty positive that more than just talking happened."

"Wait a second," Ella said. "When did I say I'd been in his room twice?"

"Well, you just admitted it in the office, and then don't think I wasn't aware of what you said when I first found you at your van."

Ella let out a sigh. She should've known Lilah would be aware of anything Ella was saying, despite the crisis going on. "Okay, fine. Yes, we had sex."

Becky let out an excited little squeal.

"I knew it," Lilah said. "How was it?"

"It was good, but..." Damn it, Ella really didn't want to talk about this. Didn't want to explain what Lincoln had said, didn't want to talk about how it fed into her deepest fears.

*Pity fuck.*

"But what?" Becky asked gently.

"I don't know." Ella gave a one-shoulder shrug. "I think it was just a one-time thing."

"Why?" Lilah asked. "Would you want it to happen again if you have the choice?"

This was getting harder and harder to explain without giving away all the details. "I don't know. I think we were both just caught up in...a moment. It feels weird talking about this not knowing how Colton is doing, so let's drop it."

"Fine." Lilah turned off the highway. "But only because we're almost to the hospital."

Ella would take the reprieve and hope it would be permanent. But her relief was short-lived when they pulled up to the hospital and found it completely packed with people obviously not there for medical attention. By the looks of all the Colton Harrison T-shirts and gear, a group of his fans had figured out where the medevac had taken him.

"Holy shit." Lilah's voice was tight. "I get that these people love Colton, but this is ridiculous. They need to get the heck out and let the doctors do their job."

They found a parking spot in the very back of the lot and made their way to the main entrance.

"Bear is going to meet us out here," Lilah said. "Colton's condition is listed as serious but no longer critical, so he's definitely still alive."

Still alive was better than nothing, but Ella wanted so much more than that.

They had to almost fight their way through the crowd to get to the door. Security was already trying to get people to disperse, but none of them wanted to go.

The outpouring of support was touching, but at the same time, these people were stopping Ella from getting to Colton. Maybe it was talking about last night a little with the girls, but she needed to see him more than ever. Needed to know for herself that he was going to be all right.

By the time they made it to the door, local police had arrived. Obviously, the hospital was feeling overwhelmed and had called them. Immediately, they started making people leave.

"Listen up, people!" one of the police officers yelled from the front of the hospital entrance. "If you are not here for medical attention or are not on the hospital visitor approval list due to a loved one being in this hospital, then you need to leave now."

The crowd began grumbling. Nobody wanted to leave. A man Ella didn't recognize came out from the inside of the hospital and spoke to the police officer. The officer was definitely interested in whatever the man was saying. A few seconds later, the man began to speak.

"Guys, I'm Tony Salaun, part of Colton's support team. I want to announce that Colton is alive, breathing on his own, and does not seem to have any life-threatening injuries from the avalanche."

Tony's words eased some of the tightness in Ella's chest, but she still needed to see Colton for herself before she would really accept he was okay. Before *she* would be okay.

"The best thing you can do to help Colton right now is to leave the hospital premises so that the medical staff can work to the best of their abilities without having to worry about an unruly crowd on their hands," Tony continued. "I will personally post updates as they are available on Colton's website. And if updates aren't available, I will still touch base with you once an hour until we all make it through this crisis."

"That's Colton's PR manager," Becky whispered.

"He's fucking good," Lilah said.

Lilah was right. The crowd was already relaxing a little. They truly just wanted Colton to be okay, and knowing that someone was going to provide them with information was making them more willing to leave.

"You heard the man, people," the police officer said. "You'll get your updates, but right now, you need to leave."

Tony continued to encourage them to go, walking into the crowd to answer individual questions as they began to disperse. He was definitely good at his job. This is exactly what was needed right now.

Now that the way was clearer, they were able to get all the way up to the door. Bear met them.

"He's awake. I haven't seen him. They are keeping everybody in the waiting room, but his dad came out and said he was awake and talking some."

Relief nearly made Ella's knees weak. Colton was *awake*.

"Full functionality of his body?" Lilah asked.

"As far as I know, yes. At least as much as can be tested at this point. It looks like maybe our boy is going to get out of this scot-free." Bear pulled open the front door, and they walked inside.

Every word he said made Ella feel better, but she still wanted to see Colton for herself. Just for a second. No need for awkward conversations.

Two hospital guards stopped them just inside the door.

"Nobody is allowed in unless you're on the list," the first one said.

Bear rolled his eyes. "Dude, you just saw me come from the main waiting room."

The guard pointed at Ella, Becky, and Lilah. "I'm talking about them."

"We're on the list," Lilah said. She gave him her name, and he nodded. Becky gave hers, and he gave another nod.

"Ella O'Conner."

The guard looked through his tablet then obviously started looking through the list again. "You're not on here."

"She's with us," Bear said. "Trust me, if she was left off the list, it was in error."

Both guards shook their heads.

"The command has come down from God himself, basically. Nobody is allowed inside this hospital unless they are here for medical care or are on the visitation list," the first one said. "I'm sorry, but we have to hold fast on this."

Ella had no idea what to say.

"Ella, let me go down and talk to Uncle Boy. Get you on the list. It's just a mistake," Lilah said.

Ella swallowed the lump in her throat, but it didn't budge. Yes, it was possible that it was a mistake, but what if Colton had specifically said he didn't want to see her? That was an option. How humiliating would it be if Lilah got down there and they told her the same thing.

"Listen, it's fine," Ella said. "You guys go and just keep me updated, all right?"

"No," Becky said. "Let us get this fixed—"

Ella leaned in to her friend so she could whisper. "Maybe Colton doesn't want to see me. I can't take the risk."

Becky reached down and squeezed her hand then she turned and looked at Lilah and Bear. "Ella is going to go home."

Lilah started to argue, but Becky held out a hand firmly. "She's going home. Give her the keys."

Lilah finally nodded and dug the keys out of her pocket, handing them to Ella.

"I'm sorry, El," Bear said. "This really is probably just an error. I know neither Colton nor his parents would leave you off any visitation list on purpose."

Ella forced a smile. "Colton is going to be okay. That's all that matters. Call me if anything changes. I'll see you guys back in Oak Creek."

She turned and walked away before anyone could see the tears falling down her cheeks.

# CHAPTER ELEVEN

*Two months later*

Colton stood leaning against the back wall of his team's conference room at their home base office just outside Denver. It was getting late, but Tony had brought the team together to see the edited footage of last week's paragliding stunt.

Colton watched himself dip and fly through the air, grinning like he didn't have a care in the world, almost as if he were watching a stranger. But he had to admit the camera footage, and what had been done to it in editing, was exceptional. Tony, as always, had known what he was doing and what shots he wanted to get. What shots people would love.

The way everyone in the room cheered as the video ended and the lights came up in the room, Tony had once again done what he did best: make Colton look like a superstar.

"And that's how it's done, people." Tony was grinning from ear to ear at the head of the conference table. Public relations and media were his show; this was his team. Colton was more than happy to let him run with everything. "You all did your job perfectly, and the results were fantastic. Good job."

The team of eight erupted into cheers, hugging and slapping one another on the backs. Tony was right—everyone had done a great job. Another successful stunt in the books.

It wasn't the first since the accident. Colton had done half a dozen televised stunts since the avalanche—rock-climbing, canyoning, BMX biking, kitesurfing, and, most recently, paragliding at dawn from the Makapu'u Cliffs in Hawaii.

All successful.

Hell, he'd even gone snowboarding two weeks after leaving that hospital. Nothing nearly as elaborate as the original stunt off Grand Teton, but enough to prove he wasn't going to let a bunch of snow get the better of him.

"You just wait," Tony announced. "This is going to get a shit-ton of views, and nobody had to almost die for us to go viral."

Everybody cut their eyes over to Colton, and he forced a grin onto his face. "The nobody-has-to-die stunts are quickly becoming my favorite."

Everyone laughed, and Tony dismissed them to get to work posting and preparing for the next event. He walked over to Colton.

"Sorry, boss, that joke too soon?"

Colton thumped him on the shoulder. "It's all good."

And it was all good. Colton hadn't suffered any long-term damage from the avalanche. A slightly sprained wrist and a bunch of bruises, but no broken bones or concussion. Yeah, CPR from his dad had been necessary, but he hadn't had any long-standing effects from that either.

Everything was fine. Better than fine.

Like he'd said: *all good.*

Colton felt his hand begin to tremble and stuck it in his pocket without looking at it. Sweat popped out on his forehead, but he forced himself not to wipe it. He happened to know for a fact that if he ignored the physiological signs of the panic attack waiting to try to overtake him that nobody would notice anything was wrong at all.

Because nobody knew about or expected them. They only knew

Colton showed up for work every day and got shit done. Just like he always had.

He turned away from Tony as the man started talking to someone else, and he walked toward the conference table, breathing in through his nose and out through his mouth.

*One, one thousand.*

*Two, one thousand.*

*There was no snow. There was no dark. There was plenty of air. He was fine. He was fine. He was—*

"You okay, Colton?" Tony asked from behind him.

"Fine." Colton forced the word out, taking a seat, keeping his back to the other man.

If tradition held, nobody would press. All Colton had to do was keep it together enough not to make anyone look too closely. It had worked for two months.

"You sure?" Tony continued. "If we need—"

"Okay. I've got the master calendar like you asked." Sheila Masters, one of the leads of the media team, entered with Rick Wynnsworth muttering behind her.

Rick was kind of an asshole, but at least their entry got Tony's attention off Colton. He clenched his hands in an effort to force the tremors to stop, but it didn't seem to work. Even breathing was becoming an effort at this point.

*Fuck.* He couldn't have a full-on panic attack right here in front of some of his team.

"We're still waiting to hear back from the Taiwanese government about the Taipei 101 stunt, but—"

Colton tried to focus on the words as the three of them discussed something about camera problems and security, but he could barely hear them over the roaring inside his head. The most he could do was nod anytime any of them looked his way.

*This is like a stunt. Breathe through the fear. Breathe through the pain.*

Colton had been facing down fears his whole life. Nobody did the sort of stunts he did without having to figure out how to center themselves in the middle of chaos.

*Do that now.*

Centering himself had never been something he'd actively had to figure out how to do. He'd always merely focused on what was in front of him and silenced the noise of everything else around him.

But how could he silence something that was inside his own mind?

Sheila laughed at something scribbled on to her tablet. Tony said something to Rick and the other man rolled his eyes, but Colton still didn't force himself to figure out the words. Instead, he clenched and unclenched his fists, focusing all his energy into that motion.

Into something he could control.

He did it over and over, until some of the roaring died, his chest easing and allowing more air through.

"What do you think, Colton?"

Colton looked over at Tony. "Yeah, just let me know when and where to be."

The air became thick with awkwardness as Tony, Sheila, and Rick looked at one another and then basically everywhere but at Colton.

He obviously hadn't answered the question correctly.

"Um." Tony cleared his throat. "Rick was telling us there's been another letter."

Colton sat up straighter, trying to salvage the situation. "Right. Sorry. I had the master calendar on my mind and sort of zoned out."

Everybody gave slightly awkward laughs, but it broke the tension in the room at least a little bit.

"Another letter?" Colton asked.

"Your stalker has struck again." Rick wafted a piece of paper in front of him. Colton could smell the perfume even from across the table.

The annoyingly sweet scent clung to the air but at least wiped out the last of the panic from Colton's body. His head cleared, his chest loosened enough for regular breathing, his hands stopped shaking.

For whatever reason, the thought of a stalker was easier to process than everyday life.

"Give me the details," Colton demanded. "Where was it found? Anything unique about this one?"

He could see the relief on Sheila's and Tony's faces that he was finally acting normally as they took seats around the table. Colton had no idea why focusing on a stalker could snap him out of an oncoming panic attack, but he would take it.

Rick perched himself on the table and handed the letter to Colton.

"This was found on your doorstep. Your cleaning lady found it and called the office."

Colton reached up and rubbed the back of his neck. "Lucy knows to do that. It must have come after I left this morning."

But the fact was it could've come at any point after about two a.m. last night. That was when Colton had given up trying to sleep —*again*—and had left his townhouse. He'd gone for a run and then a workout, hoping that would exhaust his body enough to sleep.

It hadn't. Just like it hadn't for the past two months.

So, he'd ended up in the only place that had worked for him to get any sort of decent sleep: his ancient pickup truck.

It seemed to be yet another perk of whatever fuckup his brain was having—only being able to sleep in what had to be the most uncomfortable and least-secure place possible. Go figure.

"There doesn't seem to be anything new with this latest letter," Rick said.

Colton could tell just by glancing at it that Rick was right. Tony stretched out his hand for the letter, and Colton slid it over to him. A few seconds later, the other man had images of the other letters pulled up on his tablet and then displayed on the conference room screens.

"Definitely the same MO as the other letters," Sheila said. "The theme is consistent."

"*You need someone,*" Colton said.

"*I want to be her.*" Tony pointed to another bit of similar phrasing in multiple letters.

"*We'll be together.*" Rick rolled his eyes. "*It's meant to be.* Jesus, if this person is going to go to enough trouble to stalk you, they could at least attempt to be original in some way. What a waste of time and resources. I'd like to find this bitch myself and give her a taste of her own medicine."

Tony held out a hand toward Rick. "Let's keep things professional."

Rick rolled his eyes again.

Tony turned to Colton. "But it might be time to bring in law enforcement. We're now up to six letters in eight weeks, if you count that note from when you were in the hospital."

Rick threw up his hands. "And say what, exactly? That someone has all these lovey-dovey feelings for Colton but no creativity or capacity to say anything even remotely interesting? There's no threat."

Sheila shrugged. "There's no threat until there is a threat. Anybody else see that old movie *Misery*? I hate to think of some woman kidnapping Colton and taking out his knees."

Colton sat back as the discussion about going to the cops continued, interspersed with generally inappropriate comments on occasion from Rick.

But the other man was probably right—at this point, the letters were more of an annoyance than anything else. Besides the fact that this woman was convinced the two of them were soul mates and continually said that she and Colton would be together forever, there wasn't much of a case for stalking.

Even some of the pictures of Colton that had arrived with the letters didn't suggest foul play. It wasn't illegal to take pictures of someone when he was out in public.

Creepy, but not illegal.

Colton stared up at the five letters on the screen, a feeling of detachment falling over him. He didn't care about these letters.

Didn't care about anything. The apathy was the opposite of the panic attacks, but it seemed like those two extremes were his only two ways of existing.

And neither led to anything good.

"Is that okay, Colton?" Tony asked.

Shit. How many times in one day could Colton have no fucking idea what was happening in a conversation he was a part of without everyone figuring out he was *not okay*?

His phone buzzing on the table in front of him saved him. It was Bear. His friend had always had great timing.

"I've got to take this," he told the PR team. It didn't matter that he probably would've said the same thing even if it had been a telemarketer.

Colton pressed the button to receive the video call as he stood and walked toward the conference room door.

"Bear. What's going on? How are you?"

"I had a quiet minute here, so I thought I'd give you a shout. How's everything going?"

Colton could tell Bear was inside the Eagle's Nest, the bar where everyone hung out in Oak Creek. Bear was a damn good mechanic by trade, but he liked picking up a bartending shift here and there, mostly just to interact with everyone.

He had been calling Colton at least once a week since the accident. He knew Colton wasn't at one hundred percent, but Colton hadn't shared how bad things really were. Not even with his closest friend. Not with this family. Not with anyone.

"Just going through some fan mail." Colton ignored both Tony's and Rick's huffs of air. "Everything's good."

He glanced over to find Tony watching him with one eyebrow raised, so Colton turned and walked the rest of the way out the door.

"Really?" Bear asked.

"Hey, fan mail is one of the perks of the trade." Hopefully he could keep Bear focused on that rather than wanting details about reality.

"Since when do you care about fan mail?"

He didn't normally, but he did now. "This one is a whole long brouhaha. I'll have to tell you about it."

Bear narrowed his eyes as he studied Colton but didn't press. Time to change the subject.

"Your camp's coming up in a couple weeks, right? Everything ready for that?"

Bear took the bait. "Mostly. Always more to be done, but the whole town is rallying around this, so I can't complain. Good kids. Good cause. Good activities planned."

His friend was so earnestly invested that it was hard not to be a little jealous. Damned if Colton didn't want something he could be that passionate about.

Although, hell, right now, he would take just not being batshit crazy.

"It's going to be amazing. I know it." That was nothing short of the truth.

"I think so too. I can't wait to get this first group of kids in and then hopefully make this an annual thing."

"I'm sure it will be."

"It's a lot of work, but..." Bear swung his head around. "Shit, we've got a DJ tonight, and he's starting the music back up."

A second later, music was almost all Colton could hear, along with a group of women laughing and talking as they headed out to the dance floor. Over Bear's shoulder, they came into view.

It took less than a second for Colton's focus to zero in on Ella.

She wasn't looking at Bear or his phone; she was talking to her friends and smiling.

That smile. He hadn't seen it since that night in his hotel room two months ago, but he'd definitely thought about it. Thought about her.

Moreover, the only good dreams he could remember since the accident had involved Ella O'Conner. He might've been irritated that she had snuck out after their night together, but his subconscious had been clinging to her like some kind of lifeline.

He watched as she danced with Lilah and Becky, saying something that made both women laugh. Her own soft smile crept over her face.

"Hey, I've been wondering if you need an extra pair of hands getting this first camp set up." The words were out of Colton's mouth before he was even aware he was going to say them.

Bear's eyes widened. "You?"

"Yeah, me. I've got a few weeks with no stunts coming up" — *Colton was a little surprised that Tony didn't stick his head out of the conference room and start screaming at the lie—* "and I'm thinking a little change of pace might be good for me."

Bear glanced over his shoulder at the girls and then turned back to his phone. The other man obviously knew what was going on, but he didn't force the topic.

"We could definitely use your help. Make it out whenever you can, and we'll put you to work. I've got to go, brother. See you soon."

With a wink, Bear was gone.

Colton slipped his phone back into his pocket, trying to wrap his head around what he'd just done. Tony and the team weren't going to be happy, but then again, Tony and the team were on Colton's payroll. They got paid whether he did stunts or not, so they would be fine.

But he needed to get the fuck out of here. Get away from everything.

Ella's smile flashed through his mind. He shouldn't want to see her. She'd snuck out after their sex and then hadn't even come to see him in the hospital.

So, going to Oak Creek would not be about her. It would be about helping a friend launch a project dear to his heart. A good cause. Not about Ella O'Conner at all.

And hopefully Colton could get his own head on straight in the process.

# CHAPTER
# TWELVE

"When you asked if I needed another set of hands last week, this is not what I was expecting, but I'll take it."

Colton reached out his bottle of beer and tapped it against Bear's at his words. They were both sitting leaned back against what would be the final climbing wall of an obstacle course for the kids coming to camp in a few days.

"Honestly, it wasn't what I was thinking of either, but I've had a hell of a time designing and building it."

Colton had arrived in Oak Creek four days ago, leaving almost immediately after hanging up with Bear. He'd gone home, packed his shit, put stuff in his truck and driven to Wyoming. Tony had almost had a fit—if the fourteen thousand messages on Colton's phone were any indication—but Colton didn't care. He hadn't told his team leader or any of his team where he was going. He'd just taken off.

Colton's head was still messed up, he still wasn't sleeping, he barely felt like he was hanging on... But at least if he was going to go down, he would go down here at home. Not that that changed anything.

Being here felt important and right, but he hadn't wanted to let on how much he was struggling. So, when the idea of creating some sort of fun activity for the kids got discussed the first morning Colton arrived, he jumped on the idea of designing a small but challenging obstacle course on the Linear Tactical property.

"You know your parents met on one of these things, right?" Bear asked.

"Oh yeah, I've heard the stories. Maybe at some point, somebody will consider restarting the Wild Wyoming Adventure Race."

"Please, no." Lincoln was walking around rechecking the structural integrity of everything. "You have no idea how many times I've heard the story of my dad's face being trapped in your dad's ass when that rappelling line broke."

Both Bear and Colton chuckled. The rappelling was part of the adventure race that Boy Riley had won multiple times, but in this case, there had been sabotage, and Baby Bollinger, Lincoln's father, had almost died.

Somehow when the story got told now, the danger of plummeting one hundred yards to his death got brushed aside, and Baby made it sound as though Boy Riley's passing gas in his face was the most dangerous part of that day.

"The kids are going to love this," Bear said again as Lincoln continued his study farther back on the course. "And the fact that the great Colton Harrison developed it and will be providing tips on how to best navigate it...that will be icing on the cake."

*The great Colton Harrison.* It was all he could do not to scoff.

"I'm just happy I could be part of creating it."

Colton was even more glad that he could have something on which to focus his attention. Working himself into exhaustion, first with the design and then with building the obstacle course, had kept him busy. And, more importantly, had kept everyone from paying too much attention to the state of his mental health.

He still hadn't gone into town. No one had questioned that either since everyone had been trying to help with the obstacle course and all the other final elements for the camp.

But now, it was done.

"Have you gone to see Ella yet?"

Colton glanced over at Bear, not entirely sure how to respond.

Lincoln saved him, calling out from one of the obstacles. "You know, if we change the angle of this wall, it would allow the rope swing to get greater trajectory when someone jumps and grabs it."

Bear glanced over at Lincoln to see exactly what he was talking about, and Colton took a sip of his beer to hide his sigh of relief. Because he didn't want to answer his friend's question about seeing Ella. Except for the people who had been working on the obstacle course with him, nobody even knew he was in town.

He just wasn't quite sure what he was going to say to anybody, especially Ella. Again, not that he was here to see her anyway.

His hermit-like behavior hadn't been a topic of conversation for anyone or even part of his own thinking because they'd been working from dawn until late in the evening to get this obstacle course ready. But now, that time-filler was done, and he wasn't sure what he was going to do.

Bear got up and walked over to stop their cousin from doing anything drastic like rebuilding the wall, but Colton stayed where he was.

And grimaced as he felt a tremor start once again in his hand.

Goddamn it.

He jumped up to his feet. He could not go through this again. He walked over to where Lincoln was still discussing the pros and cons of a steeper climbing wall and how it would affect the rope swing. Bear was amazingly patient with their cousin, given the fact that if the man had made his concerns known a few days ago during the planning process, there would be no need to rebuild anything now. Not that rebuilding was needed—this wasn't Olympic training; this was just something for the kids to have fun on.

But if they did change the wall, it would at least give Colton another few hours of something to do.

"Actually, Lincoln may have a point." Colton thumped his fist on the climbing wall. "It won't take very long for us to rebuild this at a steeper angle."

Bear's eyes grew wide. "Are you kidding me? You're actually agreeing to this? My to-do list is already ten thousand items long, it's eight p.m., and we've been working on this for three days straight."

"Yeah, but—"

"No." Bear's tone brooked no refusal. "There's plenty of other stuff that still needs to be done before the kids get here in a few days."

Colton knew he was right, but damn it. "Are you sure?"

Bear looked like he might actually take a swing at him. Colton couldn't blame his friend. He knew he was being unreasonable. Lincoln was pretty much always unreasonable, so that was understandable. But Colton wasn't usually in the crazy camp with him.

"Are you messing with me right now?" Bear asked.

Colton forced a smile onto his face. "Yeah. Of course I am. I'll stop."

"Good. Because I expect this sort of stuff from Linc, but there's no need to encourage him. This course is amazing just as it is, and the kids are going to love it. Now, I'm going home by way of the Eagle's Nest for a bite to eat first. Anyone interested?"

Colton knew he should rip off the Band-Aid and head into town. See everyone and get it out of the way. But he couldn't when he was walking such a fine line and didn't have control of his body the way he wanted.

"Rain check for me. I'm going to make it an early night."

Bear was distracted enough not to push it. "Lincoln?"

"Yeah, I'll meet you there in a few minutes."

Bear shook his head. "So help me God, if you guys rebuild this climbing wall…" He didn't finish the threat as he walked toward his car, looking down at his clipboard with the never-ending checklist.

Bear's car hadn't even started before Lincoln said, "I estimate that we could rebuild this in just under six-and-a-half hours if it's just you and me working on it. Roughly three hours and forty-five minutes if we can find a third person."

Colton held up a hand to stop Lincoln before he continued with exact estimates for how long it would take with five people, six, seven... No doubt he'd already done all the calculations in his computer of a mind.

"I don't think rebuilding is necessary." Although he was tempted. "Like Bear said, the kids are going to love it just as it is. Plus, if we're up half the night working on this, Bear will never let us hear the end of it tomorrow."

Lincoln continued to study the climbing wall for a few more seconds before turning to Colton and nodding. "Yes, Bear will be upset. And I do understand that there are more important things to do than this."

But the tightness around Lincoln's lips indicated he obviously didn't like it. Colton slapped him on the shoulder with a chuckle. "The kids will never know."

Lincoln's jaw clenched. "But I'll know, and I'll have to live with it."

That was obviously a line that had been said to his cousin over and over during his life. Colton wasn't surprised.

"That and the fact that I am not allowed to teach hacking skills to the children next week. Which is ridiculous. Understanding certain hacking principles will do nothing but help make them less susceptible to being hacked."

Colton laughed at the despondency in Linc's voice. "You going to catch a bite to eat with Bear?"

"Yes. I enjoy the chicken potpie the Eagle's Nest has on weekend nights. You are not going to come?"

Colton shook his head. "Nah. I'm not very hungry."

Lincoln was still studying the wall. "Ah, I misunderstood. I thought it might be because of your abnormal physiological reactions to seemingly temperate events throughout the day. Are you ill?"

Colton froze. Nobody else had noticed him trying to keep his crazy under control. But Lincoln, who had difficulty reading the simplest of nonverbal cues, had picked up on it—or at least the physical reactions his body was having. Fortunately, the other man was unable to put together that it was panic attacks.

"I think maybe I'm coming down with something. But I'll be fine. I just need rest."

Lincoln looked over at him and then nodded. "Rest is good for illness. The body is more able to heal itself when it is fully rested."

If Colton could manage to get a good night's sleep, maybe his fucked-up brain would start healing itself.

Maybe not.

"I'll catch you tomorrow, Linc."

Colton walked toward his truck, not wanting to say much else to Lincoln, lest he put together what was actually happening. He got into his truck and drove it toward the bunkhouse. He didn't know why he was staying here rather than at the place his parents still owned just outside of town.

Actually, he did. As soon as his parents found out he was staying in town, he had no doubt they'd be coming for a visit. He'd been avoiding them for good chunks of two months—only talking to them enough that they didn't initiate some sort of intervention. He wasn't ready to see them yet here.

As long as they thought he was on the road focusing on work, they wouldn't get too concerned. But if they knew he was here, they'd swoop in. He was also thankful his brother Tucker had been sent on some extended mystery mission overseas and wasn't around. Tucker tended to be a jokester, but hiding what was going on from him would've been nearly impossible.

That was the problem with being too close to your family—they figured things out damned quickly.

He parked his truck outside the tiny cabin Theo had given him to use, not that he'd been there very much. Hell, he didn't want to go in there now either. The dark looked stifling, and he knew sitting there with his own thoughts was only going to lead to a long night.

He tapped the hood of his truck as he walked by. "See you soon."

No doubt, he would be sleeping out here if he even slept at all.

# CHAPTER
# THIRTEEN

Ella wanted everything in this test kitchen to be perfect when the kids arrived in a few days.

She stood on her tiptoes to pull down a set of containers from the high counter so she could add flour to each one. That would save time when she taught the fundamentals of baking class next week.

Maybe her subject wasn't quite as invigorating or important as the other things the kids would be learning—like wilderness survival and basic automotive mechanics—but baking was still fun.

This test kitchen had been built out of one of the old houses on the Linear Tactical property last year. It contained six different work counters, complete with sinks, and just as many ovens and stovetops.

So far, it had been used by some of the therapists who brought clients out to the property, but this was the first time it would be used by Ella. She wanted everything to be perfect.

Thus, being here at nearly midnight to do more setup, when she had to be back at her shop at five a.m. At least the crazy hour gave her time to talk to her sister on the phone while she worked.

"But thank God for no more morning sickness."

Jess let out a huge, dramatic sigh, a standard response from her sister. "That's the truest thing anyone has ever said. I'm glad the National Science Board didn't send us out here during my first trimester."

"But you will definitely be home from Romania before this baby gets here, right? You know Mom and Dad will charter a plane and fly you home if they think you are anywhere close to giving birth."

Jess was a genius in every sense of the word and was a world-renowned biotechnology scientist. She was sent to all sorts of conferences and think tanks all over the planet. Had been doing this sort of thing since she was in her early teens.

"Ethan talks to Dad nearly every damn day. This baby isn't due for another two months, and I'm only scheduled to be here three weeks. But trying to convince either of them that the math is not worrisome is impossible."

Ella let out a low chuckle at the frustration in her sister's voice. "Ethan has always been protective of you, sis. I've heard all those stories about when you guys were kids and, even then, how protective he was."

"Oh, I know. And if he was protective before, it's a hundred times worse now. I thought Ethan was going to break some guy's arm because he accidentally bumped into me in a crowded elevator."

Ella stopped organizing the containers for a second. "Wow, that doesn't sound like Ethan. He's always so cool under pressure." Always had been. The calm yin to her sister's rather wild yang.

"It's the baby, I'm telling you. And I'm not going to lie... Ethan all aggressive is pretty sexy."

"You think Ethan is sexy, no matter what."

Jess chuckled. "Yes, that's true. And we both know there's someone you think is sexy no matter what, also."

Ella hadn't told her sister about what had happened with Colton. Under normal circumstances, she would've, but that night had gotten pushed to the wayside in light of the avalanche.

She knew he was back in town—Oak Creek was too small for her not to have heard the rumors. But she'd kept her head down, filling her hours between Fancy Pants and getting this test kitchen set up.

The one thing she'd always found true was the more she worked, the less time she had to sit around and think about Colton Harrison.

And she knew if she stopped working now, the very first thing she'd be thinking about was the fact that he'd been in town for at least a few days and hadn't made any effort to contact her at all. That pretty much told her all she needed to know, didn't it?

As if his refusal to let her into the hospital room that day hadn't told her enough.

"Pity fuck," she murmured under her breath without thinking.

"Did you just use the F-word? I'm gonna tell Mom."

Ella chuckled. Jess had never once told on Ella in her life. Ella could've murdered someone right in front of her sister, and Jess wouldn't tell a soul—would just help her figure out how to best hide the body.

"I just realized I was going to have to climb up on the counter to get to some of the items I need. This is what happens with the entire kitchen design team is over six feet. They needed supervision. Thus, the use of the F-word."

With her sister suitably distracted, Ella dragged a chair over to the counter so she could step up onto it and then open the highest cabinet.

"You've been listening to me talk for an hour. What's going on with you?"

Ella slid a set of bowls out of the way. Jess would be homing in on Colton soon. "I like listening to you talk. Plus, you live that jet-setter lifestyle I like to live through vicariously."

Ella had been to plenty of places when they'd been growing up. The whole family had traveled with her dad for his concert tours, and then they'd gone with Jess for some of her conferences when she was young.

While Ella liked to travel, Oak Creek was always where she'd wanted to be.

"You're a good listener for everyone, little sis. But your life is just as important as anyone else's."

"You know me, I'm good. It's a busy week between the shop, individual baking orders, and setting up for the camp."

"I was wondering why you were calling me at nearly midnight your time."

Ella winced. She should've known that her sister would quickly figure out the time difference. "Just trying to get everything done. And wanted to hear your voice since you are one of the smartest people on the planet."

"More importantly, I am sister to the wonderful Ella O'Conner."

Ella smiled. "And don't forget mother to my little niece or nephew. So, let your husband be overprotective and get home safe in a few weeks."

They talked a few more minutes before Jess had to head off to an early-morning meeting there in Romania. Ella disconnected the call on her watch and was about to get down from the counter when she realized she needed one more set of bowls.

She opened another cabinet and muttered a curse when she saw the ones she needed were along the far wall. She studied the far cabinet door, estimating her reach. It would be a stretch, but she could reach it. It would be easier than getting down, dragging the chair over there, and going back up.

She stretched, going up on her tiptoes, and realized almost immediately that she'd made a mistake as she began to lose her balance. She was going to fall.

Shit. This was going to hurt. She tried to twist so that her arm and shoulder could take the brunt of the impact, but it wasn't as easily done as thought.

Her entire body tensed as she closed her eyes, bracing for a crash into the floor, but it didn't come. Instead, a set of arms stopped her fall.

She blinked her eyes open, completely unable to believe that it was Colton holding her.

"That was not a good idea," he said.

She was so shocked that she just blinked up at him. "What are you doing here?"

"Evidently, saving you from cracking your head open."

He was still holding her in his arms. She squirmed. "Put me down. I'm too heavy."

The sound that came out of his mouth could not be called anything less than a scoff. "Please. You are insulting both of us. I could hold these gorgeous curves of yours for an hour without breaking a sweat."

They locked eyes. Honestly, Colton looked as surprised that he'd said that as she did hearing it.

But yet, he still didn't put her down.

"Are you okay?" he finally asked.

She nodded. "I was trying to get some bowls. I lost my balance."

He nodded too. "I saw that part. That would've been a hard fall."

"You're right. Thank you. I should've been more careful."

He slowly let her down to the floor. She couldn't help but be aware of how their bodies touched the entire way.

As soon as her feet were on the floor, she backed away. No doubt all this chemistry was just in her mind. She was not letting herself go there again.

"What are you doing here, Colton?" There was a bite to her voice, one she rarely used, but she couldn't help it.

"Here in Oak Creek, or here in this building?"

She shrugged and turned back toward the counter so that she could set out the bowls the way they were needed. She'd go ahead and get that done since she'd risked her life to get them.

"Both, I guess. I heard you were in town…" But he didn't come see her and hadn't made any effort to reach out, so she assumed he didn't want to talk to her at all.

"Yeah." He cleared his throat slightly. "I haven't left Linear Tactical property since I got here. I got some bright idea about building an obstacle course for the kids' camp, and that has basically filled my time twenty-four seven."

She didn't look at him. "Understandable."

"I'm telling the truth, Butterscotch."

She looked over to find him standing much closer than she'd expected. Once again, he looked about as surprised at what he'd said as she was to hear it.

"And Oak Creek is my hometown too. Maybe I just needed to be here for a while."

She closed her eyes and rubbed the center of her forehead. She was being unfair. The man had almost died just two months ago. *Had* died, if you considered that Boy Riley had done CPR on his son.

"Of course it is. You're right."

She looked over at him and felt even worse. He looked great—Colton always looked great—but also, he looked...*off*. "Are you okay?"

He tensed just slightly, but she saw it. "What do you mean?"

He *wasn't* okay. She wasn't sure how she knew that, but she did. But his being off could have to do with a number of things, including general awkwardness, given their personal situation. So she didn't want to read too much into it.

"I guess I mean, why are you in a test kitchen at midnight? That seems out of the norm for you, so are you okay?"

That wasn't what she'd meant, but it at least made sense.

"I'm staying over at one of the cabins and saw the lights on here and thought I'd better check it out."

"Oh." That made sense, although she hadn't thought this building could be seen from any of the cabins.

"What are *you* doing here at this hour?" he continued.

"I'm teaching a few classes for the kids' camp and wanted to make sure everything was ready."

"At midnight?"

She shrugged. "It was the only time I had today. And I know Bear has his hands full with everything else, so I assured him I'd take care of all this myself so he didn't have to worry about it."

"I don't think Bear would want you to be working at midnight."

"I don't mind." She poured a set amount of baking powder into each of the bowls. "And everyone's been working long hours, but it's for a good cause."

"Yes, it is."

He was closer. Just like at the hotel, he'd moved without her hearing him and was now right behind her. She kept her focus on the containers in front of her, measuring and then remeasuring when she forgot how much she'd already put in one bowl.

"I know Bear is glad to have you here. I haven't made it to that side of the property yet, but I heard about the obstacle course."

"We finished it tonight."

Why was he so *close*? "That's good. Just in the nick of time."

"Why, Butterscotch?"

She had to dump out her measured baking powder for the third time. There was no way she could do anything when he was this close.

"Why what?" Her voice was a squeak.

"Why did you sneak off that night while I was sleeping?"

She spun and found him as close as she'd known he'd be. She'd thought facing him would be easier.

It wasn't.

Even worse was that he actually looked a little hurt. As if what had happened between them had been something real.

She shook her head. "Why did I leave? I think the real question is, why did you invite me to your room to begin with?"

One dark eyebrow rose. "I thought we both wanted something to happen between us. What I didn't think was that you were a trophy hunter."

"A *what*?"

He shrugged. "I'm somewhat famous. I know there are women who get off on spending the night with any sort of celebrity. I just didn't think you were one of them."

She couldn't believe what she was hearing. "*What?*"

He shrugged again. "I thought we were friends. Even if you

weren't interested in pursuing anything beyond that night, it felt pretty shitty for you to just sneak out while I was sleeping."

She blinked up at him. "Do you really not remember what you said to me right before you drifted off for your nap?"

"I remember that you'd blown my mind and saying I couldn't wait for a round two."

Was he telling the truth? Was that really all he remembered? Nothing about Lincoln revealing that she was basically a sure thing?

Colton eased just the slightest bit closer, a predatory look coming into his brown eyes. "Was it not as good for you? Hell, I'm nowhere near God's gift to women, but I don't usually have complaints. If it wasn't good, we could've tried again—or tried *something else*—right away. You didn't have to sneak out."

Without a doubt, he'd already thought about what the *something else* could be. Her throat went dry. "I— No. It's not that it wasn't good. It was amazing. But I…"

She let the sentence fade off. She didn't want to bring up what she'd thought that night. There was no way she could force the words *pity fuck* out of her mouth in front of him.

"Explain it to me, Butterscotch. Explain why you left when I wanted you again so badly."

"I…"

He was going to kiss her. And she wanted it. Even as she knew it was the biggest possible mistake she could make, she still wanted it.

She would never not want to kiss Colton.

He eased in, lips skimming against her temple. "At least give me the chance to show you round two now."

She felt his breath against her cheekbone then down her jaw. This was a bad idea. She'd been depressed for weeks after what happened last time. Letting it happen again would just lead her back to that. She'd lose the ground she'd fought so hard to gain.

But she knew she wasn't going to stop Colton. She'd never been able to make herself keep distance from him.

He circled her hips with his hands and drew her closer. She tried to block out the fact that she'd gained five pounds since he'd last seen her—feeding her depression, even though she knew better.

"Colton, I—"

"Let me kiss you, Butterscotch."

As if she was going to say no to kisses or anything else from him. "Yes."

But his lips didn't even make it to her before the door opened, startling them both.

Two men walked in, giving Colton a friendly wave.

"Hey, boss," one of them said. "We've been looking all over for you."

# CHAPTER
# FOURTEEN

THE NEXT MORNING, Colton sat at the Frontier Diner across from Tony and Rick. He'd gotten over the urge to strangle them both after they'd walked in on him and Ella at the most inopportune moment the night before.

"You shouldn't have left without telling us where you'd be." Tony took a bite of his pancakes. "You know we'll work with you and help with whatever you need, but we lost two days thinking you were just hiding out in your townhouse."

"Which would definitely be better than here," Rick interjected. "I looked up one-horse town, and lo and behold, it was a picture of Oak Creek. What can there possibly be to do around here besides watch the grass grow?"

"Shut up, Rick." Tony shot a look at the other man. "This is his hometown."

Rick rolled his eyes. "What? I'm just saying it's small and in the middle of nowhere."

Tony gritted his teeth, obviously about to lay into Rick, but Colton held out a hand to stop him and then took a sip of his coffee. He was well aware that to people outside of Oak Creek, the charm and appeal could be lost.

"You guys know me," he said. "Sometimes I need space. We didn't have anything on the schedule, so I just took off."

Tony cut into another bite of pancake. "I get it, but now's not a great time to disappear. We want to capitalize on your uptick in popularity since the avalanche. Continue to use it for growth and get you to the next level."

"I had plenty of followers before the avalanche, and to be honest, I'm not interested in those who just started to follow me because they are tragedy-chasers. That's not what we're all about."

Tony nodded. "I know that, but if we are able to convert some of those people into true fans, then we can double your base and have even more options available to us. Hell, man…films, TV series. Next-level stuff."

And none of that interested Colton even the slightest bit. For him, doing stunts had always been about the love of the outdoors and pitting himself against nature. He'd been very blessed that he could make a living doing that, but making himself into some sort of social media superstar had never been his goal.

"I haven't taken a break since the accident. I'm taking one now."

Rick scrunched up his face so much he looked like a cartoon character. "Here? You're going to take a break *here*? Why don't you take a break in Rio or on an island in Fiji or, hell, somewhere that has an actual chain restaurant rather than this diner."

Now, Colton was starting to get a little bit offended.

But before he could say anything, Tony slid Rick's plate away from him and stood so the other man could get out of the booth. "Why don't you go inventory the equipment we brought with us, Rick?"

Rick made a face. "Dude, we only brought like three cameras and some basic editing stuff."

Tony gestured toward the door. "Then you should be able to count it multiple times and think about how not to be an asshole while doing it."

Rick muttered under his breath as he slid out of the seat and walked toward the door. Tony sat back down, shaking his head.

"Sorry. Rick is a hell of a cameraman but obviously not much when it comes to tact."

"Thanks for getting him out of here before I had to do it myself."

"He's just young and stupid."

"As I once was myself." Colton held up his coffee cup in salute to Tony.

"Same, my friend." The other man picked up his water glass and clinked Colton's cup. "Also, Rick is a little stressed about the stalker situation. Another reason you probably shouldn't have just run off. You got another letter, and then no one knew exactly where you were."

Shit. He hadn't thought about how this whole stalker thing might affect his absence for everyone else. Generally speaking, he'd always been able to just get up and go for a couple of days whenever he wanted to, and as long as there hadn't been a stunt scheduled, nobody cared.

"I'm sorry if I worried you or anybody else. That wasn't my intent. Was there anything different or special about the letter that came?"

Tony took out his tablet and spun it around so Colton could see a picture of it.

"Not much, except for the fact that it was twice in one week. And, unless I'm mistaken, her phrasing is starting to get a little stronger."

Colton nodded while he read. "A little more desperate."

"Exactly."

---

*My dearest Colton,*

*I dream of you nearly every night now. And thank God every day that you are alive. I know that's true because we are supposed to meet and because we will be together forever.*

*It won't be long now. I can feel it, can't you? I wonder if you dream of me also. You do, don't you? That's the way it's meant to be.*

*I can't wait until we can hold each other forever. One lifetime isn't enough with you. But it's a start.*

---

"There's still no threat." Colton handed Tony back his tablet. "Creepy as fuck, but still no threat."

"Drenched in the same perfume and placed outside the office doors this time."

Colton grimaced. "She's doing her research. Finding out more about me."

"I'm not sure whether to be truly worried, but I think you should watch your back. And definitely don't take anyone you don't know back to your hotel room."

"I don't plan on it, but not necessarily just because of the stalker." There was only one person he wanted to consider taking back to his room, and she definitely wasn't a stranger.

"Because of Ella O'Conner."

"You know about her?"

Tony shrugged. "I saw the way you two were talking at the wedding reception. Plus, I heard rumors. And then last night…"

"I'm not sure exactly how things stand between her and me."

"But she's part of the reason you're here."

Very definitely, but he wasn't going to get into that with the other man. Time to change the subject.

"I know we want to capitalize on…everything." Tony would probably want to post about Colton's panic attacks on social media if he knew about them. "But I've got a friend who's starting a camp for kids, and I'd like to be here to help him get this first one off the ground."

Colton explained some of the details behind the camp.

Tony's eyes lit up. "Actually, that sounds amazing and would be something your fans would love to see. Why don't we film it?"

"No." Colton didn't even have to think about it. He'd already offered to use any of his media clout to help with fundraising or awareness, but that hadn't been what Bear wanted. This was about a group of kids getting attention that they never did in day-to-day life. Bringing in a crew, and to record Colton with the kids, would be no different from the normal lives they led with their siblings getting so much time and attention.

"I get your hesitancy, but it could be tasteful." Tony gripped the table. "We could show how you were getting to know the kids and how important they are too."

"Not this time, Tony. I know you mean well, but no."

Tony sat back, crossing his arms over his chest. "Okay, you're the boss. And, you're right, you deserve a break. Maybe a week here will refill the well for you. I'll make sure this whole week is clear."

"Actually, let's go ahead and clear the whole month."

Tony raised an eyebrow. "A month? That's a long time to go without any sort of new stunt. It's going to affect popularity ratings."

Colton didn't care. "Then we'll just have to replay some stuff from past stunts. And honestly, I'm not sure when I'm coming back."

Despite Tony's grimace, it felt good to say those words out loud. A month would be much longer than the camp, but it might be just the right amount of time to see if what was happening with Ella was something real.

He'd been on his way outside to sleep in his truck again when he'd seen the lights on in that building. He hadn't had anything better to do than to go turn them off—no need to waste electricity.

He hadn't expected to find Ella inside that test kitchen. And he definitely hadn't expected not to be able to keep his hands off her.

He shouldn't want her after what had happened between them that night she'd snuck out, but that hadn't seemed to matter to his libido one bit.

Even now, he had to be thankful he was sitting down so no one could see what sort of physical reaction he was having to the thought of touching her last night. Of catching those soft curves as she fell. Of breathing in the scent of her skin right before a kiss that was interrupted.

"Does all this have to do with Ella?"

Colton reached back and rubbed his neck, wishing his fingers were touching Ella's skin instead.

"It has to do with a lot of things. But mostly, it has to do with helping kids who deserve it. That's why I'm here, and that's what I want to concentrate on."

It was definitely true that those kids deserved it, and it was even true that he wanted to give them the attention they deserved.

He wanted to help them.

And if he happened to get to spend as much time as he wanted with Ella O'Conner in the process, even better.

# CHAPTER
# FIFTEEN

"I don't think I was ever this quiet and well-behaved my entire life."

Bear chuckled and looked up from his clipboard. "Well, we've always been rowdy, so no surprise there."

They looked around at the twelve boys and girls between the ages of ten and fourteen who had arrived for the camp. They were truly so well-behaved, it was a little unnerving. Polite, quiet, and respectful.

"Our parents used to send us to camp because they wanted a little peace and quiet." Colton shook his head. "And we just got wilder once we arrived there. These kids could do a workshop on politeness and maturity. Honestly, I'm a little intimidated."

Bear chuckled again. "This is the very reason why I wanted to have a camp for these particular kids. Some of them have spent their whole lives in the shadow of their terminally ill sibling. And instead of acting out to get attention, they just learn to be muted and take up as little space as possible so that their parents don't have to worry about one more thing."

"That makes them pretty damn amazing."

Bear nodded. "That was exactly why I wanted to do the camp."

The campers had shown up right after lunch, politely and

calmly said goodbye to their parents and then maturely waited to be told what to do.

Today, they were highlighting many stations, giving the kids a taste of what they would be doing for the next ten days. Becky and Eva, since they were both vets, had shown them the different therapy animals used at Linear Tactical—everything from horses to rabbits and even a llama that had been acquired in the past few months.

Admittedly, that had almost gotten a kid-like reaction out of the campers.

Lilah and Theo, both of whom worked at Linear, talked about wilderness survival and what they'd be learning—how to make shelters, how to start a fire, and even how to track wild animals.

Lincoln was going to be teaching anyone who was interested about coding—mumbling under his breath the whole time about no hacking. A couple of kids were obviously going to gravitate to him. Bear was going to teach them basic mechanics. The tiny adults had appreciated the usefulness of that also.

And Ella had brought treats around for everyone. Not cupcakes or cookies as one would expect for this age group, but perfectly designed macarons in different colors and flavors. When she told them they'd be learning how to make these, quite a few of them had definitely perked up.

Colton wasn't sure exactly how to relate to these kids, but Ella didn't have that problem at all. She basically sat down in the middle of them and incorporated herself into their little circle as they ate. At first, they'd kept their distance, but Ella hadn't let that deter her. She just stayed there and kept talking to them. She hadn't demanded anything, hadn't tried to be cool, hadn't tried to fit in unnaturally.

She'd just been Ella, and the kids had responded to her authenticity. Colton wasn't surprised at all.

Bear's phone chimed, and he looked down at it. "Perfect timing. Now, we get to show these kids a little excitement."

That meant Bear's brother Derek was on his way with the helicopter. They hadn't wanted to mention it to the kids as a possibility until they were sure that the Teton Helitak crew wouldn't be in the middle of an emergency, making the helicopter unavailable. These kids had probably been disappointed enough over the course of their lives with plans and activities constantly having to change due to their siblings' illnesses.

But there would be no canceled plans today. Derek and the helicopter were on their way.

"We'll split the kids into three groups so they can all have window views. I'll catch you later."

Clipboard in hand, Bear headed toward the Linear Tactical helicopter pad.

Colton walked back toward where the kids were still going through the multiple stations. They'd decided to keep the obstacle course as a surprise for later in the week. So today, he was moral and physical support as needed—as a matter of fact, he was wearing a ball cap pulled low on his head in an effort to blend in and not be recognized. Not that any of these kids were likely to be extreme sports fans anyway.

Not being recognized wasn't a problem for Colton. It was refreshing.

He spotted one of the campers standing over by himself near the snack table and went to talk to him—a boy, early teens.

"Hey. You over here picking up more of the macarons?" Colton asked the boy. "In my book, that makes you the smartest person out here."

The kid studied Colton with serious eyes. "They are good. I'm looking forward to learning how to make them."

"Is baking your thing?"

The kid shrugged, looking out at the rest of the campers. "I haven't really done much baking, but my little sister would really like all the different colors. So, I'd like to learn how to make them."

"Your little sister—she sick?"

The kid nodded. "Leukemia."

Damn. "That sucks. I'm sorry. But you know, the next ten days is supposed to be about you enjoying yourself and not having to worry so much about your sister."

He shrugged. "Maybe. But that doesn't change the fact that she's still going to have leukemia when I get back, and if I can do anything that helps take her mind off that for a little while, I'll do it."

Shit. This kid was more mature than most adults Colton knew. Being the sibling of a terminally ill child caused someone to grow up quickly.

"I'm Colton."

"Marshall. And yeah, I know who you are. I recognized you right away. I'm a huge fan."

Colton raised an eyebrow at him. "No offense, kid, but you don't act like a huge fan. I met quite a few of those, and they tend to be a lot more ridiculous and obnoxious."

Marshall shrugged again, looking more like a forty-year-old than a kid. "Honestly, there's not a lot of room in my life for ridiculous and obnoxious."

"How old are you? Thirteen?"

"Fourteen."

Kid was fucking fourteen years old. At that age, Colton and his brother Tucker had still been playing outside and almost blowing themselves up with fireworks. Their biggest concerns had been whether they could talk their mom into letting them have two desserts and whether girls thought they were cute.

"Well, Marshall, I'm honored that you know who I am. Maybe we can spend some time together this week. Sometimes fans have questions about some of my stunts, and I'd be happy to answer anything for you or maybe teach you some things if you're interested."

Marshall's eyes lit up for a second, the first age-appropriate response Colton had seen. "Yeah, okay. I mean...if it works out. I know sometimes things don't work out."

Kid was obviously used to disappointment. "How about we make sure it works out?"

Marshall nodded, but Colton could tell he was still slightly skeptical. He'd obviously learned to manage his expectations at a young age.

They both took another of the bright cookies and turned to look as the helicopter appeared in the distance, making its way closer. Marshall studied it silently until it became obvious it was going to be landing nearby.

"Is someone being evacuated?" Marshall asked.

Of course that's what he would think. Probably the only time the kid had ever seen a helicopter was when it was medically transporting someone.

"Nope. That's Derek Bollinger. He's Bear's brother and one hell of a pilot. He works for a helitak team. Do you know what that is?"

Marshall shook his head, eyes still glued to the helicopter.

"Basically, search and rescue and firefighting. They do a little bit of everything."

"That's so cool."

*Finally.* Finally, the kid was acting like a kid.

"Derek's not here to do any sort of rescue or transport. He's here to take you guys up in the helicopter."

Marshall's eyes got big. "Really?"

"Yep. And you better strap in, because I'm sure Derek's going to show you some of the rescue moves he has to do sometimes."

"That's awesome! I'm going to go ahead and get in line." He started to run off but then stopped and turned back to Colton. "Unless you needed to talk to me about anything else."

Colton grinned. "Not at all. You and I can touch base later. Right now, go do some really cool shit."

The corners of Marshall's mouth rose at the curse word, just like Colton had hoped they would. Kid needed to learn how to be a kid.

As he ran off, Colton knew he had a new mission in front of him: helping Marshall let loose over the next ten days.

It didn't take long for the rest of the kids to figure out that the helicopter was for them too. The excitement was contagious. Colton and the other adults helped get them situated. He looked over and found Ella grinning from ear to ear. She wasn't the least bit offended that riding in a helicopter was more exciting than her macarons.

Although Colton would've chosen the macarons if he had to choose.

Her green eyes met his before quickly looking away. That had been happening all day. She was keeping her distance but, like him, couldn't ignore this spark between them.

It was there, and it wasn't going away.

Between that and working with the kids, he realized his system felt calmer than it had since the accident. No shaky hands. No feeling like the pressure on his chest would stop him from breathing.

He wasn't focusing on himself, and that felt really fucking good.

Right up to the point where Tony and Rick showed up on the Linear Property. Immediately, tension flooded Colton's body. He beelined toward their car.

"Was I unclear about something last night? Today is not about me or filming or fans." He pointed over at the last set of kids, including Marshall, who were getting into the helicopter. "I thought you guys were going back to Denver."

Tony shook his head. "We are, I promise. We stopped by your cabin to drop off some stuff so you would have it."

Now, Colton felt like a jerk. "I'm sorry. I should've asked what you were doing here rather than just assume. I just don't want to make today about me."

And damned if his hand wasn't starting to tremble just slightly.

"It's not like this would be very exciting to film anyway," Rick muttered. "Kids petting horses and going for a ride in a helicopter isn't exactly going to go viral."

Tony ignored the younger man. "When we went by the cabin, there was a problem."

"What? Look, whatever that place lacks in luxury doesn't matter to me. I'll handle it. It's not something you need to worry about."

The cabin was simple, containing only the very basics. No TV, no computer. But Colton didn't care. And while he wouldn't expect his team to live that way, he had no problem with it. Liked it, actually. He might be used to certain luxury, but there was something satisfying about living much more simply.

"Unfortunately, it was another letter from the stalker," Tony said. "It was on the door of your cabin."

Now, they definitely had his attention. "What? How the hell did that woman know I was here?"

"I don't know, but she does," Tony replied.

Rick slapped him on the back. "And now, it's starting to look like she's pissed. So, you better watch your back."

Colton looked between the two other men. "How do you know she's pissed?"

Tony crossed his arms over his chest, his face pinched. "Because this one contained a picture of you and had a knife stuck through it."

# CHAPTER
# SIXTEEN

CALLUM WEBB HAD BEEN the sheriff in Oak Creek for as long as Colton could remember. He'd worked with Ian DeRose and Zodiac Tactical—stories Colton had heard all his life—before moving here.

He'd had a wife at some point, but she had died. Colton had been a self-involved adolescent at the time, so he couldn't remember much in terms of details, but he thought it was cancer.

The man had always been *grumpy Sheriff Webb* to Colton. The one he and his friends had to keep an eye out for when they were planning stuff as teens they knew would get them into trouble. Hell, Callum had been the one who had delivered Colton and Bear back to their parents when they'd gotten caught underage drinking.

All half dozen times.

In Colton's mind, Callum had rarely been more than a one-dimensional law enforcement figure. Someone set in place to keep all others from having any fun.

But looking at him now as they studied this new letter from the stalker, Colton realized Callum wasn't one-dimensional at all. That vision of him had been Colton keeping the older man trapped in the past—filtering him through a child's eyes.

Hell, Callum wasn't even that much older than Colton. He'd

always assumed that Callum was his parents' age, but really, the man split the difference in the Oak Creek generations. There was no way he was any older than his midforties.

"So, this is the first time there has ever been a knife. That means something, right?" Rick asked, pacing back and forth excitedly. The younger man might have been hesitant to bring in law enforcement before, but now that the sheriff was here, Rick had all sorts of stuff to say. He pretty much hadn't stopped talking since Callum had arrived.

"Like a... What is it called...?" Rick continued. "You know, when things are getting worse and worse."

"Escalation," Callum muttered without looking at Rick.

Rick snapped three times and then pointed his fingers at Callum. "Yes, exactly! The stalker is obviously escalating. I have a lot of theories. Maybe it's someone who knows Colton. Right? An ex-girlfriend or something. That would make sense. Or—"

Callum stepped back from his study of the note that was pinned to the door with the knife.

"Nick—"

"Rick," the other man corrected, "but it's cool, man."

Callum gave a tight nod. "Rick. Look, you've obviously given this a good deal of thought."

Rick nodded, fairly buzzing with excitement. "Yeah, I have. I really have."

Callum slapped him on the shoulder. "I need someone like you, someone who has really thought through this situation, to be a sort of unofficial deputy for me. Do you think you're up for that?"

Rick's eyes got wide. "Yes. Yes, sir. I definitely am."

"That's good to hear. I'm wondering, since you're so close with this case, if you'd be willing to walk around the property and look for anything out of place. The stalker had to get here somehow and maybe left a clue that could help us. Would you be willing to scour the area and look for anything you think might be of any importance?"

Rick took a step back, still nodding. "Absolutely. You can count on me. Do you, like, need to swear me in or anything?"

Callum shook his head. "I don't think that's necessary for this. And I don't want to waste time. Time is of the essence, right?"

"Yes, sir. Yes, it is. I'm going to start right now."

Rick bounded off the porch.

"Be thorough and methodical," Callum called out. "Start very far back and work your way slowly closer."

"Yes, sir!" Rick didn't slow down as he said it, running around the back of the house.

Callum crossed his arms over his chest once Rick was out of earshot. "Okay, now we can try to figure out what's going on here."

Colton chuckled. "You got rid of him on purpose."

Callum shrugged. "That kid has way too much energy, and I need to think."

"Why didn't you just tell him to get lost?" Tony asked.

"Kill two birds with one stone. Maybe he'll actually find something useful. You never know."

The older man was astute, Colton had to give him that.

"Is that what you were doing that time Mrs. Boyd's dog got lost, and we all wanted to help you find it?" Colton could remember Callum lining them up and assigning them all sections of town to search.

"Did we find the dog?"

"Yeah."

Callum grinned and looked years younger. "Then I stand by my methods."

They all turned back to the embedded note on the door, much more serious.

"I don't want to make a big deal out of this, Sheriff," Colton said. "Not right now, not while the camp is going on. Those kids are what is important."

"Understood. This has nothing to do with them, and the Linear Tactical property is expansive enough that there shouldn't be an issue."

"Rick was right about one thing he said." Tony pulled his ever-present digital notebook up so Callum could see it. "There have been multiple letters, and this really does seem like an escalation."

Callum took a moment to look through the copies of the letters on the tablet. Then he turned his attention back to the note.

"First of all, just because the letters are about love and they are drenched in perfume does not mean this is a woman. It could be a man covering his tracks."

Colton nodded. "That makes sense."

"But it could be a woman, right?" Tony asked.

"Yes, and honestly, it probably is. But I just wanted to make sure we noted that that might be an error. But for now, we'll refer to the perp as a she."

Colton looked over at Tony, who shrugged and nodded.

"Okay," Colton said. "She, unless proven otherwise."

Callum crouched down to a small bag near his feet, pulled out a camera, and began taking pictures of the note and the knife.

"Shouldn't you have a crime scene team or something?" Tony asked.

"This is a small town. I am the crime scene team. We have one for Teton County, but I don't know that this merits a call out to them."

Callum finished taking his pictures, then put on a pair of gloves and pulled the knife out of the wood of the door.

"It wasn't in very deeply, so that's another sign that it may be a woman." Callum marked the hole the knife had made with a Sharpie marker. "But a tall one."

"How can you tell?" Colton asked.

"Think about where you would put a message up. Knife or not, you would put it up in what would be your direct line of sight. This letter is a little high, so we can pretty much eliminate shorter women as suspects."

"How do you know she didn't just reach up and stab the paper?" Tony asked.

"Because of the angle of the knife—pointing down. If she were reaching, it would've been pointing up."

"That's pretty damned impressive detective work," Tony said.

Callum kept working. "I wasn't always a small-town cop. So, I do know a thing or two."

"The fact that you knew how to handle Rick is impressive enough for me." Colton looked out and saw that the younger man was walking slowly and methodically, looking for clues.

Callum chuckled.

"That knife looks pretty small, right? Like something a woman would use," Tony said, studying the knife Callum was holding in his gloved hands. "As much as a knife could be masculine or feminine."

"I agree," Colton said. "It's definitely not something that screams manly."

Callum nodded. Then he placed the knife in an evidence bag. "We'll check it for prints, of course. Although, if the stalker is dumb enough to leave their prints on something like this, then you probably don't have anything to worry about to begin with. Can you show me those other letters again?"

Tony got out his tablet and showed Callum the rest of the notes that had been found over the past two months. The sheriff studied them carefully, asking questions about where each one was found and the circumstances surrounding them. When he reached the last one, he leaned back against the porch railing and scrubbed a hand down his face.

"I'm afraid your excitable friend is right. This is an escalation."

"Because of the knife being stabbed through a picture of me?" It definitely had gotten Colton's attention. The letters had been a sort of flattering annoyance up to this point.

"Yeah, a knife is never good, but honestly, there's something about this picture that is suggesting the escalation more than just the knife."

"What about it?" Tony asked. "She sent a couple of other pictures with the letters. You saw those, right?"

"Yeah." Callum held up the photo from today from inside a clear evidence bag. "But those other pictures were different."

"How so?" Colton thought of all three images. "They're all of me. All relatively recent."

"I know. As a matter of fact, objectively, you look better in the other two photos than you do in the one for today."

Colton couldn't help but laugh. "Thanks."

Callum gave a wry smile. "I just mean that those other two photos are you at your most picture-worthy best. You look like the superstar you are known for being."

"It's not like he looks *bad* in today's picture," Tony said.

Callum shook his head. "No, not at all. I'm sure you probably can't take a bad picture of anyone in the Harrison family. But in this picture, Colton's focus is different. Do you happen to know when this was taken?"

Colton took the evidence bag Callum was holding out and studied it with Tony. "You're wearing a collared shirt. That doesn't happen too often."

Callum was right. The picture was not typical of the ones taken of Colton. "This was at the wedding. The one the night before the accident."

Tony shook his head. "I don't think so. You were wearing a suit. In this shot, it's just a button-down shirt."

"I took off my jacket. Toward the end of the night."

All the pieces fell into place. Colton knew exactly when this picture had been taken, and he knew exactly why he had the slightly predatory look on his face that he did.

He'd been looking at Ella. Getting ready to make his move. He'd known what he wanted, and he'd been about to go after it.

But none of this was something he wanted to share with the other two men. It felt like it would be a betrayal of Ella's trust and their night together.

He had no idea how the stalker had gotten this photo, but he understood now what Callum was talking about.

"In this picture, I'm looking at something real and important to me. In the other two pictures, I was just putting on a show."

He looked up from the picture to find Callum watching him, nodding.

"I agree, and I think your stalker friend saw that too." Callum held up the other bag with the knife. "And she definitely didn't like it."

# CHAPTER
# SEVENTEEN

ELLA WATCHED the kids leave her class through one of the open test kitchen windows. She shook her head at them. Still so orderly as they walked toward the vehicle they'd be piling into to head farther back on the Linear Tactical property.

No shoving. No goofing around. None of the obnoxious behavior normally expected from young teens. Just once, Ella would have liked to laugh with exasperation and tell them to calm down because they were acting up during a demonstration.

But she had to admit she saw more smiles now than she had four days ago when the kids arrived. They were loosening up, getting more comfortable. Finally starting to act a little more like kids.

She swallowed a yawn. One she felt like she'd been swallowing all week. She loved working with the kids; she truly did, but she also had a business to run in town. Fancy Pants seemed to be continuously growing. Ella loved her shop, loved coming up with new recipes and treats to surprise her customers. Plus, catering for parties and small events had really taken off in the past couple of years. It was exactly where she wanted to be as a small business owner, making it on her own.

But man, she was tired. She needed to finish cleaning up here, then hopefully, she could catch an hour-or-two nap before heading to the bakery to get more prep work and baking done tonight for what was needed tomorrow. Then make it back here for some more classes.

"Something smells pretty darn good in here." Dr. Annie Mackay stuck her head into one of the open classroom windows.

Ella smiled at the older woman she'd known all her life. Dr. Annie was Becky's mom and an emergency room doctor here in Oak Creek.

"Because I have some pretty fantastic students learning how to make naan bread. I wanted them to know that baking doesn't need to be just about sweet food."

Dr. Annie took another deep breath in. "Well, I think they definitely mastered that lesson."

Ella took some of the pans out of the industrial washer in the back corner and put them over to dry on the counter. "Plus, this will be bread that they can make and use in their wilderness survival training next week. Naan packs very well."

She looked around the classroom. She didn't have as much left to do as she had thought. The kids had spent a lot of time cleaning and straightening before they left.

Ella shook her head. "I sure do appreciate how helpful these kids are, but…"

Annie let out a low chuckle. "But also, you wish they would break some stuff and mouth off to you a little bit?"

Ella grinned over at her. "I know. That's ridiculous, right? But I so want to see them let loose."

"When Bear first told me about this plan and his vision, I have to admit I was a little skeptical. But meeting these kids and seeing how much of the load they carry… I'm a believer now. Just want them to have as much fun and freedom as they can handle."

Ella wiped down a countertop that was already pretty spotless. "I could see Bear's vision right away and felt connected to it from the beginning. Honestly, I feel even more connected to it now. Feel connected to these kids."

Dr. Annie crossed her arms on the windowsill. "Because you are them, Ella."

"What?" She folded a towel and hung it neatly over a rack. "I've never had any terminally ill siblings."

"But terminally ill siblings are only a by-product of what we are trying to provide them relief from. It's actually the fact that these kids don't ever demand—or probably get—much attention. In a lot of ways, you grew up the same way. You had a famous dad and a genius sister, both of whom end up getting a lot of the focus from everyone."

Ella shook her head. "It's not the same."

Annie shrugged. "No, not the same, but similar. And you never acted out either. Like these kids, you just did what needed to be done to help your family. You never tried to make things about you."

"Maybe." The other woman was probably right. Maybe that was why Ella felt such a connection to these kids. She knew what it was like to feel invisible, but then to feel guilty for even having those feelings, given how many blessings she had.

"How did your workshop go?" Ella asked. A change of subject seemed like a good idea.

Annie stood back up and stretched her arms over her head. "Good. I was surprised they were as interested as they were. I was concerned that these kids had been around medical stuff for so long that learning CPR and a few first-responder basics would either be too simple or too much of a downer for them."

"But it wasn't?"

"For a couple, maybe, although they were still polite and attentive. But for a few of them..." The older woman smiled. "I saw *the gleam*."

"Ah, maybe a couple of future doctors in our presence."

"Having a sick sibling certainly motivates young people sometimes. They either want out completely, or they want to be a part of the solution."

"It feels pretty damn amazing to work with these kids, doesn't it?" Ella's exhaustion had vanished, rejuvenated by Annie's insights. Maybe she could find a way to include a couple more cooking workshops for them, for at least the ones who were most interested. Bear had mentioned allowing the kids to specialize and hone in on some of the workshops for their last couple of days.

"Absolutely. I —"

Annie broke off from what she was about to say when they heard cheers in the distance. Both women looked out the window in that direction.

"What in the world?" Annie asked. "Are those our campers, squealing like...dare I say it? *Kids*."

Ella broke out in a grin. "The obstacle course. It has to be. Come on, let's go over there."

They rushed to the truck and a couple minutes later were pulling up at the obstacle course that had been built on the far side of the Linear Tactical property. Ella had heard about it, and she knew that Colton had designed and helped build it. But she hadn't made it over here to see it yet.

"Wow," she whispered. It was amazing. Of course, it was amazing. Colton had designed it, and there was nobody who knew adventure better than Colton Harrison.

And it wasn't just the obstacle course itself that was so impressive. Colton was out there helping and demonstrating.

"Now, that is a man who knows how to command an audience," Annie said as they got out of the truck and walked over to observe more closely.

She was right. The kids were aptly focusing on Colton and what he was telling them, which right now looked to be how to get a stronger vertical jump from one of the ledges to reach a swinging rope.

He was demonstrating how to use muscles in the legs, but she couldn't stop thinking about those arms that had caught and held her so easily the other night. The same biceps that strained against his T-shirt now as he helped the campers.

Colton had never been overly muscular. His stunts required

more than mere muscles. He needed balance, agility, and mental focus. Ella remembered a talk he'd given about that very thing to a sold-out auditorium in Denver a couple years ago. The need to hone the strength of your mind, not just your body. It had been a wonderful speech.

She hadn't let him know she would be there. Hadn't let anyone know. She'd just wanted to see his face and hear his voice in person. Admitting that to anyone just felt pathetic.

And now she had no idea where she fell on the *patheticity* scale.

She and Colton hadn't talked since that night when he caught her and they'd almost kissed. Yeah, she had been avoiding him a little bit. Because…what could she say? She had no idea where things stood between them or if he was interested in her at all.

But she'd definitely seen him looking at her. Like, all the time. Like, whenever she felt eyes on her and looked up, it was Colton.

"Now I'm seeing *the gleam* again," Annie said.

Ella tore her eyes from Colton. "Afraid I'm going to become a doctor also?"

"Not that gleam. The gleam you get when you look at Colton."

"It's not like that. We're not together." Dr. Annie probably didn't know anything about the one night she'd spent with Colton, but in a town as small as Oak Creek, Ella couldn't be one hundred percent certain of that.

"You are not together *yet*. Don't forget, I was once the near-invisible girl in love with the alpha warrior. So, I recognize that look when I see it."

Ella didn't even have it in her to deny her feelings to the other woman.

"Well, I'm very glad it worked out for you and Mr. Zac so that my best friend ended up being born."

Annie walked over and rubbed Ella's back gently. "I got my hero. Becky got hers. Neither of those were simple situations either. But I have a feeling when this is all said and done, you are going to have your hero too."

There was nothing Ella wanted to believe more desperately. "I wish I could believe that, but I just don't think Colton Harrison thinks of me that way, Dr. Annie."

Colton chose that moment to glance up from where he was standing on a ramp. He saw Ella and Annie looking at him and gave the handsome grin he was so famous for, before winking at Ella.

Dr. Annie laughed out loud, the sound pure and joyful.

"Oh honey, if that's what Colton looks like when he's *not* taken with you, then I'd hate to see the look when he is." She reached over and squeezed Ella's arm. "I'll catch you around later. I see my own hero right now."

Dr. Annie walked over to where her husband, Zac Mackay, and some of the other original Linear Tactical members were standing, watching the kids laugh and carry on on the obstacle course.

Ella couldn't stop watching Colton. Everything he did seemed to draw the kids in more. They were laughing and cheering and yelling more than she'd seen them since they'd gotten here.

She desperately wanted to latch on to what Annie had said about Colton's feelings for her, but she wasn't going to let herself. Colton was here, and yes, they seemed to gravitate toward each other more and more.

But in another week, the camp would be done and Colton would be gone. She didn't fit into his world. She couldn't let herself forget that.

# CHAPTER
# EIGHTEEN

Ella closed her eyes and rubbed her temples as the five industrial mixers whirled in front of her. It was late, nearing midnight, and she was tired. She'd had an exciting day but was now regretting staying to watch the obstacle course for so long.

Kind of.

She'd completely enjoyed it at the time. Hell, it had almost been like a reunion, so many people had shown up. The kids had gotten as many turns as they wanted, and then the adults—both the former Linear Tactical founders, the current Linear Tactical employees, and all their loved ones—had wanted a turn.

Ella had not been interested in going on the obstacle course. No need to reemphasize how much slower, chunkier, and nonathletic she was compared to everyone else. But she'd had a blast watching everyone else.

Now she watched, bleary-eyed, as mixers continued their spinning in front of her. Her gaze fell on a note she'd made for herself on the giant whiteboard over the prep table.

*Hire someone.*

That note had been up there for months now. She had hourly employees who worked the counter and register for her, but for some time, Ella had known she needed to hire someone with an affinity for baking. Someone with actual experience. It was all becoming too much for Ella to do on her own.

Fancy Pants was hers. She had bought it from Violet Teague when the other woman had retired. It had been a labor of love for Violet and was a labor of love for Ella also. But this was *her* company. Except for when she'd bought it, she hadn't dipped into her family money at all.

And she loved the business. Even as exhausted as she was, she still loved it. Not to mention since she was a business owner, people were more content with allowing her the lack of a dating life. Nobody expected you to be a social butterfly when they knew you were the sole proprietor of a small business. That had kept the questions about Colton at bay for many years. For both other people and for Ella herself.

Normally, she didn't mind the long hours; she truly didn't. But tonight, something felt off. She glanced over at the windows at the front of the shop. She could almost swear she felt eyes on her.

That had to be the exhaustion. This was Oak Creek in the middle of the week. There was very little chance someone was out at all, much less watching her bake. That was about as exciting as watching grass grow.

She shook off the feeling, but it was back a few minutes later. She shut off one of the mixers and sucked in a breath when she swore she saw a shadow passing along one of the windows.

There had been a fire here at Fancy Pants before Ella was even born. It had almost killed two people, and they'd later found out the fire had been set deliberately.

But that was a long time ago. Why was Ella feeling the same sort of bad-guy vibes again now?

She turned off all the mixers so that she could hear more clearly. Surely she was just letting her exhaustion get the better of her. She walked out into the front and looked around. Nothing. She was imagining things.

She closed her eyes and took in a deep breath, calming herself.

She needed to refocus, get this done, and get some sleep. She blew out the breath and opened her eyes, ready to restart.

And she saw a face in the window directly in front of her.

She jumped back, letting out a scream. She couldn't see who it was, someone wrapped in a black hoodie. A split second later, the face was gone.

She ran over to grab her phone on the counter, not even sure who to call. Sheriff Webb? Nine-one-one? And say what—that someone had looked in her window?

But she'd seen enough horror movies to know that she wasn't going to stay here by herself and wait to get killed. She may be many things, but too stupid to live was not one of them.

Calling Sheriff Webb probably made the most sense. He lived outside of town but could get here relatively quickly or would know if there was a deputy he could send. She hated to inconvenience anyone in the middle of the night, but she would also hate to wind up in a serial killer documentary.

Especially when a knock on the shop's back door sounded out a few seconds later. Her heart rate ratcheted up again. There was no way she was opening that door.

She opened her phone to find Callum's number and was startled into screeching again when her phone buzzed in her hand.

"Oh shit." She dashed for the walk-in chiller. She could at least bar that on the inside if someone was breaking in.

Of course, if someone was setting a fire like years before, it would also be her death sentence.

She stopped when she saw the reason why her phone had buzzed. A message from Colton?

> I'm at the back door of your shop if you would like some company.

She stared at the phone. Was that really him? She decided to call, stepping into the walk-in chiller as she did so.

"Hey," he answered. "Did you get my text?"

"Are you really at the back door of my shop?"

He muttered a curse under his breath. "I'm sorry. I knew this was a bad idea."

It had been Colton at the window. Thank God. She ran from the chiller toward the door. "No. No, I'm glad you're here. You just scared me."

She made it to the door as she finished her sentence. She ended the call as she opened it.

"I'm so glad it was you. You scared me to death in the window." She held open the door and stepped backward so he could come in. She was still a little shaken, so she immediately locked the door behind them.

"What window?"

"When you stuck your face right up to my front window! I wasn't expecting it, so it scared me to death."

"I wasn't anywhere near your front window. Scout's honor."

She looked at him more closely. He definitely wasn't wearing the black hoodie like the face she'd seen.

"There was somebody there. Freaked me out."

Colton instantly stiffened. "I'm going to go check it out. You stay here and lock the door behind me."

She grabbed his arm. "It was probably just somebody walking by and saw my light on."

"I'm still going to check it out."

He was walking out the door before she could make an argument. She kept her phone in her hand so she could call Sheriff Webb if needed. But Colton was back just a few minutes later.

"I didn't see any sign of anyone out there. Did you get a good look at the person?"

"I just saw a guy in a black hoodie. It startled me pretty badly, so I didn't catch any details."

"Are you positive it was a man?"

She hadn't been expecting that question. "I think so, but I can't say with absolute certainty. Why?"

"Just wondering." He shook his head. "Don't worry about it. What are you doing here so late anyway?"

She went back over to the mixers, took a breath, and started pulling ingredients to begin the next batch of cake batter. "I'm a little behind on my work, so I needed to get caught up before tomorrow morning."

"Anything I can do to help?"

Ella took a closer look at him now that she had calmed down. Colton looked rough—like he had that first night when he'd caught her. Whatever was going on with him, he needed something to do. Fortunately, she could help with that. Not to mention, she could use all the assistance she could get.

"Let's rinse out this mixer, and here's the recipe card. Basically, combine the ingredients and follow the instructions."

She knew she'd done the right thing when she saw the relief in his eyes. He turned to the mixing bowl and immediately got to work.

She turned her attention to her own mixing bowl. "Did you just happen to be in town?"

He stiffened for a second. "I have trouble sleeping sometimes. It's been better since I've been in Oak Creek, but tonight just wasn't good. So, I decided to go for a drive. When I saw lights on here…"

"You decided to make sure I wasn't falling off any countertops again?"

He relaxed slightly. "Something like that, yeah."

They worked in silence for nearly half an hour. While she had no problem with the quiet, she'd never known Colton not to talk for that long. The longer the silence stretched out, the more concerned she became about him.

"Are you sure there's nothing you want to talk about? How are things really going with you?" she finally asked.

He immediately stiffened again. "What do you mean? I'm fine."

"Colton, I mean that you are at my bakery at nearly midnight. That's not normal."

He shrugged but did not look up from the batter he was mixing. "There's not really anything to talk about. I'm fine."

She took a chance. "You nearly died two months ago. That's no small thing."

"And I've done plenty of stunts since then. Hell, I've even gone snowboarding and skiing since the avalanche. I'm fine. Same old, same old."

He obviously didn't want to continue to talk about this—everything about his body posture and his word choice basically screamed it. But there was one thing Ella knew was true, regardless of how many times he said it.

Colton Harrison was not *fine*.

Her mom had always taught her to trust her instincts. So, she did that now.

"And the panic attacks?"

That was a wild guess. She had nothing to base it on. Except for the fact that she'd always been connected to him in a way that she'd never really understood. She knew something wasn't right.

"Panic attacks?" He fairly scoffed the words. "Why would you think I'm having panic attacks? Yeah, I have a little trouble sleeping every once in a while, but that's not a panic attack."

Saying the words three times in one remark did not reassure her.

"All I'm saying is that it would be completely understandable if you were struggling after what happened."

"And like I said, I've been doing my stunts with no problem. I'm fine. It's not like you really know me, so why don't you just let it go."

It was like an actual slap in the face. "I overstepped. I apologize."

She blinked back tears as she walked to the mixer farthest from his. He was right; she didn't truly know him, did she?

And the connection she thought she felt with him was—and always had been—something she created in her mind. It wasn't real, and she still needed to stop pretending that it ever would be.

She focused on the task in front of her as silence fell over the bakery, the only sound being the whirr of the mixers. The batters were almost done. The baking would be completed in the morning by the opening staff. She'd planned to do one more recipe tonight but now decided not to.

She just wanted to go home.

"Butterscotch…"

She shook her head and held up a hand to stop him without turning around. "Like I said, I overstepped."

She poured the batter from the mixing bowl into the storage container and walked it into the fridge. When she came out, Colton had done the same and was washing out his bowl. She added her utensils to the pile of dirty dishes. "They'll do that in the morning. Don't worry about it."

He kept scrubbing the bowl.

"Did you hear me? I have staff who comes in specifically to clean what I do at night."

"Okay."

He still didn't stop washing. As a matter of fact, he was scrubbing even harder now.

"Colton, you just said okay."

"I meant okay, you're right. I've been struggling pretty badly, and yeah, panic attacks have been a big part of it."

# CHAPTER
# NINETEEN

COLTON HAD no idea why he just said that. Actually, he knew exactly why he'd said it. Because he couldn't stand the look that had crossed Ella's face when he'd shut her down a couple of minutes ago. Couldn't stand to hear the hurt in her voice and know that he'd been the one who'd caused it.

How the hell had she noticed in such a tiny bit of time what his entire team—people he worked with day in and day out—hadn't noticed in weeks?

Still, he didn't want to talk about it. He set the bowl to the side and walked back over to the other mixers. He was almost done with the final batch he was working on.

"Colton..."

He held out a hand to stop her. "I know what I said, but I don't really want to talk about it."

"But—"

"It's not you. It's just not something I have anything to say about right now."

"Yeah, but—"

He didn't want to hurt her again, but he didn't want to chat about his emotions either. "Seriously, Ella. Just let it go."

She let out a sigh. "All I was going to say was that you need to combine the wet ingredients together before adding them to the dry ingredients. I'm not sure if that's in the instructions or not."

"Shit." He ran his forearm across his brow as he looked over at her. "I'm an asshole. I'm sorry."

"Don't worry about it. It's fine."

That was Ella, wasn't it? The peacekeeper. Always quick to forgive and to include others. She'd been that way for as long as he could remember, even when they were kids.

But for the first time tonight, he could see that maybe she paid a price to be that way. That she opened herself up and it hurt her when people stepped all over her feelings. As it should. Everyone was just so used to Ella not demanding anything that they took her gentle spirit for granted.

He stepped back from the mixer. He was in a shit mood, and staying here would only lead to him hurting her more. "I should go. I'm not in a good place, and I shouldn't have come here. I'm sorry I hurt you."

He was so lost in his own thoughts, he didn't realize she'd walked over to stand beside him. She touched his arm. "If you need to go, I understand. But you don't need to do that for my sake. If you don't want to talk about what's going on, I'll leave it alone."

He didn't say anything as he finished the batter, and true to her word, she didn't ask any more questions. It wasn't long before they were stacking the rest of the mixing bowls and containers into the washing pile.

"Thank you for your help. You saved me a lot of time—"

"Why did you leave that night?" Another thought out of his mouth he wasn't expecting. But he wanted to know. Everything he knew about Ella did not gel with the theory that he was just a sexual trophy for her.

"You know why," she said softly.

He rubbed the back of his neck. Maybe he'd been wrong. "Because I was a notch in your bedpost? Look, I'm not judging, if that's your thing. You wouldn't be the first woman who'd come to my hotel room because they'd wanted to be able to say they'd slept with a quasi-celebrity."

"*What*? No. No, that's not it at all. Honestly, I've never thought of you as a celebrity. Around here, you're just…Colton."

"Then why did you leave?" He took a step closer to her. Hearing her say she hadn't been using him for his celebrity status eased something in him.

And it made sense. That wasn't Ella. Thinking about it now, it was ridiculous to even consider that as her motivation.

"You know why I left. You're the one who brought it up in the first place. What you said that night."

He racked his brain to figure out exactly what she was talking about. "What I said? When?"

What could he have possibly said that would make her sneak out?

"Right before you fell asleep?"

He looked over at her. He had no recollection whatsoever of saying anything bad that would've caused that reaction from her. But studying her now, he knew she was telling the truth. Her brow was furrowed, and she was wringing her little hands together.

He took a step closer, reaching out to stop the nervous movement. "The only thing I can remember was how amazing our lovemaking was and saying I needed a break in order to recuperate for round two."

"Not that." Her voice was quiet. Too quiet.

"Whatever I said, I didn't mean it the way you took it, Butterscotch."

"You confessed that you were with me because Lincoln told you I had a crush on you."

"What?" He remembered that conversation with Lincoln at the wedding, but that wasn't what he'd been expecting her to say.

"You told me about it right as you fell asleep. That you were glad he'd let slip I had a crush on you."

"And I was."

She tried to pull back, but he wouldn't let go of her hands. He didn't know why she was so upset about this, but he was going to get to the bottom of it.

"That's why I left. Because Lincoln—and I get it, he didn't do anything on purpose—but he basically set me up as some sort of sure thing for you. Like some sort of…" She faded off and looked away.

"Some sort of what?"

"It doesn't matter." She still wouldn't look at him. "Once you said that, I just knew that you hadn't necessarily invited me to your room because you wanted me."

"*What?*" This conversation was getting more off track by the second. "What part of that night made you think I didn't really want you? The way I pounced on you in bed and lasted such a short time that I was mortified?"

She shook her head, still staring down at the floor. "You don't have to pretend with me, Colton. I know what that night was."

"Enlighten me, then."

"A pity fuc—"

His lips were on hers before she even finished that filthy phrase.

Not that he had a problem with the F-word, but he was absolutely floored by the fact that she could possibly think that. The only thing he could focus on now was erasing that thought from her mind.

Because nothing on earth could be further from the truth than him thinking of her as a *pity fuck*.

He ravished her mouth. He might not have been able to find the words to set her straight about what had happened that night, but he could damn well show her.

He reached under her armpits, not caring a bit how unsexy it was, and hoisted her onto the counter. He slid one hand into her hair, gripping it hard—because damn it, he was fucking pissed—holding her in place so that he could plunder those lips. The other hand, he slid down to her hip and yanked her to the edge of the counter so that he could press up against her.

"Don't you dare ever call yourself that again." He slid his tongue deep into the recesses of her mouth before nipping at her bottom lip. "Ever. Do you understand me? There's nothing pitiful about you in any sense of the word, and most definitely not when it comes to you and me making love."

"But—"

He nipped at her lip again. "No buts."

He hated that this was why she had left that night, but it explained so much. And it changed everything, at least for him.

She hadn't been using him. And somewhere, he'd always known that—it was completely opposite of what he knew of Ella O'Conner's personality to think she had used him in that way. He should've followed through weeks ago. Demanded to know why she left that night, rather than to have assumed the worst. If it hadn't been for the accident and those damned panic attacks, he probably would have.

He pressed up against her, loving that sigh that escaped her.

"Lincoln telling me that you were open to some sort of advance from me just gave me the freedom to do what I'd always wanted to without risking alienating a precious friend. Trust me, there was no pity involved in that night. Only heat. Passion. Explosive chemistry." He punctuated each word with a kiss.

"Really?"

"I don't think I'm going to be able to accurately tell you this with words. Will you let me show you instead? Pick back up where we should've left off that night after my nap?"

Those green eyes looked up at him. "Okay."

He couldn't stop the grin that broke out on his face. "Do you still have the place upstairs?"

She shook her head. "No. I bought a little house down the street a couple years ago."

"Can we walk?" As soon as she nodded, he slid her off the counter. "Get what you need."

He waited, not at all patiently, as she grabbed her bag and shut down the lights. She kept shooting him somewhat wary looks, but each time she caught him still looking at her, she blushed and looked away.

She liked it. Liked that he was beside himself with the need to get her into the nearest bed. Good. It was good right now that she didn't want soft and romantic.

"Because all I'm going to be able to give you is hard and fast, Butterscotch. This unquenchable need I have for you isn't going to allow for much else."

She blinked over at him, not responding to the fact that he was obviously having a conversation in his mind. And only making part of it verbal.

The walk to her house didn't take very long—thank God—and he didn't let go of her hand the whole time. He wasn't sure he could've forced himself to stop touching her, so he was glad he didn't need to.

She got the door unlocked, and they walked inside. "This is it. It's not much, but it's—"

He kissed her again. Without breaking the kiss to respond, he swept an arm under her knees and lifted her up.

"Colton." She let out a nervous laugh. "I'm too hea—"

"Don't you dare even say it. Just point in the direction of the bedroom, or else I'm going to take you right here against this wall."

He knew she was skeptical, and there was nothing he would like more than to prove that he was more than capable of doing exactly what he threatened. As a matter of fact, he would definitely be proving that to her—first, that whatever she thought her weight problem was, it wasn't a factor, and also, that he was more than capable of handling every ounce of her.

Lying, sitting, standing…he'd take her all the ways he could get her.

But tonight, he really wanted her in a bed. So, when she pointed down a small hallway, he headed in that direction.

"I should have never taken a nap that night. Shame on me." He laid her on the bed.

"I actually liked that you needed a nap. It was just when I thought the other was true that I…"

"In case I haven't made it abundantly clear, that night, this night, every night we have together… None of them will ever be out of pity." He unbuttoned her blouse. "Unless it's you taking pity on me."

He moved his lips across her jaw and down her throat, paying attention to where her breath hitched. Interesting how his sweet little Ella liked pressure that almost bordered on pain. Liked it when he grazed his teeth against her neck. Liked it when he made quick work of her bra and sucked hard on one breast and then the other. She gripped his hair, pulling him closer to her.

"I want you inside me."

"Don't worry, I'm going to be. But I want to taste you first."

He unzipped her jeans and slid them over her hips and down her legs, leaving her gloriously naked, laid out on the bed.

"I made way too many tactical errors last time."

Concern fell over her pretty face. She shook her head. "No. No, it was amazing for me."

"I'm glad, although it couldn't possibly have been as good for you as it was for me. But what I mean is that I didn't take my time and appreciate you the way I should have. I assumed we had all night, when I should not have taken that for granted."

"I'm sorry I left without giving you a chance to talk things out with me."

He reached over and trailed his fingers gently down her cheek. "I'm mostly sorry that those thoughts went through your head at all, Butterscotch."

He was going to do his damnedest to make sure that never happened again.

He made short work of his own clothes then reached down and ran a hand up her leg, starting at her ankle. She was shy, trying to close herself off to him.

His mouth began to follow the same trail his hand had taken. "Too late to get shy on me now, Butterscotch. I want to see you. I want to taste you."

He eased her thighs open, wishing he could make her understand how beautiful she was to him in every possible way. All he could do was show her.

And that was exactly what he did.

## CHAPTER
# TWENTY

COLTON COULDN'T GET his eyes to close. He wasn't sure if it was a result of the two bouts of amazing sex they'd had, still processing that Ella had actually thought he'd considered her a pity fuck, or the residual stress that had led him to her shop in the first place.

"You're not sleeping," Ella said, softly snuggled up against him long minutes later.

He tightened his arm around her then trailed his fingers up and down her spine. "Maybe I'm making sure you don't sneak out again."

She chuckled. He loved the sound. "If I promise no sneaking out, will you go to sleep?"

He probably wouldn't, if previous nights when panic attacks had woken him up were any indication, but there was no reason to keep her awake also. "Yes, since I don't have to keep watch on any little runaways. Go to sleep." He kissed the top of her head.

He lay there in silence, staring up at the ceiling. Having Ella here was better all the way around. No, maybe he wouldn't get sleep, but at least he had her close by.

He didn't tend to be very woo-woo, but it felt like somewhere her peaceful aura was combining with his—lending some of her gentle strength.

"You're still not sleeping, are you?" she asked after a long time.

He'd thought she had been out for a while now. "It's okay. You don't need to stay awake."

"Okay, but you know you're going to have to talk about what's going on with you with somebody. Like you said, I don't actually know you very well, so it doesn't need to be me. But…someone."

"I had a panic attack earlier tonight. That's how I showed up at your shop."

"Are the attacks bad?"

"Sometimes. Tonight was bad mostly because the last few days had been so good. I thought I was turning some sort of a corner, maybe. I had actually gone to sleep, and this one woke me up."

"The ones that wake you up are worse?"

"Yeah. The ones that come on during the day are frustrating as hell because I can't seem to stop them, but at least they give some sort of warning—shaking hands, muffled hearing, tunnel vision. I can't necessarily do anything about them, but they at least aren't on me so suddenly." He honestly hadn't planned to talk about this, but now that he'd started, he found that he couldn't stop. "But the ones at night are on top of me when I wake up and…"

He didn't really have the words to explain it. It was like waking up underwater, drowning. Unable to breathe and with no way of knowing which way it was to the surface.

"When you wake up in that state, you're trapped in it," she said softly.

"Yes. Trapped like I'm underwater or…" *Shit*. "Or like I'm caught under that avalanche."

And it was like that every single time—the panic, the inability to breathe…

"The helplessness," he said. "That's the worst thing about the panic attacks, and it was the worst thing about being in that avalanche. The helplessness. There doesn't seem to be anything I can do to stop what's happening, just like I couldn't at the time either."

"You know that developing PTSD is natural for someone who

went through what you did. If it were anybody else, you would have nothing but sympathy and patience for them."

He stared up at the ceiling. "Yeah, probably. But I'm frustrated because it's not like I'm scared. I was telling the truth when I said earlier that I'm still able to do stunts, even ones involving snow. I am."

"And so, because you faced your physical fears, you expect that everything should be okay and that your brain should treat this as if nothing happened."

"No. Not necessarily." But the more he thought about it, the more he knew she was right. "I don't know. Maybe. All I know is that there were a shit-ton of people watching me those first couple weeks after the accident. Everyone was wondering if I was going to get back up on the horse. They all wanted to know if I could still do stunts or if I was going to retire."

And he would never forget the look of relief on face after face as he completed each stunt. The knowledge that Colton Harrison was back, that jobs were secure, that the adventure would live on.

"Did you want to retire?"

"I didn't want to let that avalanche beat me."

"And you haven't."

"It doesn't feel that way sometimes. It feels like I'm no longer in control of my body."

"Some of that may pass with time."

He rolled over and scooted her under him. She's said some things he needed to think about, but for right now, he just wanted to *feel*. And since they were both awake anyway...

"I'd rather it pass by me spending time with—and *in*—you."

She smiled up at him. "That works too."

---

Ella woke up just before her alarm went off, a fairly common practice even when she was burning the candle at both ends.

What wasn't fairly common practice? Colton Harrison sleeping in the bed next to her.

She switched off her alarm and then shifted onto her side so she could look at him. She didn't want to wake him up; he needed the rest, especially after all the energy they'd expended last night. But also, she needed to get over to Fancy Pants to make sure everything was ready there.

She wished she could take the whole day off and just stay in bed with him, but that couldn't happen today. Too many private orders, plus the shop itself was always packed on mornings as the week went on.

But a smile crept up over her face. She was lying in bed with Colton after having the most wonderful night of lovemaking. She could definitely say now that she'd misread the situation last time. He'd gone out of his way to prove that she was not any sort of pity fuck.

As a matter of fact, he had described in great detail what he would do to her if she ever called herself that again around him. Of course, he had to have known that the *punishment* he was threatening couldn't be taken very seriously—especially when it involved him tying her up in his bed completely naked.

The thought had her squirming a little, which should be impossible, given how they had used each other to exhaustion last night. She needed to get out of this bed before she found herself kissing her way up his body.

She eased her way backward, aware that she was once again sneaking out. This time, she would at least leave a note for him.

But she didn't even make it out of bed. "Sneaking out again?"

He pulled her in for a kiss, and she ran her fingers along his hard jaw. "I wanted to let you sleep."

"What time is it?"

"Early. Before six. It really is okay for you to go back to sleep. I need to go in to the bakery."

"I thought you said you had someone who did the cleanup for you."

He looked so grumpy, it was pretty endearing. "I do, but today, I'm needed there for other things, to make sure there are no hiccups. There's a big catering order being picked up. The shop staff can't handle that and all our normal business."

He trailed his fingers up her arm and across her collarbone. She couldn't stop her shivers. "You work too hard."

"I'll admit it's been a little hectic with trying to fit in my classes with the campers. But that's temporary, so I'll get caught up on my sleep soon."

He slid back, stretching as he sat up. "I'll come with you."

"You really don't have to. No need for both of us to get up this early."

He reached over and grabbed her wrist, tugging her to him. "It's still a little dark outside, and I'm not letting you walk over there alone. So, if I can't talk you into staying in bed, I'm coming with you."

He kissed her, and it was all she could do not to lose her resolve. If it weren't for this catering order, she would definitely leave her shop workers to manage on their own.

"Trust me." Kiss. "There's nowhere I'd rather be than in this bed with you." Another kiss.

She felt the outline of a smile in his lips against hers. "In that case, you better get going, or we're definitely not making it out of this bed."

Twenty minutes later, they were on their way down the block to Fancy Pants. It was still early enough that there weren't many people out, but all it would take was one person glancing out a window and seeing them walking together at this hour, and the cat would be out of the bag. Oak Creek was many wonderful things—but at the end of the day, it was first and foremost a small town. Gossip reigned supreme.

"You do have coffee at that place, right?" Colton threw an arm around her shoulder. That definitely wasn't going to help if anybody saw them, but she had no desire to move away from him.

"In abundance. Every type you could want. And all sorts of breakfast foods too, so I think you'll survive."

She let out a squeal as he slapped her on her ass. She planned for them to go in through the back, but she saw something sticking out of the front door where the customers would come in. How had she missed that last night?

"Hang on, let me see what that is." She pointed toward the front door and jogged that way.

She heard Colton call her name just as she realized that the object wedged in the crack of the shop's front door was a knife.

"Ella, don't touch it," Colton said from behind her.

She wasn't really listening to him. She was too busy studying the weapon. Why was it there? Why would somebody leave their knife jammed into her door? Maybe it had fallen on the ground, someone had found it, and this was their way of getting it back to the owner?

No, that didn't make sense. Why would someone do that? Small children came to her shop all the time. This could be dangerous. She was mad. She moved more quickly toward the door, ready to grab the knife before someone got hurt.

Colton's hand on her arm stopped her. "Leave it."

"Why? Somebody might get hurt. We have children who come—"

She stopped when she saw the picture the knife had speared to her door. One of Colton, although you couldn't really make out his face because the blade had gone straight through it.

She looked over at him. He was taking this way too calmly. "What aren't you telling me?"

"Apparently, I picked up a stalker over the past couple of months."

"Is that what you've been talking about with Callum when I've seen him around Linear Tactical?"

Colton nodded, still studying the knife. "Yes. The stalker has been sending me letters, and then she graduated to pictures a little more recently. There was one a few days ago in the door of my cabin, similar to this one. We need to call Callum and get him here."

Colton was already on his phone, contacting the sheriff. Ella was trying to wrap her head around all of this.

"A stalker?" she asked once Colton finished his brief conversation with Callum. "Is she dangerous? Are you safe? Why didn't you tell me about this?"

She could feel her hysteria rising. Evidently, so could Colton. He turned and cupped her cheeks. "It's more of a minor annoyance than anything else. An overzealous fan who has too much time on her hands. You don't have to be scared."

"It's not that I'm scared as much as I hate the thought of this happening to you when you're already under so much stress. Maybe this is part of the reason behind your panic attacks."

"Honestly, the stalker stuff doesn't seem to affect me that way. It has actually given me something else to focus on besides what's happening inside my mind."

She had to admit, he looked a lot calmer and more focused now than he had last night when he'd shown up at the bakery. That made sense if she thought about it. The thought of danger wasn't what caused Colton's panic. It was the thought of helplessness that brought it on.

Still, she didn't like this at all. "But—"

He squeezed her cheeks gently. "I wasn't trying to hide it from you. I was wrapped up doing much more pleasurable stuff with you than worrying about this. Why don't you go inside and handle what you need to? I'm sure Callum is going to have some questions for you."

"For me?"

"Your mysterious person in the window with the black hoodie last night? That's probably the closest thing we have to any sort of solid lead."

"That's why you asked me if I saw a woman. Because your stalker is a woman."

"Yes. And if you can remember any details of her face, it would really help."

"I don't know that I remember anything at all."

He reached forward and kissed her. "That's okay. Like I said, an overzealous fan. She'll eventually wear herself out. I don't think we have any real reason to be concerned. It's going to be fine."

The knife stabbed through a picture of Colton's face certainly did not make it seem that way.

# CHAPTER
# TWENTY-ONE

DESPITE WHAT HE said to Ella, Colton was truly concerned about his stalker for the first time now.

"This picture was taken yesterday, Callum. That's on the obstacle course. How the hell did someone get there without any of us noticing a stranger?"

Callum studied his copy of the picture from where he sat behind his desk. "It looks like whoever took it was right there with the crowd, but it's probably just a very clever zoom."

Colton scrubbed a hand down his face and leaned forward in his own chair. "I still don't like it. And I particularly don't like the fact that I was looking at Ella in this picture."

He'd looked over and found her watching him, and he hadn't been able to stop himself from doing a little pose and winking. It seemed his stalker had caught that for posterity. "Whoever this stalker is, I don't want her deciding that she can't get to me, so she'll go after Ella instead."

He was relieved when the sheriff didn't blow off his concerns. "I agree. I don't think it's to that point yet, but it's logical to think the stalker will be upset if she realizes your attention is focused somewhere else, particularly on another woman."

"Do you think the sketch artist will be able to get anything from Ella?" She was in working with the county's sketch artist right now.

Callum shrugged. "To tell the truth, probably not. Given that Ella thought it was a man until finding out you have a stalker of the female persuasion, I doubt that she actually saw enough to be helpful. A sketch artist can't do much if the memory isn't there."

Colton had pretty much feared the same thing. He shifted and rubbed the back of his neck. "I don't like this letter either, Callum. I know there's nothing concrete that makes it feel more like a threat, but both this one and the one at the Linear Tactical cabin feel stronger to me."

"A knife tip through the face can do that, too."

Colton gave a wry chuckle. "True. But honestly, the first letters I got from this woman, and even when she started including pictures, I didn't really feel like it was a threat. Did I want to be trapped in an elevator with this woman? No. But I truly felt like we were in the *fantasy* realm, not the *danger* realm."

"But that changed when you got here?"

Colton shrugged. "Yeah. I can't pinpoint exactly why, but it definitely put me more on edge."

He looked down and read his copy of the letter again.

*My dearest Colton,*

*I dream of you nearly every night now. And thank God every day that you are alive. I know that's true because we are supposed to meet and because we will be together forever.*

*It won't be long now. I can feel it, can't you? I wonder if you dream of me also. You do, don't you? That's the way it's meant to be.*

*I can't wait till we hold each other forever. One lifetime isn't enough with you. But it's a start.*

. . .

"I don't know. Maybe I'm paranoid. Can you see a difference in the earlier letters and these last two?"

Colton chuckled as Callum patted around his desk before he finally found the reading glasses he was searching for. He flipped Colton off as he placed them on his nose.

"I'm not really sure," he said after reading the letter. "There is nothing overt that makes it more of a threat, but I can understand why it feels more…immediate. Almost more calculating."

Colton nodded. "Yes. Calculating is a good word for it." And he didn't like it at all.

"Your team is most familiar with all of this and, realistically, has the most to gain by getting this taken care of as quickly as possible. Maybe it's time to call them back to Oak Creek."

Colton's jaw tightened at just the thought. He appreciated everything Tony and his team did for him, but he didn't want them around.

"Yeah, maybe."

Callum wasn't fooled. "I get it, they're a lot. But they seem to have your best interests at heart. Although Nick is a pain in the ass and a little too obnoxious for my taste."

"Rick. But yeah."

Colton felt a slight tremor take over his hand, and he gripped it into a fist to stop it, before standing up and walking over to the window. He needed to keep it together. He wasn't going to let the thought of his stalker cause him to lose it right here in the sheriff's office.

But Callum wasn't fooled. "You okay?"

Damn him for being so observant.

"Yeah, I'm fine," Colton lied, jamming his hands into the pockets of his jeans. "I just want to be able to do something, you know? I'm fucking tired of twiddling my thumbs and waiting for the stalker to strike again."

"Well, I actually have an idea, so I'm glad to hear you say that."

The trembling in his hand stopped immediately. He pulled them out of his pockets. "I'm all ears."

"Your stalker is here in Oak Creek, but she may not have taken into consideration that everyone in Oak Creek knows everyone else."

"You're thinking of setting a trap." He walked back over and sat down, anxious to hear what the man had to say.

Callum gave a low chuckle. "It probably won't end up being quite that cloak-and-dagger, but yeah. What if you were at the Eagle's Nest having a drink at the bar by yourself? It might be catnip for your stalker, the perfect time to initiate contact or at least snap a picture."

"You think she would just expose herself like that?"

Callum crossed his arms over his chest. "I wish we could get that lucky, but no, probably not. But what I do think is that we can use Oak Creek to our advantage. Have people we know and trust set up around you with eyes for anybody unfamiliar."

Colton sat up more fully in his chair. "That might actually work. She'd be comfortable enough in a crowded place that she wouldn't know that almost everyone else knew each other and that she's an odd man out."

Callum grinned. "Exactly. We can get your Linear Tactical buddies out here. They aren't law enforcement, but they can handle this sort of sting operation, for sure."

"In between them and people we know from town, we should recognize just about everyone who's not a stranger."

"There may be a few tourists around, but we can try to vet them on the fly."

"You know who can help with that."

Callum rolled his eyes. "Yes, I'm very aware that Lincoln is the best thing since sliced bread when it comes to computers. It's not like he would ever let anyone forget it."

Colton tried to hold back his smile, but he couldn't. "Linc doesn't do it on purpose, you know that. In his mind, he's just stating a fact when he lets everyone know that he can do damn near anything having to do with software."

Callum's face was comical. "Fine. We can have him run any strangers we think fit the bill and hopefully get this taken care of."

Colton pushed out of his chair. "Let's do it tonight. In a couple of days, everybody's going to be needed to take the campers out in the wilderness, and like I said, I'm tired of just sitting around here with my thumb up my ass, waiting for the next letter or something worse to happen."

"It'll be tight to get everything in place by tonight. This'll have to be more off the books than I want, although that happens with your little buddies more than I would like anyway."

"I can make some calls and get everybody in place by nine o'clock tonight. It's worth a shot."

Callum stood up. "I agree. I don't want anybody thinking they can come in and cause trouble in my town just because they want to."

Colton winked at him. "Yeah, that privilege belongs to those of us who were raised here. So, let's get this handled."

There was no shaking in his hands now.

---

"For Christ's sake, you guys are like a bunch of fucking toddlers."

Snickers went through the various comms units at Callum's words later that evening.

So far, their sting operation hadn't produced anything much worthwhile. Colton had been sitting at the bar for the past thirty minutes. The Eagle's Nest was fairly busy, but so far, nobody who fit the bill of the stalker—female, relatively young, and a stranger in Oak Creek—had been spotted.

So yeah, Colton's friends who were helping out were a little chatty. He could see why Callum was frustrated, although the other man knew everyone would immediately focus if needed.

"Maybe if Colton had worn a tighter T-shirt, he'd look more approachable," Lilah said into the comms unit.

Colton turned his head and glared in her direction where she was sitting at the far end of the bar. Or at least as discreetly as he could since they weren't supposed to be noticing each other at all.

"Don't you think his biceps would burst through the seams if his shirt were any tighter?" Theo's voice rang in his ears. "Do they make that brand in adult sizes, Colton, or is it just for kids?"

Colton now turned to glare at his friend who was sitting in a far booth with Derek Bollinger. Meanwhile, Lilah nearly spewed her drink, barely covering the mishap with a cough.

Colton reached up and scratched his cheek deliberately with his middle finger, spinning slowly on the stool under the guise of looking around casually so all his friends could see the gesture. "Always a pleasure to be back home," he muttered behind his hand.

"You guys want to lock it down?" Callum asked. "Anybody with an IQ over sixty is going to be able to tell something is going on if you're not careful."

"Roger that," Theo said. "Let's get serious."

Callum was right. If the stalker felt like something was off, she might not approach Colton, or hell, she might not even come all the way into the bar at all.

As Callum had feared, Ella hadn't been able to remember any details about the face in the window, outside of the black hoodie. So the forensic artist hadn't been able to come up with any sort of sketch. Colton had taken Ella home from the sheriff's office and tucked her into bed so she could rest. She'd been so tired, she hadn't even pressed when he'd told her he needed to meet his buddies for something tonight. Becky and Eva were with her right now.

All his friends had been down to help with this sting operation, once he'd explained about the stalker and how the situation seemed to be escalating. They'd come up with a plan where Colton would be by himself at the bar, to look approachable. Lilah would monitor from the other end. Derek and Theo would have eyes on the back of the room.

Of course, anybody from Oak Creek would wonder why the four buddies weren't sitting together as they normally did. But for tonight, they would just give the gossipmongers something to feast on—let them assume they were having a big fight or something.

All of them had comms units, discreet and top-of-the-line from Linear Tactical. Everyone could talk and hear one another with tiny electronic pieces inside their ears. His friends all knew what they were looking for. Bear knew too, although he wasn't on comms. He was working a shift behind the bar like he sometimes did.

As a matter of fact, it was Bear who gestured with his chin when two women walked in the door. Colton glanced at them without making it obvious.

"We got two possibilities entering," Lilah said. "Both female, roughly age thirty, five foot eight and five foot six, both slim build."

"I'll come inside and get a shot of them and run them through my system," Lincoln said. He'd been quiet on the comms unit so far. Small talk wasn't his forte.

"Be discreet, Linc," Derek told their cousin.

"They'll never know."

Colton had to admit, Lincoln was right. He had some sort of pen that was able to take a digital photograph. He walked by the women as they were still figuring out where they wanted to sit and then walked back out the door.

Lincoln walking in and then deciding to leave without saying anything to anybody actually wouldn't tip off anyone from Oak Creek as being unusual. He did that sort of thing all the time.

Lincoln was Lincoln.

Colton was careful not to stare at the women. He didn't want to do anything to tip them off. Lilah, Theo, and Derek were in much better positions to observe.

"So far, it doesn't look like either of them is taking much interest in Colton," Theo said.

"Just keep an eye on them," Callum said. "There's a couple who just parked and are on their way inside. Using the date as a disguise would be a smart play, so don't write this woman off just because she's with another man."

Callum and Lincoln were out in a van in the parking lot so that

Lincoln could utilize his computer system on images of anybody unfamiliar. It wouldn't definitively tell them if they'd found the stalker, but Lincoln had set up parameters in his system to provide them details that would be useful.

"Somebody else get me pictures of the couple while I'm running these two women," Lincoln said. "I need eighty-seven seconds to finish and get the info."

Nobody doubted that when he said eighty-seven seconds, he meant it exactly.

"I can get them," Lilah said. "Hold and I'll send it."

She signaled over to Bear so that he walked to her, then pulled out her phone like she was taking a selfie of the two of them. Colton had no doubt that her camera was actually facing the direction of the couple and she was getting the shot she needed.

"Okay, I'm fairly certain we can eliminate these two women. Neither of them has any social media accounts—public or private—that are associated with Colton. Neither of them has been at any of his stunts or gotten caught on camera, nor does either of them have travel records to anywhere he's been in the past two years."

"This is so fucking illegal," Callum muttered.

"Technically not," Lincoln argued. "All I'm doing is searching what people have made public. It's amazing how many details of their lives people post on the internet without thinking about the ramifications. Now, I can slip into illegal territory if you guys want me—"

"No." They all said it at the same time.

"I didn't think so." They could hear Lincoln typing on his computer at a speed faster than most humans on the planet. "Looks like the couple is relatively clean too. The guy has watched a couple of Colton's bigger stunts—including the avalanche—but not enough to raise any red flags."

Colton sipped slowly at his beer and talked to a few townspeople who came over to him throughout the next hour. He kept the conversations short, not wanting to scare away anyone else wanting to strike up a conversation, but it didn't seem to matter.

The team found a couple more people who Lincoln put through his system, but none of them fit the profile nor had any seeming attachment to Colton. Moreover, none of them seemed to pay him any attention at all.

It was getting close to eleven when Colton finally decided to shut it all down. There was no point in making the bar stay open later just to continue this.

"I'm calling it," he said into his comms. "If she was coming, she'd have been here by now. Either she didn't show up at all, or she got spooked somehow."

"Probably got spooked by a grown-ass man wearing a child's shirt," Lilah said.

Callum ignored her. "I concur. I'll have one of my deputies monitor those two women who came in at first since they best suit our profile. But my gut says it's not either of them."

"My software says that too, which is better than any gut." Lincoln's tone dripped defensiveness—the concept of trusting a "gut" was completely foreign to his computer of a brain.

"Regardless, just to double-check," Callum said.

One by one, everyone took off, keeping the ruse in place in case they happened to still be watched, no matter how unlikely it seemed.

Colton wasn't sure what he was going to do now. The stalker was still out there, and there didn't seem to be anything he could do about it.

# CHAPTER
# TWENTY-TWO

ELLA WOKE up inside Colton's old truck. She vaguely remembered his waking her before dawn and shuffling her in here in a blanket. He hadn't said where they were going, and she'd been too tired to ask—then she'd promptly fallen back asleep as soon as the engine had started.

"Is this a kidnapping?" She popped a hand over her mouth when the last word came out as a yawn.

He smiled over at her. "Maybe, since you've been unconscious for a couple hours. It was starting to feel that way."

She un-cocooned herself from the blanket so she could stretch. "I can't believe you still have this truck. You were driving this thing around back in high school. It's ancient."

"Hey, now. Respect your elders. This truck is my most prized possession."

She smiled. It had been his most prized possession back in high school also. She reached up and patted the dashboard. "I apologize, beautiful."

Colton nodded in approval. "Good. Now she might get us there without breaking down."

"Where are we going?"

"One of my favorite places on the planet. Garnet Bend,

Montana. I have a lot of friends here. It's home of the Resting Warrior Ranch, although that's not where we're going."

She blinked, looking out the window. "It's beautiful here."

"I decided we needed a break, away from everything. Lilah is going to cover anything you need at work, and Bear has given us the full day off from camp."

Just for a second, she almost argued but then decided he was right. They did need a break.

"How long have we been driving?"

"A while. But it will be worth it, I promise."

That sounded fine to Ella. Honestly, merely driving with him was a treat. She wished she hadn't slept for so long, but she knew she'd needed it.

"Do you want me to drive? I've gotten more sleep than you have."

He smiled, reached over, and grabbed her hand. She told herself not to read too much into that, but the gesture made her want to break into a grin.

"No, I'm fine. We are almost there now anyway."

A few minutes later, a little town seemed to pop out of nowhere in the middle of the mountains. Garnet Bend was charming—had the same small town appeal of Oak Creek.

"Are we stopping here?" she asked.

"Nope."

"Aw, man. I'm disappointed." She craned her neck to look out the window as they passed out the other side of the little town. It truly wasn't very big.

"How about if we come back another time?"

"Deal. But if we're not stopping here, then where are we going now?"

"To a cabin in the wilderness."

Her eyebrows shot up. "You do know we have those just outside of Oak Creek, right? In our billion acres of wilderness surrounding the town?"

She giggled as he poked her in her ribs. "You just wait, smartass. You tell me if it's worth it when we get to our destination."

She knew it would be even if he was taking her to the most unremarkable place in the country. They were together, they were laughing, and Colton, despite not having gotten much sleep, seemed relaxed and nowhere near any sort of panic attack.

So, whatever cabin it was, she was sure it would be great.

About twenty minutes outside of Garnet Bend, he pulled off on a side road and took them way up into the middle of nowhere, before parking. "We need to walk from here. But not too far, so don't worry."

He grabbed a small bag from the truck and held it up. "A change of clothes for both of us."

"I don't guess you have a picnic basket in there also?" She didn't necessarily like highlighting that she needed food, but she wasn't one of the size-zero models he'd been known to date in the past. She was already a little hungry.

"There will be some stuff in the cabin."

She was careful to keep her face neutral, but she grimaced internally. She'd been raised in Oak Creek, so she had spent a little bit of time in various hunter's cabins as a kid. Yes, they tended to have some canned goods and emergency rations. They weren't very tasty, but they would suffice. Or hell, it wouldn't kill her to fast for a day.

They walked for about twenty minutes and finally came up to the cabin.

Yep. There were definitely cabins just like this scattered all around Oak Creek. But she wasn't about to say that to Colton.

But evidently, she didn't have to. "Oh, ye of little faith."

But his eyes were bright as he punched in a code on the cabin door, and it opened. The fact that there was a code on the door should've clued her in, but she was still expecting the sparse provisions of a normal hunter's cabin as she walked inside.

She could not have been more wrong.

When Colton flipped on the light, Ella's jaw dropped in amazement. The inside of the cabin was small but beautifully styled.

There was a decent-sized kitchen area, along with a couch, side table, and a large fireplace, then a very comfy-looking king-sized bed on the other side of the room.

But the most impressive fixture was the steaming hot spring nestled in the corner, inside the actual cabin.

"Oh my gosh." She couldn't stop spinning slowly in circles and taking it all in. "Wait. How is there electricity here?"

"A mix of solar plus clever usage of the spring that also flows out back. And the spring is also a natural heat system."

"It's magical." There was no other word for it.

"It started out as a very simple cabin around a hot spring decades ago and then the Resting Warrior guys have been steadily improving it for years. I try to come here as often as I can."

"I can see why. It's beautiful and so romantic."

This was where he brought his women. It had to be. She closed her eyes and pushed away the thought. Even if this was where he brought women, she wasn't going to let that ruin the time they had together in this magical place.

"Hey." She opened her eyes as his fingers traced up her arms that she had crossed over her chest. "What just happened?"

"Nothing. It's silly."

"Tell me."

She shrugged. "You bring your lady friends here. I don't blame you. This is a great place."

He pulled her against his chest and wrapped his arms around her. "You're the only woman—the only person at *all*—I've ever brought here. This is my haven I come to when I want to get away from everything else and think."

She rested her head against his chest and sighed. "Even if you had brought women here, it would be okay."

"I know the press—and hell, Tony and the rest of my public relations team—try to make me out to be some sort of player or ladies' man, but that's not how I am."

"It's okay. Someone of your popularity is bound to have a lot of—"

He shook his head, cutting her off. "They want to make it seem like I'm with a different woman every night because it perpetuates the *adventurous hero* stereotype—" he made exaggerated air quotes with his fingers "—but I have no interest in that. For a while, it was fun, but it hasn't been that way for a long time."

She felt bad that she was making him defend himself. "Colton—"

He pulled back so that they could look each other in the eye. "I haven't been with anybody since you at the wedding. And even before then, it'd been months. I don't want you to get the idea that I think of women as disposable. And I very definitely don't think of you that way."

With those chocolate-colored eyes locked with hers, it was impossible to doubt the sincerity of his words. She reached up and cupped his hard jaw with her hands. "Thank you for bringing me here. Now, let's get into that hot spring."

He smiled and the tension was broken.

Once their clothes were off, they didn't make it into the steamy water right away, and even once they did make it in, they couldn't keep their hands off each other. Not that Ella was complaining at all.

Colton sat with his head leaning back against the edge of the spring, eyes closed. Ella was on the other end, also lying back, loving the feel of their legs entwined and how he gently rubbed his foot up and down her calf, as if he couldn't stand the thought of not touching her, despite the two rounds of lovemaking they'd just had.

"This is the best cabin ever," he muttered. "I suspected that was true before today, but today cemented it for me."

"I wish we could stay here and let all our problems figure themselves out back home. Speaking of, how did the sting operation go?"

He explained what had happened and that they hadn't had any luck.

She immediately knew the issue. "Well, the problem was that you were sitting there alone."

He shrugged. "We were trying to make me seem approachable in case the stalker got the nerve to come up and talk to me."

Ella sat up a little straighter in the water. She wasn't law enforcement or any sort of profiler, but she did know what it was like to be someone who couldn't get Colton Harrison out of her mind.

"I'm not sure that approaching you is her endgame, despite the letters."

"What do you mean?" His eyes popped open.

"I feel like everything she's doing may be more to feed the fantasy in her mind than it is to actually meet you."

He stopped rubbing her leg with his foot. "Honestly, that was my thinking too, until recently, when all this took a turn for the more crazy. I might not have ever really pursued catching her at all if it weren't for that. The knife through the pictures and the talk about being together forever."

"If you want to catch her taking a picture of you, I think you're going to have to be doing more normal stuff. Sitting alone at a bar isn't normal for you."

"Normal, like going on a date?"

Ella nodded. "Sure. As a matter of fact, that might get her jealous enough to force her into action. Maybe you have a lady friend that you can call up and ask to help you out?"

The thought gutted her, but if it got the stalker out in the open, then that was the only thing that mattered. Plus, it wasn't like she and Colton had any sort of commitment to each other.

"A lady friend I can call up?" He cocked his eyebrow nearly to his hairline.

"Yeah, you know, like an ex-girlfriend or someone."

He held his hand up to his face, his pinkie at his mouth and his thumb at his ear, simulating a phone. "Hi, is this Ella? I was just wondering if you would go on a date with me tonight. A date to catch a stalker might be a little untraditional, but at least doing it with you would make it amazing. Please say yes and save me from a maniac."

She laughed. "You know I'm not your normal type of date. I'm not sure of your normal type at all."

She didn't want to spend too much time thinking about his normal type: thin, leggy blondes.

He "hung up" his phone and swam over to her, placing his arms on the edge of the rock ledge on either side of her, trapping her in.

"*You* are my normal type now. So, if you don't have any plans for tonight, let's get back to town and see if we can catch a bad guy."

Maybe not the most traditional of dates, but she would take it.

# CHAPTER
# TWENTY-THREE

ELLA KNEW this was a fake date, but it still felt real.

They'd driven back from Montana earlier this afternoon, Colton calling the team and setting everything up as they drove. They decided that going back to the Eagle's Nest would probably make the most sense—that was where Colton would take a date here in town.

She'd gone home and dressed in her cutest little sundress. She figured that was probably stupid, pretend date and all, but when Colton had shown up at her door, he was wearing a nice sweater and khaki pants. Also a little dressy. He hadn't needed to make the effort, but it meant a lot to her that he had.

It meant a lot that he'd ordered a bottle of wine for their table as if this were a completely real date too.

At the very least, they were fooling everyone in town, if all the knowing looks and smiles were anything to go by. Nobody was bold enough to come up to them and ask outright what was going on, but Ella had no doubt they would be the subject of much gossip.

She'd already been ignoring all of Lilah's suggestive texts. The woman was sitting at the far side of the Eagle's Nest, and Ella didn't dare make eye contact with her since she was sure it would lead to rude sexual gestures. Lilah was Lilah.

The rest of the team was here again just like they had been last night. Callum and Lincoln were outside; Lilah, Derek, and Theo were here inside.

So, yeah, a date with Colton, but it didn't really count when all your friends were surveilling you.

Colton reached over and took her hand in his. "You look a little nervous. Because of the stalker? I promise you're not in any danger."

She gave a shrug. "No, that's not it. I'm not worried about that."

"Then what? Talk to me, Butter—"

He broke off in the middle of the endearment and pointed at his ear, reminding both of them that he was on the comms unit with the rest of the team. And that was the problem, wasn't it?

"Tell me what you're thinking," he began again.

"This is our first date," she finally said.

She wasn't sure exactly what she'd been expecting, but it definitely wasn't him tilting his head to study her and then nodding. He touched something on his ear. "I'm going off comms. You guys can handle this. Right?"

Whatever response he got had him slipping the small device out of his ear and into his pants pocket.

"Why did you do that?"

"You're right. This is our first date. I don't want to have everyone listening. I want to be with you. The team can handle it if any stranger shows up who fits the profile. Being with you is more important to me."

She couldn't stop the smile that crept up over her face. This wasn't some ruse. He wasn't acting.

Colton Harrison really wanted to be here with her on a date. Nothing could have made her feel more special.

They ordered food, and soon, Ella was forgetting anyone else was around except the two of them. They talked about their favorite memories from high school and different places they both traveled since they both had celebrity fathers. Their food was delivered as they talked.

"Are you ready for our wilderness adventure tomorrow?"

Ella took a bite of her chicken and let out a groan. "I guess so. Although my role is to show the kids that even non-outdoorsy people can do wilderness survival stuff too."

Colton chuckled. "Those kids are a unique blend, aren't they? Some of them would rather be inside on a computer with Lincoln, and some of them we'll have to drag out of the wilderness because they want to stay."

"I can't believe the camp is almost over. I met a baking buddy. Her name is Ashley. She wants to know if she can come back when she's in high school and do an internship at Fancy Pants. She's definitely got the skills for it."

"Yeah, I've seen her. I've been spending a lot of time with Marshall, and I think he has a little crush on her."

A smile tugged at Ella's lips. "I think the feeling is mutual, although both of them are so guarded that camp will be over and they won't do anything about it. But I'll bet they'll stay in touch afterward. Maybe we can help them spend some time together while we're camping."

He laughed as he took a bite of his steak. "Look at you, the little matchmaker."

"I just like watching their eyes light up when they see each other and then pretend like neither of them really cares. It's cute."

Colton kept her entertained and laughing as they finished their meal. There had been no word from anybody on the team, so she assumed nothing was going on that they needed to know about concerning the stalker.

"Do you think this is another dead end?" she whispered when their meal was over and the waitress had cleared away their plates.

"Hell no."

"But surely the team would've told us if anybody was around who fit the bill."

"Yeah, I mean the chances that we're going to catch the stalker tonight are probably slim, but that definitely does not mean this night has been a dead end. The opposite, in fact."

She could feel herself blushing. "Good, I'm glad you feel that way. And I'm hoping maybe we can have another date at some point that doesn't involve most of our closest friends keeping an eye on us."

"Bet on it."

"Should we pack it in? Do you want us to hang out here longer? I'm good either way."

Colton looked out toward the middle of the bar where some couples were dancing. "How about a dance?"

"Do you think that will help with the stalker?"

He winked at her. "Probably not. But if having a stalker gives me an excuse to dance with you, then I'm thankful for every letter that psycho has sent me."

She wanted nothing more than to believe he was telling the truth. "Okay, you have a debrief with the team. I'm going to go to the restroom really quickly."

"Hurry back."

She was walking on air as she headed to the bathroom, so caught up in her own happiness that she forgot she was walking by Lilah, who was sitting at the bar. The other woman smacked her discreetly on the ass and winked when Ella jumped and looked over. "Looks like you're having a good time. I'm so happy for you, Elly-Belly."

Even the dreaded nickname couldn't pull Ella from her happiness. "Anything happening on your guys' end?"

"Nothing so far. But if you two are having a good time, we're happy to merely be along for the ride. Now, get out of here before you blow my cover. Although it would probably be more suspicious if we hadn't stopped to talk."

Ella wanted to tell her friend all about what she was feeling, how much fun she was having—despite potential stalker issues—but it would have to wait. Not only were they in the middle of an op, Lilah would need at least a couple of hours to congratulate herself on getting Ella and Colton together.

Ella chuckled to herself as she left Lilah and continued to the bathroom, glancing at herself in the mirror as she walked in. God, she was flushed, but it looked good on her.

It felt good on her too.

Yes, she wished this date were under different circumstances, but she was having the most wonderful time. Most people didn't spend the day making love in an isolated cabin and *then* go out on their first date, but she couldn't bring herself to care. And the biggest thrill of all was that the night wasn't over yet.

She went into the stall to use the bathroom, and a few moments later, two other women walked in. Ella was about to flush the toilet when their words stopped her.

"I mean, that is Colton Harrison, right?"

Ella froze. Could this possibly be the stalker? She peeked through the crack in the stall. One of the women she recognized as a local. Susan or Sarah—something like that. Ella didn't know her well. She was younger, maybe twenty-one or twenty-two, and worked part time at the grocery store. The other woman who brought up Colton's name was the same age. Ella didn't recognize her at all.

"Yeah," Susan/Sarah said. "He grew up here, but he's not around very often."

"He's super hot."

Maybe this woman *was* the stalker. She was definitely homed in on Colton. Maybe she had befriended *Samantha*—yeah, that was the grocery clerk's name—to have a legitimate reason for being at the Eagle's Nest.

Ella squinted at her through the crack in the stall, trying to force her brain to remember if this could've been the person in the black hoodie. It was possible. Ella tried to memorize as many of the woman's features as she could this time. Brown hair, freckles, wide-set eyes.

"Yeah, he's hot," Samantha agreed. "But he always hangs out with his group of Linear Tactical friends, so I wouldn't get your hopes up about anything happening."

"Who's that woman he's eating with? His sister?"

Samantha chuckled. "You wish. That's his date. Her name is Ella."

The other woman's eyes got wide. "Really? That's his *date*? That woman—all plus-size of her—is not who I expected Colton Harrison to be taking on a date."

Samantha smacked at her arm. "Jesus, Crystal, be nice."

Crystal. Ella tried to focus on getting as many details of Crystal's appearance as possible and not on the woman's unkind words. That wasn't what was important.

"Don't tell me that everybody out there wasn't thinking the same thing."

Samantha shrugged. "From what I've heard, Ella has had a crush on him, like, forever."

Ella could feel her face heating for an entirely different reason now.

Crystal pulled out some lipstick and dotted it on her lips. "It's so nice of him to take the time to go out with someone like her. I mean, I guess it makes sense while he's here in this tiny town to give the ordinary girls some attention too."

"It looked like they were having fun."

"Oh, I can imagine *she* was having fun. But Colton? I mean, he's basically an actor, right? So maybe he's using this as practice for facial expressions in future stunts. You never know when the *I need to pretend like I'm interested in this not super-attractive person* look is going to be needed for a stunt."

"Jesus, Crystal, you're such a bitch."

Ella watched Crystal put her lipstick away. "I just call them as I see them. Colton's being nice to that woman now, but I'm sure he'll be back to his normal caliber of dating as soon as he is out of this town and has more options. That Ella person won't keep his attention long."

The women finished their makeup touch-ups then left.

Ella stayed where she was long after they were gone, even when other women came in and out.

Was this what people thought about her and Colton?

Even more importantly, was it the truth and she was just blinding herself to it? Would he be back to dating his normal "type" as soon as he was gone from Oak Creek?

It was only the thought that Crystal could possibly be the stalker that finally had Ella leaving the bathroom. She washed her hands then immediately went to find Lilah.

"Damn, girl. Are you okay? You were in there a long time."

Ella spotted Samantha and Crystal then twisted around until her back was to them and Lilah would be able to see them over her shoulder. "Do you see those two women behind me? I'm wondering if one of them, her name is Crystal something, could be the stalker. She was talking about Colton in the bathroom."

Lilah pressed the comms unit at her ear. "Lincoln, are we sure that the Crystal woman you ran earlier is clean? She was talking about Colton in the bathroom."

Ella couldn't hear Lincoln's response, but Lilah shook her head. "We'll dig into her more deeply, but Lincoln is fairly certain she's clean."

Lilah made a face at something that was said in her ear. "Lincoln would like to state for the record that Crystal is not the stalker. Evidently, his software is God and knows all things."

Lincoln obviously had something to say to that in Lilah's ear because she rolled her eyes.

"Okay. I just wanted to make sure," Ella said. Her shoulders slumped. She couldn't help it. If Crystal had been the stalker, then maybe she could've written off what the other woman had said.

"You okay, honey?" Lilah asked.

*No.* "Yeah. I think I'll be wanting to turn in soon, so we might have to wrap up the search for tonight."

"Oh, I thought Colton said you guys were going to dance."

She couldn't stand thought of eyes on her right now and what everyone might be thinking if they were dancing together. "I'm tired, and I'm a terrible dancer anyway."

"Elly-Belly…"

God, she hated that name. "I'll catch you later, Li. Thanks for being here tonight and helping Colton out."

She didn't see Colton at their table and wasn't sure where he'd gone. She let out a surprised yelp when an arm wrapped around her waist and pulled her against a hard body. "Dance with me, Butterscotch."

She couldn't seem to find the words to say no, so she let him pull her onto the dance floor. It was a slow dance, so he tucked her against him.

She could feel eyes on her. Knew everyone was looking and wondering and judging.

"Hey. You okay?" he asked.

"I..." She had no idea what to say.

"Whatever it is, just tell me. It's better for us to talk it out than let—"

She wasn't sure what he was going to say because Theo rushed up to them.

"Colton, Callum just caught someone putting something on your truck. It's a foot chase outside."

"I'm coming." Colton squeezed her waist. "Stay here. I'll be back soon."

With that, he was gone, walking as fast as he could out the door without causing a huge scene.

Leaving Ella alone on the dance floor with everyone looking at her.

# CHAPTER
# TWENTY-FOUR

As soon as he and Theo hit the door of the Eagle's Nest, they were running. Colton got the comms unit out of his pocket, flipped it to automatic so he could talk freely, and stuck it in his ear.

"Somebody update me."

"Suspect moved toward your truck," Callum said. "We didn't realize what we had on our hands until she stuck a letter and picture in the crack of the door. She took off when we approached. Heading south on Grant Street. I'm in my vehicle. Lincoln is on foot."

"She's fast." Lincoln's labored breathing punctuated the words.

If Lincoln was saying she was fast, it was no joke. The other man might be a computer genius, but he also kept himself in top physical shape.

"There's only so much I can do in a vehicle," Callum said. "Too many side roads and alleys in town."

"Theo and I are coming on foot." Colton pushed himself for more speed. He wasn't going to let her get away, no matter how fast she was.

"I had Derek and Lilah stay at the bar with Ella, just in case." Theo was right next to Colton, step for step.

Knowing Ella was protected allowed Colton to just focus on the chase. This woman might be ahead of them—and fast—but she didn't know Oak Creek the way they did. They would use that to their advantage.

"Linc, see if you can get her to cut down Broadmoor. That will eventually lead to a dead end," he said.

"Colton is right," Callum added. "Lincoln, actually, if you get her to cut down any side street south of Main, I'll be there to cut her off."

"Roger that," Lincoln responded. "I think she's going to—*shit*."

"What?" Lincoln wasn't one to express frustration in curse words.

"She just cut down Lexington," the other man said.

They all muttered curses. The stalker had just gotten extremely lucky—Lexington gave her more exits out of town than any other street she could've picked to dash down.

"We're going to have to split up." Colton ran the options in his head.

"Agreed," Callum said. "I'll stay on Grant in the car in case she spins back around. Theo, you go down Baxter Road. Lincoln, try to force her west. Colton, you come around from the east side and box her in."

They muttered agreements and pushed for speed.

"She's not slowing down," Lincoln said. "And I'm not making any gains on her."

Just their luck his stalker was some sort of Olympic sprinter.

Colton and Theo split off from each other without a word. They both knew where they needed to go.

Everyone ran in silence for a few moments before Lincoln's voice came through the comms system again. "She turned south on Branch."

Colton muttered another curse through labored breath. Damn it. This woman was making all the right choices—her change in direction down that road would also give her a way out of town. So much for trapping her.

But Colton knew a shorter way. It required him to cut through an alley and leap over a damn trash can, but he did it.

"Almost to you, Lincoln." Colton could hear the clanging sound of someone trying to climb the fence and knew that they had her now. He turned the corner, and, sure enough, the woman—and in a black hoodie, no less—was climbing up a chain link fence. If she made it over that, she'd be pretty much home free.

Colton didn't think about it; he leaped—landing hard against the woman and then pulling them both down to the ground, knocking the wind out of himself.

*Shit, that hurt.*

It didn't feel any better when the woman swung her fist out and caught him in the jaw. "Goddamn it."

Colton wasn't one to hit women, but neither was he one to sit there and get his ass kicked just because she was female. But Lincoln caught up to them and did a flying tackle of his own, taking her down completely so she was face first on the ground, Lincoln pulling her arms behind her.

"Get the fuck off me, man."

Wait. That wasn't a woman's voice at all. *What the hell?*

A knife clattered out of the guy's pocket as Lincoln flipped him around so they could see his face.

Hell, not a woman, but not really a man either—a fucking *teenager*.

Colton kicked the knife out of the way, and Lincoln pulled him so he was sitting up against the fence. Colton and Lincoln stood there for a long minute staring down at him, trying to catch their breaths and figure out what the hell was going on.

"Colton, Lincoln, come in." Callum's voice came over the comms. "Update."

"We're at the end of Adams Street. We caught our perp," Colton got out, breathing almost normally enough to talk in full sentences.

"Okay. I'll be there in less than one minute. Don't do anything to her."

"Oh, believe me, we won't do anything to her."

"Teenager, what is your name?" Lincoln asked.

"My name is *Fuck You, Man*," the kid spat out.

Lincoln narrowed his eyes. "I'm fairly certain that is not your actual name."

"Lincoln, he's baiting you. Just ignore him."

Colton watched as the teen's muscles tensed. He was about to make a run for it. Colton squatted down closer to him. "If you make me run after you again, I will catch you. But you won't like it when I do."

"I don't even know why you guys were chasing me in the first place. That's why I was running. What was I supposed to do?" The kid was lying, but his muscles relaxed, so at least he wasn't about to take off again.

"We were chasing you because we told you to stop, and you ran," Lincoln stated.

Colton shook his head. Talking reasonably with this kid wasn't going to get them far, but reason and logic were the only things Lincoln knew.

Sure enough, the teen turned to Lincoln, eyes wide. "I'm just a kid, man. I see grown men running toward me, and yeah, I'm going to take off. How did I know you weren't going to kidnap me or something?"

Colton could see that Lincoln was about to debate the issue with him. "He's baiting you again, Linc. Trying to distract us so he can make a run for it again."

"Are you fucking kidding me right now?" Lincoln was stopped from arguing with the kid further by Callum walking up behind them. "Jeremy Ritter?"

"Shit," the kid muttered.

"You know him?" Colton asked as he stood back up.

Callum raised an eyebrow. "Jeremy and I go way back. A couple of misdemeanor B&Es, underage drinking, and recreational drug use."

Colton scrubbed a hand down his face. "There is no way this is my stalker. Hell, even if we got the gender wrong, there is no way this punk is my stalker."

"Got anything to say, Jeremy?" Callum asked.

"Dude, these guys were chasing me, and how was I supposed to know if they were going to take me back to their love cave or something."

Lincoln and Colton both rolled their eyes. Even Lincoln could recognize the absurdity of this statement.

Theo arrived in a rush a few seconds later, saw the kid, and immediately surmised the situation. "Great."

"Who put you up to this, Jeremy?" Callum crouched down beside him.

"I don't know what you're talking about."

"Somebody paid you to put a knife and the picture on that truck, right? If you tell me who did that, we could pretend like there's no problem."

Jeremy shrugged. "I have no idea what you mean."

Colton reached over and grabbed the knife off the ground, holding it by the handle in front of the kid. "Let me guess, you were supposed to use this to put the letter and picture into my truck door, but you decided to keep the knife for yourself."

Jeremy looked away, and Colton knew he'd discovered the truth.

"Who was it?" he pressed. "Who told you to do this?"

The kid caved. "Look, I don't know. I got a text earlier today, offering me some money to deliver some stuff. I didn't know what it was I'd be delivering."

Callum shook his head. "Let me guess, you thought it would be drugs? You know you're only a half step from juvie, Jeremy."

He shook his head. "No. As a matter of fact, I was very clear that I couldn't do anything illegal. So yeah, when I heard it was just putting a love letter and a picture on a truck, it seemed like easy money."

"And the knife?" Colton asked.

Jeremy shrugged. "Seemed like a waste to just leave it there if I could get the letter and picture to stay attached to the truck without it. Listen, I didn't know any of this was illegal."

"Who paid you?" Callum asked. "Did you get a name?"

"Well, I asked for a business card and a few references, but..." Jeremy rolled his eyes. "No, man, I didn't get a name."

Colton didn't know whether to smack the kid or laugh at him for being such a wiseass. But he didn't need to ask him any more questions to know that this was probably going to be a dead end.

"Was it a woman?" he asked.

Jeremy shrugged. "I couldn't tell by the texts."

"How did you get paid? Electronically?" Lincoln asked.

"No, actually, there was cash in the bag with the stuff I was supposed to leave on the truck."

Lincoln grimaced. "I was hoping our stalker had paid him through some sort of app—I could've traced that, no problem."

Jeremy looked over at Callum. "Like I said, I really didn't think this was something illegal. Yeah, I got a little spooked when you guys started chasing me, but I wasn't trying to get into trouble."

Callum looked over at Colton while rubbing his neck. "Technically..."

"Yeah, I know," Colton responded, knowing what Callum was going to say. Jeremy was right that he hadn't actually broken the law.

"Do you still have the text that started this whole thing?" he asked Jeremy.

Jeremy pulled out his phone. "Yeah, right here."

Lincoln reached for it, and none of them protested. "Give me a couple hours with this phone, and I'll see what I can find. But it looks like it was a third-party app that hides identification, so I'm not terribly hopeful."

"I'm going to take Jeremy back to my office, and we'll go over this again," Callum stood up, pulling Jeremy up by the arm. "If anything comes of it, I'll let you know."

Colton handed the older man the knife, and Callum led the kid off in the direction of his car, the kid whining the whole time.

Colton began walking back toward the Eagle's Nest with Theo and Lincoln.

"She somehow knew this was a sting," Theo said.

Lincoln was still studying the phone in his hand. "Either that or she has always used someone else to deliver the messages."

Colton shook his head. "That's possible, but I've always felt like part of her MO was to deliver them in person. To try to get as close to me as possible. At least, that's what it felt like until I got to Oak Creek, when things started to take a turn for the more vicious."

"She doesn't like that you're here," Theo said.

"Seems that way. And I don't want to be bringing trouble to the people I care about the most. Maybe it's time for me to leave, at least until this is settled."

But hell if that was what he wanted. But what he wanted didn't matter. Making sure Ella was safe was what mattered.

"Maybe," Theo agreed. The other man knew what it was to need to keep his loved ones safe. His wife Eva had had her own stalker who had nearly cost her her life. "But why don't you see if Callum or Lincoln can get any further info first? Let's take the kids on the wilderness adventure—there's no way some stalker is going to find you there. When we get back in a couple of days, maybe we'll have more info to go on."

Colton wasn't very hopeful, but neither was he going to back out on Bear and those kids. Everyone had really been looking forward to this, especially Marshall. Colton couldn't renege now and miss it.

But no matter what, this stalker was going down.

# CHAPTER
# TWENTY-FIVE

COLTON ARRIVED at the Linear Tactical property the next morning with gritty eyes. It had been a long night. He'd been in touch with both Callum and Lincoln multiple times as any sort of update came in.

Unfortunately, all the updates tended to lead nowhere when it came to the identification of the stalker.

Jeremy Ritter was pretty much a punk kid who didn't know his ass from his elbow. The thought of making a couple hundred dollars had been enough to not ask many questions.

Electronics hadn't helped either. As far as Lincoln could tell—and that was pretty damn extensively—the communication to Jeremy had come from a burner phone as well as a third-party app. That meant it could be pretty much anyone, anywhere.

Callum felt certain that the kid was telling the truth when he said he'd had no actual contact with the person who'd hired him. Both Lincoln and Callum were going to keep at it, but neither was very hopeful.

About an hour ago, Colton had finally called Tony and told him about last night's incident and the note found at Fancy Pants. He could tell his PR manager was not happy about being left out of the loop for so long, but Colton wasn't going to apologize for that.

Tony also wasn't happy that Colton didn't have any sort of long-term plans for stunts. But honestly, Colton couldn't even think about that until they had this stalker situation under control. He told Tony to put any and all resources they had toward figuring out who this stalker was. That had become Colton's number one priority.

Because he couldn't keep doing this to Ella. By the time he'd made it back to the Eagle's Nest the night before, Lilah had already taken Ella home. Colton went over there as soon as he could, hoping to find Ella already asleep. She'd been so tense with him out on the dance floor before he'd run out to chase Jeremy that he was crushed he couldn't tell her they had caught the stalker.

He'd hated seeing that pinched look on her pretty face.

But it had still been there when he'd gotten to her house, and she'd still been wide awake. He'd explained what happened and she seemed to take it in stride, but he could tell she was still upset. Or maybe upset wasn't the right word. She'd almost been…sad.

Not afraid, which he would've expected. Not angry, which would be slightly out of character for sweet Ella, but he could understand.

*Sad.* That, he didn't quite know how to wrap his head around. All he knew was that a stalker wasn't what she'd signed up for when she'd gotten involved with him.

He'd held her all night, but except for when she had finally fallen asleep, she'd been stiff in his arms—not pulling away, but like she couldn't quite decide if she fit there or not.

When she'd left early this morning to go to the bakery, the tension in her body had still been there. He'd wanted to go with her, but since they'd already arranged for Lilah to come keep an eye on things at Fancy Pants whenever Ella was there, he decided to just stick with that plan. But there was no way he was leaving Ella alone until the stalker was caught.

He was going to figure this out. But first, these kids. The next two days belonged to them. He'd seen their eyes light up when he'd arrived. Marshall had rushed over to say hello, shaking Colton's hand like the little adult he was.

Bear walked over. "Lincoln told me about last night. Sorry to hear it was a dead end also."

Colton slapped his friend on his back. "Thanks, but I'm not going to worry about it. Right now, I want to focus on the next two days and these campers."

Bear's face relaxed, and he broke into a grin. "That's exactly what I want to hear. I overheard the kids talking, wondering if you were going to be here. Your presence means a lot."

"A chance to hang out with them means a lot to me too."

"Plus, you don't have to worry about your stalker finding us out there. Nobody but our personal circle knows where we're going. And you know Dorian and Ray will handle anybody in the vicinity who doesn't belong there."

Dorian Lindstrom—whose code name had been Ghost when he'd served in Special Forces—and his wife Ray were Theo's parents. They had lived in the wilderness surrounding the Linear Tactical facility for most of Theo's life. A necessity, given that Ray Lindstrom was a listed enemy of the United States government and also officially dead.

"Hopefully Aunt Ray asks questions before shooting anybody with her crossbow." Although Colton wouldn't mind if Ray just took the stalker out.

Bear left to go see about some last-minute supply organization as Ella pulled up in her car. Lilah got out and walked toward Bear, but Ella walked toward Colton.

Her face was still pinched.

"Everything situated at the bakery?"

"Yes. I'm ready to brave the wilderness." She smiled, but it didn't reach her eyes. Colton couldn't stand this.

He trailed his fingers up her arms. "Butterscotch, you don't have to be scared, I promise."

"I'm not scared."

Maybe she wasn't scared, but the look on her face made it

obvious that she still wasn't okay. If he'd had any doubt about leading the stalker away from Oak Creek, that made up his mind for him.

"I'm going to leave town after we get back from the wilderness."

It wasn't what he wanted, but he was determined to get this stalker out of Ella's life and put a happy look back on her face.

"Oh."

"So you're not going to have to worry about the stalker anymore."

"I—" She looked down at the ground.

He cupped her cheeks in order to force her gaze back up to his. "I'm sorry all of this has happened. But for right now, let's just focus on the kids and this excursion. We are one hundred percent safe out here. Nobody here but our inner circle and these kids."

Her eyes brightened. "You're right. Nobody out here but us. That's good."

Seeing the stress slide away from her features just reaffirmed to Colton what he needed to do.

Get himself out of Oak Creek to make sure Ella was safe.

―――

Compared to the people out here right now, Ella was never going to be a wilderness survival expert. Outdoor activities had never been her thing. She preferred cute dresses and desserts over dirt and campfires.

But she knew her presence here proved that anyone could do what the experts were teaching. Granted, Ella had been raised around Oak Creek, so she had been more exposed to outdoor stuff than a lot of people, even though it hadn't been her forte. So, she had her own hiking boots and backpack and knew enough basics that she could keep herself alive if it came down to it.

But she wouldn't like it. She preferred her comfy bed over a sleeping bag, and a three-course meal over food cooked on a campfire.

Regardless, she was glad she was here, even if it was only to see how much the kids were enjoying this. They were finally really loosening up. Her little buddy Ashley had stuck with her for most of the four-hour hike that had gotten them to the main campsite. Ella had enjoyed talking to the girl—had loved all her questions about recipes and flavor profiles. But Ella had also been glad when Marshall had come over to talk to Ashley. The two obviously had crushes on each other, and it was sweet to behold.

Bear and Lilah had used the hike as a teaching opportunity. They pointed out wildlife, poisonous plants, and different types of trees that would be good for fires and shelters. The kids not only were asking more questions now—not afraid to take up space that was rightfully theirs—they were cracking jokes and laughing. This was what Bear had envisioned for these kids, and she was so thankful he was getting to see it come to fruition.

And if she had to hide that she was a half breath from falling apart, so be it.

Colton was leaving. She'd known that was coming from the beginning so she shouldn't let it upset her, but somehow it did. His casual announcement that he'd be leaving town, combined with what she'd heard in the bathroom, had made it clear exactly where she stood.

She'd always known this was temporary. Colton had never made any sort of indication otherwise. Yes, they had good sex. Yes, they had fun together.

But he'd probably had that with a hundred different women. He didn't think of her in the same way as she thought of him. Never had. Never would.

But damn it, she was not going to fall apart here. This time was for the kids. There would be plenty of time to fall apart when she was back on her own.

Not to mention, if these were the last couple of days she had with him, she wanted to soak in this time. There was nobody around to judge like Crystal and Samantha in the bathroom. Nobody around to say he was slumming it by being with her.

"Are you okay, Miss Ella?" Ashley walked over with a hot dog that had been cooked on a stick. "I made this for you."

The kids had been absolutely thrilled to learn about making fires. They'd each been in charge of collecting their own tinder and kindling, and then they had been required to use flint and steel to get a flame started.

Ashley had been one of the last ones to get a fire going, but everyone had cheered her on and encouraged her until she did.

"Did you eat a hot dog?"

The girl nodded enthusiastically. "Yes. And I don't know what it is about Wyoming hot dogs, but that was the best thing I'd ever eaten."

Ella winked at her. "Either that, or it has to do with the fact that you cooked it over a fire that you made with your bare hands."

Ashley's grin got even bigger. "Yeah, maybe. It felt really good to do that. I've never been camping before in my life, because my sister…" She faded off, and her smile fell away.

"Because your sister can't, right?"

"Cancer has taken so much from her."

Ella grabbed the stick with the hot dog Ashley had brought for her. "Cancer has taken a lot from you too. It's okay to acknowledge that and be frustrated. It's okay to feel a little cheated."

"But I'm not the one who is sick." Ashley sat down next to her.

"But you still got dumped with a set of circumstances you didn't choose. Just because you don't complain about it doesn't mean it doesn't suck. It's okay to be angry about that sometimes."

Ashley shrugged one small shoulder. "Sometimes I am angry. But mostly, I try to stay focused on the positive."

Ella wrapped her arm around the girl. "Then you're more mature than most adults, so congratulations."

She took a bite of the hot dog. "That's one of the best I've ever had. And I don't think it has anything to do with this meat being from Wyoming."

She expected the girl to get up and head back over to the other kids, but she stayed there on the log. Ella caught her glancing at

Marshall once again. "Are you going to try to keep in touch with Marshall after the camp?"

A blush crept up over her face. "Yes. Do you think that's okay?"

"Of course! Marshall is a great guy. Even just keeping him as a friend would be completely appropriate."

She let out a small sigh. "We live pretty far from each other, but we could text and talk on the phone. I like that he's just...*mine*. Do you know what I mean?"

Yes, Ella knew exactly what the girl meant. But it was probably better to get her to explain it so she was sure about it herself. "Tell me more."

Ashley rubbed a pattern in the dirt with her foot. "That he doesn't know my sister or my family. That he doesn't look at me like the kid who can't do a lot of stuff because her parents are always gone for medical purposes. He doesn't feel sorry for me."

"And even better, he totally understands your situation. And probably feels the same that maybe you can just be...*his*."

A soft smile broke out on Ashley's face. "Yeah, I like that."

Ashley was thirteen and Marshall was fourteen. They both had very complex lives and lived in separate states. The chances of them "making it" as a couple were slim to none.

But Ella still hoped they did.

"I tell you what—you go over and talk to Marshall. Spend as much time together as you can in the days you have left with him. You won't regret that. And, at the very least, even if it doesn't work out, you'll still have some very precious memories that you can keep forever."

Yeah, she was definitely talking to herself just as much as she was talking to the girl.

"Do you think Marshall will mind?"

Ella had to laugh out loud at that. "He's looked over at you half a dozen times in the ten minutes you've been sitting here. So no, I don't think he will mind one little bit."

"What about you and Mr. Colton? Is he your boyfriend?"

"I'd like to think so."

Ella stiffened at the sound of Colton's voice behind them. Ashley spun around to grin up at him. "Good. You guys are cute."

With that, she ran off, straight toward Marshall.

Colton sat down next to Ella. "You didn't have to say that."

He narrowed his eyes at her. "Maybe I wanted to say that."

She wasn't sure how to respond. Just a few hours ago, he'd told her he was leaving, and now he was talking about boyfriend-girlfriend stuff. She had no idea what to think.

"What's really going on, Butterscotch? Are you still this concerned about the stalker? I promise you, we're going to get that handled."

She wasn't worried about the stalker, although she wanted that bitch gone so that Colton didn't have to worry about any of it any longer. But right now, she was providing a nice scapegoat for Ella not having to tell Colton what was really wrong.

"I know you will. I don't doubt that for a second."

"Are you sure? Last night and this morning, you seemed so upset."

He was looking at her so earnestly, she almost told him the truth about the bathroom. But what would that do? Maybe if they were going to start an actual relationship—be the boyfriend he was pretending to be in front of Ashley—she would try to talk it out. But without that, explaining the details of what she'd heard in that bathroom would just add to the patheticity.

She was saved from having to answer by Bear announcing that everyone needed to come over so he could demonstrate how to build shelters.

She stood up. "Let's just focus on these kids and helping them have fun. If they liked making fire, I have no doubt they're going to love making their own shelters."

He wrapped an arm around her waist and yanked her up against him, studying her intently. "I know you're avoiding something, but I'll let it go for now."

"I just want to enjoy the moment."

"Then let's go build shelters. But you plan on sleeping under mine with me. We won't do anything inappropriate, but I want you next to me, Butterscotch."

What was she supposed to say to that? "Okay."

He winked at her, and everything inside her body went soft and gooey. Good thing there were a bunch of kids around.

He let her go, and they turned and walked toward the group together. A number of the kids had noticed the moment between them, as well as Lilah, who was waggling her eyebrows. Ella just ignored them.

They could think what they wanted, but Ella needed to keep focused on the truth: what she had with Colton was temporary, and soon, he'd be gone.

# CHAPTER
# TWENTY-SIX

"IN THE WILDERNESS, we have what's called the rule of threes."

The next morning, Colton sat back and listened to the lesson Bear was teaching around the campfire as the kids ate breakfast. It wasn't anything Colton hadn't already heard before, but watching the kids listen so raptly had renewed Colton's interest in the basics also.

"The human body can survive for roughly three minutes without oxygen. So, that's for if you're trapped underwater."

Or under snow, but Colton didn't interject.

"We can survive about three hours exposed to extreme elements," Bear continued. "You can survive three days without water, and three weeks without food."

One of the kids laughed and shook his head. "I'm pretty sure I couldn't survive three weeks without food."

Bear grinned at the kid. "Actually, you can probably last quite a bit longer than that, but it wouldn't be fun."

Marshall raised his hand. "Which of these aspects is the most dangerous? Which type of exposure tends to kill the most people?"

Bear rubbed his hands together. "Great question. Anybody want to take a guess?"

The kids immediately started discussing the ramifications among themselves. The general consensus was that lack of water tended to kill the most people.

"Actually, it's exposure to the elements that takes out the most hikers and wilderness enthusiasts. That's why we spent so much time yesterday discussing how to make shelters and fires. It's why you should always have different types of clothing layers in your backpack when you go camping, as well as a tarp and an emergency blanket."

Lilah nodded next to Bear. "Especially around here in the mountains, the weather can change drastically and quickly. You have to be aware of what's going on around you." She pointed up to a set of clouds in the distance. "I'm keeping my eye on those. Right now, it looks like the storm will miss us, and that's great. But if anything changes, what would I want to do to prepare for a possible incoming storm?"

Hands shot up all around the campfire.

"Build a shelter," one kid said.

"Absolutely," Bear nodded. "And what's our rule about shelter?"

"Higher is drier," the kids all called out together.

Bear grinned. "Yep, if rain is coming, you don't want to end up in a flash flood area."

"What else?" Lilah asked. She pointed to Ashley.

At first, Ashley didn't look like she was going to respond but found her courage. "Getting some tinder together and keeping it dry so we can restart the fire after the storm."

Lilah ran over and gave the quiet girl a high five. "Brilliant. I sometimes keep some dried grass and tiny sticks wrapped up in my jacket when I see a storm is coming. Nothing worse than trying to rebuild a fire when you're cold and everything is wet."

Bear and Lilah fielded all the other questions and comments from the students, then they went back over certain knots and fire-making techniques that had been discussed briefly the day before.

Colton listened while occasionally glancing over at Ella. She seemed to be relaxing more with each hour they were here in the wilderness. He'd loved having her sleeping beside him in their primitive shelter. They hadn't even so much as been touching, but just having her nearby had felt right. He'd slept nearly the whole night.

The kids prepared another meal over fires they'd built then they split into groups for the afternoon's activity: a wilderness scavenger hunt.

The groups were based on the degree to which the campers had expressed true interest in wilderness survival. Those who were completely interested—about half the students—were going with Bear, Theo, and Lilah. They'd be learning more advanced stuff and finding harder items on the scavenger hunt list.

Those who weren't as interested in the finer nuances of survival would be sticking around the less-expert instructors like him and Ella.

It was all going to be fun no matter who the students and instructors were paired with, but Colton couldn't help but keep an eye on which group Marshall decided to place himself in. It looked like he was heading toward the more advanced group until it became obvious Ashley was going to stick with Ella.

"Tough call, little man," Colton muttered. But he wasn't surprised when Marshall grabbed his backpack and headed toward the two ladies when it was time to go.

Colton did the exact same thing.

For a couple hours, they were with other campers and adults—everyone working together to find the items on the list: a yellow flower, a smooth rock, various types of edible plants. But as Ashley and Ella slowed down to take in more of the scenery and colors around them, Colton and Marshall found themselves falling back with them.

"I'm a little surprised you didn't go with the advanced class," Colton remarked to Marshall while the girls were over looking at a meadow of flowers and were out of earshot.

Marshall shrugged one shoulder while organizing the list of

items he'd found. "I knew Ashley wouldn't be interested in the advanced group. She likes learning about this stuff, but it's not really her thing."

"But is it your thing? Are you afraid you are missing out?"

"No offense, but all the survival stuff I can find online—videos, books, articles, interviews. Yeah, learning in person is optimal, but I have other options available." He glanced over at Colton, probably to see if he'd just offended him.

He hadn't.

"And since you can get that information other places, you'd rather spend the time you do have getting to know Ashley."

"Yeah, exactly." Marshall nodded solemnly. "Do you think that's dumb?"

"The opposite. You can do a lot of things on your own, but spending time with that special someone is not one of them. Sometimes choosing the less exciting route is actually the more exciting route."

The gals happen to look up and over at them at that very second. Both he and Marshall gave them a wave.

"Thanks for understanding," Marshall said.

Colton understood much more than the kid could possibly know.

Since they were both at an unspoken agreement that they would be learning at the girls' pace and helping them have fun rather than focusing too much on the scavenger hunt, everything seemed to slow down for them just to enjoy themselves and the company. Colton still tried to teach as much as he could—indicating more edible and dangerous plants, animal tracks as they saw them, and even a few critters here and there that were brave enough to show themselves. Ella and Ashley pointed out different colors and what baked goods were modeled after those different hues. Everyone talked and laughed and enjoyed themselves.

It was sort of like being on a mini double date. Colton had been all over the world with all sorts of famous people and wasn't sure he'd ever had as good a time.

"Look at those—they're gorgeous." Ashley rushed off the path toward a group of flowers growing in tall columns in all different colors. "Can I pick some?"

"No!" both Colton and Ella called out before the girl could touch them. She turned around to them, eyes wide.

"Those are larkspur," Ella explained. "Beautiful, but toxic."

"Pictures only. Touching them will make you break out. Ingesting them?" Colton ran a finger across his throat in an exaggerated manner before making choking sounds and falling to the ground with his eyes closed.

Ella shook her head. "Guess he's dead. Let's leave him here for the animals."

She squealed when he got up and chased her, tickling her until she begged for mercy when he caught her.

Her laugh was the most beautiful sound he'd ever heard.

It was almost time to head back to the main camp when Colton finally had a chance to talk to Ella alone as Ashley and Marshall stood on some large rocks overlooking the edge of the fast-flowing river. They'd slipped off their backpacks—Marshall helping Ashley —then climbed up to a high boulder.

"I would remind them to be careful, but they're both more responsible than I am, so it seems like overkill."

Ella laughed. "They are definitely little adults. It's really nice to watch the two of them, isn't it? Young love."

"I don't know about Ashley, but Marshall is definitely smitten."

Colton glanced over at Ella as she watched the kids. Marshall wasn't the only one smitten.

"I think it definitely goes both ways. I saw how Ashley's eyes lit up when you guys agreed to stay with us rather than go with the more competitive groups."

He trailed a finger down her arm, unable to stop himself from touching her. "No place either Marshall or I would rather be."

Her soft smile had to be the most beautiful thing he'd ever seen. He tried to figure out a way of telling her that without sounding completely pathetic.

"You're so damn beautiful, Ella." Actually, he didn't care if it sounded pathetic. Because it was the goddamn truth.

"Somebody told you, didn't they?" The smile fell away from her face. "Somebody overheard or something, and they told you. That's why you're telling me I'm pretty."

He had no idea what she was talking about. "The word I used was *beautiful*, and I used it for a reason. Those larkspurs we were looking at were pretty. You're so much more than just pretty."

She shook her head. "You don't have to say that."

"Butterscotch, what are you talking about? I know I don't have to say it. I'm saying it because it's true, because I—"

His words were cut off by Ashley's scream.

Both he and Ella turned just in time to see Ashley fall off the boulder toward the icy water below. Marshall grabbed for her, catching her, her momentum slamming him belly-first onto the boulder as he attempted to hold all her weight with one arm.

Colton sprinted for the kids, Ella right behind him.

"No, Ashley, hang on!" Marshall let out a pained cry as his body slid closer to the edge, trying to hold Ashley's weight at an awkward angle that put way too much pressure on his shoulder socket.

But still he held on to Ashley.

"Fuck. He's not going to be able to hold her." Colton recognized how things were going to go before he was even halfway to Ashley and Marshall. He immediately spun and started running in the opposite direction.

"What?" Ella yelled as he passed back by her.

He didn't stop running. "They're both going to fall in."

Colton hit the shore again and started running downstream. Sure enough, just a couple seconds later, he heard Marshall and Ashley each let out a scream as they plummeted toward the water below.

Colton dove out as far as he could into the river, knowing the kids would soon be flowing right by him. The cold sucked the air out of his lungs, but he ignored it as he moved forward, and he felt something hit him.

Ashley.

He gripped the girl's arm and dragged her back toward the shore.

"I've got her." Ella grabbed Ashley out of his hands, waist-deep in the river herself. She began dragging the girl the rest of the way to the shore as Colton dove back into the icy water.

He saw Marshall's head bob up out of the water for a split second, and he pushed himself in a swim toward the boy. The rushing rapids poured over him, and for just a second, panic poured over him also.

In his mind, it wasn't water closing in around him, it was the snow from the avalanche. There was no air, only cold. No way to escape.

He stopped swimming, his muscles feeling trapped like in the snow.

Colton gritted his teeth and shook off the thoughts. If he gave in to panic now, it was not only going to cost him his life, but Marshall's too.

No. Not today.

He forced himself to start swimming again, though his arms felt frozen. If he didn't get Marshall out soon, the rapids would take him downstream and Colton wouldn't be able to save him.

"Make yourself as big as possible!" he screamed at Marshall. Hopefully that would slow him down a little in the water.

Marshall somehow heard him and threw one arm up in the air, trying to get more vertical. It slowed him enough that Colton was able to reach him after a few moments of pushing for as much speed as he could.

He wrapped an arm around the boy's chest and swam with all his might back toward the shore. Marshall did what he could to help, but they were both frozen and exhausted.

When they made it far enough that they were out of the river's pull, Colton flopped over on his back. They weren't out of danger—not with both of them being so cold, but there was nothing else he could do.

It was all up to Ella now.

# CHAPTER
# TWENTY-SEVEN

This had just gone from being an exercise in wilderness emergencies to an actual wilderness emergency. Ella pulled Ashley all the way out of the water. The girl was shivering, which was actually a good sign. It meant that she wasn't hypothermic. At least not yet.

Ella dashed up to their backpacks and grabbed all four, carrying them back down to where Ashley still sat on the shore. She took out a mylar blanket and wrapped it around the girl.

"Stay here. I'm going to help Colton with Marshall."

"H-he—he tried to catch me." Ashley could hardly get the words out around her chattering teeth.

Ella squeezed her shoulder. "Colton will get him."

She prayed that was true. That Colton would be able to reach the boy. That he wouldn't be hit by a panic attack at the cold of the water—that would be understandable, but deadly.

She hoisted her own backpack on one shoulder and Colton's on the other, then ran down the shoreline toward where they had floated.

At first, she ran in silence, but when she could find no sign of them, she began to get a little panicked herself. What if they hadn't made it out?

"Colton!" She pushed herself to run faster but was careful not to injure herself. A sprained ankle right now might be deadly on multiple levels. "Colton!"

She stopped and attempted to hear past her labored breathing.

"Ella…" It wasn't loud, but she heard it.

"I'm coming!"

She found both Colton and Marshall still partially in the water. Shit. That wasn't good. She dropped down beside Marshall and pulled him the rest of the way onto the shore, knowing Colton wasn't going to let her help him until she helped the boy. She needed to get his wet clothes off him, but she wanted to get Colton out of the water first.

Once she deposited Marshall, she ran back into the river for Colton.

He shook his head as she reached for him. "H-help Marshall."

"I will, as soon as you're out of the water. You want to help him? Then help me get you out."

Colton obviously wanted to try, but he had no strength left. She wasn't going to be able to drag him directly out the way she had Marshall. Colton was too heavy, and she wasn't strong enough.

She would have to use gravity to her advantage. She got behind Colton and hooked her hands under his armpits. Then she threw all her weight backward, landing hard on the ground, for the first time thankful that she had more extra pounds than most women. The maneuver moved Colton much closer to dry land. She did it again, and then again, ignoring the bruising pain on her tailbone from throwing her weight like that. All that mattered was getting Colton out of the water.

By the time she did, she was fighting exhaustion herself, but she knew she couldn't stop yet. They were nowhere close to being out of danger.

"We've got to get you guys out of those wet clothes." She pulled off Colton's shoes and then Marshall's. "Try to take off your shirts."

She pulled off their pants as they worked on their shirts. It was tough getting any of the wet material off their bodies, but they managed. Ella was wet herself, but all the movement was keeping her warm enough to stave off hypothermia. She pulled out one of the mylar blankets and wrapped it around Marshall's narrow shoulders. She started to wrap one around Colton, but he shook his head. Muttering a curse, she wrapped the second blanket around Marshall's legs.

She understood his point, she really did. Colton had a lot more muscle mass on his body than Marshall that would help him to regulate his temperature more easily. But it still didn't mean he was out of danger. She grabbed the final mylar blanket and shot him a pointed look. "You get this one."

He didn't seem too thrilled with the idea but didn't argue as she wrapped it around him.

"Ash—Ashley?" Marshall got out.

"She's okay. I left her a little farther upstream, but she was out of the water and was—"

"I'm here."

They all looked up and found the girl walking toward them. She was still wrapped in the emergency blanket and carrying the backpack Ella had left with her. Her steps were a little unsteady, but her color looked relatively good.

At least they were all here together.

"Ashley, you come sit here with the guys."

The girl plopped down next to Marshall, and they immediately huddled together.

"I'm going to make a fire." Colton looked like he was going to get up and help, but Ella pointed at the ground and shot him a look. "Don't even think about it. I will handle this."

Because goddamn it, she could handle this. She grabbed the fire flint and knife out of Colton's backpack then scrambled away from shore to find what was needed to start a fire. Thank goodness she'd just had a refresher course over the past day and a half.

She gathered all she needed and set her fire supplies down in neat little stacks—dry grass and moss for the initial stages, then smaller twigs, then a few bigger branches. Once all that was lit and going, she would have time to go get more twigs and logs.

All three of them watching her from where they were huddled in the thin metallic blankets made her feel pretty self-conscious, but she ignored it. Every minute counted. Yeah, they were out of immediate harm's way, but this was the Wyoming wilderness... Things could change at a moment's notice like Lilah had said that morning.

It took Ella a couple of attempts to get the fire started, but once the small tinder caught flame, she knew it would be okay. It was just a matter of building. She did so, slowly and methodically, until there was a large blaze in front of them.

It felt good to see them all scoot closer, some of the tightness in their features easing as they felt the warmth from the flames.

She found some protein bars in the backpacks and opened one for each of them. "Eat. Your body needs the calories to help keep itself warm."

Nobody argued. Ella got one for herself too. They all ate while silently watching the fire. It wasn't until she'd finished her bar that Ella realized Ashley had started crying.

"This is my fault. And Marshall is hurt."

Marshall shook his head. "It was an accident, it's not your fault. I'm sorry I wasn't able to pull you back up."

"Neither of you has anything to be sorry for," Colton said quietly. "You did what you could, you kept a calm head, and we're all going to be fine."

Ella nodded. "Let's finish getting warmed up, dried off, and then we'll head back to the camp."

Colton looked over at Marshall. "Shoulder?"

For the first time, Ella realized that the boy was holding himself at an awkward angle. He was hurt. She'd totally missed that, but Colton hadn't.

"I'll be okay," Marshall muttered, then glanced quickly over at Ashley before meeting eyes with Colton again.

He obviously didn't want to make a big deal out of being hurt in front of Ashley—either to not look weak or to not make her feel bad. Fortunately, Colton realized what Marshall was communicating.

"Fine. But it's going to be pretty standard for us to get checked out by medics when we get back to town. Bear and the team are going to want us to head out tonight."

Marshall looked relieved. If he had some sort of broken bone or dislocation, he'd want to get some painkillers as soon as he could.

It wasn't long before they all felt warm enough to start heading back toward the camp. Colton was quick to take Marshall's backpack so that it wasn't even a question of whether he could carry it or not. Ella smiled as Ashley arranged herself on Marshall's good side and slid her hand into his.

Ella did the same with Colton.

"You were amazing out there," she whispered. "You didn't even hesitate to dive into that icy water. It had to have been hard and brought back some hard memories."

"Only for a split second. There was no way I was going to let either of those kids drown if I could do anything about it—panic be damned."

She squeezed his hand. Maybe he'd turned a corner with panic attacks and they wouldn't torture him so often.

"What you did was just as important, so don't discount that," Colton said. "If you hadn't been able to get us out of that water and warmed up, we would've been in trouble. We make a pretty good team."

# CHAPTER
# TWENTY-EIGHT

THE NEXT MORNING, mind on food, Colton drove into town and parked at the Frontier Diner. It had been a long night.

Once they were dry enough, they'd walked back to camp, which, fortunately, hadn't been too far away. Bear and Lilah had immediately surmised something was wrong. Colton had been about to tell the story but then realized that this was Marshall and Ashley's chance to shine, so he let them tell it instead.

The rest of the campers were enthralled to hear about the near-death experience and why wilderness survival skills were so important.

Marshall didn't mention that his shoulder was hurt, but both Bear and Lilah had realized it by the way he was holding his arm. While Marshall and Ashley fielded questions about everything from how cold the water was to whether they'd thought they would die, Colton told the leaders that the kid definitely needed to be checked out by a doctor.

When Bear explained to the campers that it was necessary for Marshall and Ashley to go back, the rest of the kids banded with them and packed up to go too.

It had been a really nice moment.

Once they got Marshall to the clinic, the kid had still been a trooper as they reset his shoulder. Didn't mutter a word. Having had a similar injury more than once, Colton had expected Marshall to be more relaxed once the joint was back in its socket since the pressure and pain eased dramatically once it was back in place.

But, if anything, the kid looked more upset.

"Are you all right?" Colton asked. Maybe he had more injuries than he'd been letting on.

Marshall shrugged with his good shoulder. "Yeah, I'm okay, I guess."

"No offense, but you don't look very okay. Are you sure your shoulder was the only thing that was hurt?"

"Yeah. Just…"

Shit. Marshall looked like he might cry.

"Hey. What's going on?"

Marshall slumped over on the examination table. "Is being a hero something you can only do as an adult?"

He was taken aback by the question. "No, I think you proved that today."

Marshall shook his head slowly. "No, I didn't. I dropped Ashley. I couldn't hold on. A hero would've held on. Wouldn't have let her fall."

Colton raised an eyebrow. "No offense, but that's bullshit."

"But—"

"But *nothing*. You held on to her even after your arm had been ripped out of its socket. That's more than most adults—hero or not—would've done."

"But I couldn't get her back up. She almost died because of me."

He slid an arm around the boy's shoulders gently. "Listen, a lot of things could've gone really wrong today and would've ended up in disaster. Starting with, if you hadn't caught Ashley and held her as long as you did, there is probably no way that I could've gotten to her, and we would've lost her in that river."

"I still wish I could've pulled her back up."

"And maybe you work toward building your upper body strength so that if you're ever in a situation like this again, you can. But make no mistake, being a hero has nothing to do with physical strength and everything to do with your willingness to help others even if it hurts yourself. You're definitely a damn hero—don't tell yourself otherwise."

The boy nodded solemnly. "I'm glad everyone is okay."

"That's always the most important thing."

When they made it back to Linear Tactical, it was obvious that Ashley considered Marshall to be her hero also. She zoomed right to his side and stayed there until it was time for the campers to go to their respective cabins.

Yeah, Marshall was more of a hero than most of the grown adults Colton knew. Ella was one also. He knew wilderness survival wasn't her expertise and that she was only on the trip as a personal favor to Bear, but she had done everything damn near perfectly. Hell, even getting him out of the water had been difficult—throwing her body weight around like she had had left her with multiple bruises.

The woman was fucking amazing. The more he was around her, the more he wanted to be around her. And as soon as this stalker situation was handled, he and Ella were going to have a very important talk. One he was very much looking forward to.

His mood couldn't be higher as he walked into the Frontier Diner, until he spotted Tony and Rick sitting in a back corner booth of the diner. He tried to turn and back out, but they saw him too quickly. Tony waved him over. Gritting his teeth, Colton made his way across the restaurant.

"What are you guys doing here?"

"We've actually been staying in Reddington City in case you change your mind about anything." Tony at least had the good sense to look sheepish at the admission.

"Change my mind about what?"

Rick slid over, and Colton sat down next to him even though he really didn't want to.

"Pretty much anything," Rick muttered.

Tony shot the younger man a look. Obviously, Rick had been told not to be confrontational.

"Good thing we were so close by. I keep hearing about how you are a hero. Saved some kids from drowning."

"I'm not a hero." He caught the waitresses and signaled for a cup of coffee. "I just happened to be in the right place at the right time."

"Maybe," Tony said. "But you know this is something we could spin to our advantage."

Colton took a calming breath. "I'm not interested in spinning anything. These kids are not to be used for us to gain traction with social media."

"Maybe if you would look at how your social media numbers are dropping, you might listen to reason." Tony once again shot a look at Rick at the younger man's words.

"I've never been one to pay much attention to those types of numbers—it's not what I'm about."

Rick threw up his hands. "Well, not all of us have the assurance of a bank account the size of yours. We don't come from parents who were already wealthy and famous. So, we sure as fuck check the numbers pretty regularly."

"Enough, Rick," Tony said, before turning to Colton. "Asshole here is not making his point in a wise way, but he does still have a point. None of us wants to see you lose your status, partially because it means we'd be out of a job, but also because you worked hard to get to where you are."

He worked hard because stunts had always been what he loved to do ever since he was a kid here in Oak Creek. And he wouldn't lie...the perks of fame and having people cheer you on while you did what you loved was something he enjoyed.

But stunts for him had never been about social media views or numbers of likes.

"I'm not going to change who I am in order to be more popular on social media."

Tony nodded. "Absolutely and we one hundred percent support

that. Nobody wants you to change who you are. But what we do want is for you to share who you are with the public. For example, if I had been able to film you saving that kid…"

"My interaction with these kids is not for public amusement." He took the cup of coffee from the waitress and ordered the breakfast special—two eggs, bacon, and hash browns. It hadn't changed much since when he used to get it as a kid in high school when they'd come here every semester before final exams.

Tony held out his hand in a gesture of peace. "Yeah, I get that. I was just using it as an example. My point is, you don't have to change who you are—your fans just want a glimpse into your life."

"Maybe not all of it," Rick muttered.

Colton crossed his arms over his chest. "What does that mean?"

"Shut the fuck up, Rick."

Colton shook his head and cut off Tony's warning. "No, are you referring to something specific?"

Now the younger man looked uncomfortable. "Forget it."

"No. Is it Oak Creek? Town is too small and you think my fans will be bored? That's exactly the point I'm trying to make. There are parts of my life not meant to be public. Let my fans see the public parts—the stunts."

"You know how it is," Tony said. "The public wants to feel like they know you."

"And the town isn't the problem," Rick said. "Or it's not *just* the problem."

"Goddamn it, Rick." Tony scrubbed a hand down his face.

"What?" Rick threw up his hands. "You know it's true."

"What's true?" Colton stopped as the waitress brought his plate of food and set it down in front of him. He forced a smile at her even though he didn't feel it.

"What's true?" he asked again once the waitress left.

"Nothing," Tony responded. "Our resident asshole is being exactly that."

Rick rolled his eyes. "Fine. Right. I'm the asshole for saying what all of us are thinking."

"If somebody doesn't tell me what the hell you're talking about right now, everybody is going to be fucking fired."

Tony held out a hand to stop whatever Rick was about to say. "There's a little bit of concern about how some of your closest friends will be perceived by your public."

"In what way? I'm not planning on putting any of them on public display."

Tony nodded. "But sometimes you don't get a choice. Especially with those who are closest to you."

The bacon he was chewing went tasteless in his mouth.

"Ella." They were talking about Ella.

"Yeah, exactly, man. Compared to the women you've dated in the past, she's not exactly hot, you know?"

Colton looked over at Rick at his words. The guy actually thought he wasn't being offensive.

"It's time for you to go." Colton managed to keep his words even when all he wanted to do was take Rick's head and bash it against the table.

"Listen, man. I know you've known her a long time and she's important to you. We get it. All I'm saying is that, comparatively speaking—"

"I already heard you, Rick. And if you want to make it out of this restaurant with all your teeth still in your mouth, I suggest you leave right fucking now." He stood up so the other man could pass.

"Whatever." But Rick wisely slid off the booth seat and walked out.

Colton sat back down and pushed his plate away. He definitely wasn't hungry now.

"Before you tell me to fire him, you should know that he's an excellent camera operator and has a wonderful eye for shots."

"I'm pretty sure I don't give a shit about those things right now."

Tony leaned back against the booth. "Rick knows what people want to see, and as much as you may not like to hear this…he's right that Ella does not look like the other women you've dated."

He didn't give a shit about that. "You do realize that you're just making my point, right? This is why I don't want to film my personal life."

"I get it. Your personal life is your own. We can make that happen."

Tony pushed the plate with Colton's uneaten breakfast back over to him. Colton picked up his fork.

"Good." He was only a couple bites into his meal when he realized Tony still had more to say. "Just say it."

"I know that you like it here. I know this is home. I know you've been struggling more than you let on."

Colton shrugged and put another bite of food in his mouth.

"Both Rick and I want to make sure you have a career left to come back to when you decide you're done here."

It was on the tip of Colton's tongue to announce that he wouldn't be leaving Oak Creek and that if he was going to have a career in extreme sports, they were going to have to figure out a way around that.

They were going to have to figure out how to work his *image* with Ella by his side.

But none of that could happen yet. "I'm more concerned about us catching this stalker."

"That's my number one concern too. And hear me out... I think the best way to do this is to get you back into the public eye. None of this cloak-and-dagger stuff you've been up to trying to catch her."

Colton managed a smile. "You heard about that?"

"My friend, it's my job to know everything about you."

Colton hoped not *everything*.

"I just want the stalker handled as quickly as possible. It's important, Tony."

"Then we'll make it happen. Whatever gets you back to your old self."

*His old self.* He wasn't even sure who that was anymore.

# CHAPTER
# TWENTY-NINE

ELLA MADE at least one trip into Reddington City each week, usually more. At just over forty-five minutes away, it was the closest big city to Oak Creek. She had multiple vendors there that carried items that just didn't get delivered to Oak Creek regularly enough.

Normally, the trip to Reddington City was a tedious job she tried to pawn off on anybody she could. But not today. Today, Colton was with her.

He insisted on coming even though that wasn't necessary, which she knew had to do with the stalker. He had been on and off his phone the entire drive, talking to one of his team members, Tony, the two of them bouncing ideas off each other about the next steps in how to catch her.

"I don't want the stalker to weigh on you anymore." Colton slipped his phone into his pocket as they got out of the car. "I hate that this worries you so much. That you are so afraid."

Ella pretended to arrange something in her purse so that she wouldn't have to look at him. She wasn't afraid. It sucked that he had a stalker, and yes, she wanted the stalker gone as soon as possible, but the stalker wasn't what had made her tense and a little bit distant.

She didn't know how to tell him about her insecurities and how self-conscious she felt. Moreover, she didn't know if there was any point. Colton hadn't mentioned anything about continuing their relationship. He'd only talked about needing to leave. So rambling on about her dating discomfiture seemed like it was jumping the gun.

As they walked into the store, Colton pulled out his phone again as it buzzed. He looked at it in what could only be called disgust.

"Tony again?" she asked.

He shook his head. "Another member of my team. Guy named Rick. He was sending an apology."

"What did he do?"

Colton looked uncomfortable. "It's a long story. He's a hothead. But a great camera operator."

She didn't push for more info. Managing a team wasn't always easy; she knew that from her own experience at the bakery. Having someone who disrupted the flow could be difficult, even if they were talented.

"But let's not worry about that right now." He took a cart and followed her farther into the specialty baking store.

Colton was fun to shop with. He was witty and entertaining and almost like a kid. He kept putting things they didn't need into the cart.

She laughed as she took the items—*rainbow sprinkles,* for goodness' sake—and put them back on the shelf.

"You're missing the chance to make the world's greatest dessert." He shook his head in mock sadness.

"The world's greatest dessert involves rainbow sprinkles?"

"Hey, you never know."

They turned down the next aisle where she picked up the specialized flour she needed. She couldn't stop laughing as he listed, mostly incorrectly, all the desserts that would be made better with rainbow sprinkles. There was no way she was selling a dessert with multicolored sugar pellets all over it.

But she did give in to his request that she make something with butterscotch. That, she couldn't resist. Especially not when his eyes lit up and he pulled her in for a kiss right there in the middle of the baking supply shop aisle.

"I think I'm going to keep coming with you on these supply trips until I can talk you into the sprinkles." He pulled away and started pushing the cart toward the cashier.

Ella just stood there staring at him as he walked away. What did that mean? She had no idea.

He glanced at her over his shoulder and gave her a wink and a sexy grin. "You're thinking of rainbow sprinkle recipes, aren't you?"

She was more thinking that there was no way she was getting out of this with her heart not broken into thousands of pieces.

---

"Do you mind if we stop at the sporting goods store?" Ella asked a couple hours later when all the errand-running for the shop was over. They'd stopped and had a great lunch at one of her favorite little bistros.

He'd told her about Marshall and his concerns that he had let Ashley down by not being able to stop her from falling into the water. She'd been quick to assure Colton that Ashley already had a huge crush on the boy, and that had only grown with his heroic effort. Ella had been relieved to hear that Colton had pretty much told Marshall the same thing.

Talking about Ashley and Marshall had been a safe topic. Hell, even talking about the stalker had been a safe topic.

The only topic they'd avoided had been talking about them. No man ever wanted to have the *where is this relationship going?* talk. Colton Harrison was no different.

"You're asking *me* if I want to go to a sporting goods store?" His eyebrows shot all the way up. "Do you know who you're talking to?"

She laughed. "Yeah, I'm sure you can keep yourself entertained."

"That depends. Do you think they have rainbow sprinkles there?"

He reached over and grabbed her hand on the steering wheel and pulled it over into his lap. And just like that, she was back to thinking that maybe there was something really *real* between them. "What are you looking for at the store?"

"I ruined my hiking boots in the river incident."

He grimaced. "Trying to get me out of the water."

"I promise they were on their last legs anyway. I think I've had them since high school."

"I still insist on you letting me replace them."

She pulled into a parking space. "You really don't have to do that."

She turned to open the door, but he wouldn't let go of her hand.

"I want to." He smiled. "And that way, I can make sure you get the best pair possible."

As if there was any way for her to resist him when he was smiling so charmingly and had run errands with her all afternoon. "Fine. I'll rely on your expertise."

"That's my girl."

She couldn't even think about what that phrase did to her insides.

They got out of her car, and he once again grabbed her hand as they walked toward the entrance.

"Most of the time, I try to shop at mom-and-pop-type places. But I have to admit I love this chain. I mean, come on, they have a Ferris wheel inside." He was grinning like a little boy.

They went inside and quickly found the women's shoe department, and he dragged her over to the wall displaying all sorts of brands and fashions of hiking boots.

"You want to make sure you have Gore-Tex waterproofing, no matter what style you decide to go with. I prefer over-the-ankle boots for wilderness like what we have around Oak Creek."

"Why?"

"I'd like to say it's because of support and durability, but actually, it's more because I'd like to think if I stepped on a snake, I'd have something durable between its fangs and me."

"Not a fan of snakes?"

"Let's just say me and Indiana Jones have a lot in common."

He then proceeded to get serious and point out the pros and cons of different brands—he'd had experience with a lot of them. When a salesclerk came to ask if Ella wanted to try any on in her size, Ella was careful not to pick the most expensive brand. She knew Colton had plenty of money—hell, *she* had plenty of money—but somehow, it just didn't feel right.

"I see through you, by the way," Colton said when the shop worker walked away to get the shoes. "I noticed you didn't want to try on the most expensive ones. Good for you. They're overpriced anyway."

"I know money is not an issue for either of us, but I still don't want to waste it. And it's not like I'm out in the wilderness as much as you are."

"True, but—"

"Excuse me, but are you Colton Harrison?" A second store worker interrupted them with a sheepish smile.

Colton handled it in stride. "Yes, I am. What's your name?"

The young man looked like he would burst from pride. "My name is Terrence. I work here."

Colton didn't mock him at all for pointing out the obvious. "Nice to meet you. I'm just doing some shopping."

"I don't want to disturb you, but we are all big fans in here, and I was wondering if you'd consider letting us take some pictures of you over by a display we have on the second floor."

Colton glanced at her before shaking his head. "I'm not really here to—"

"Colton, it's fine," she whispered. She didn't want him to miss a chance to interact with fans or disappoint the employee who was obviously thrilled at the thought of getting some pictures with Colton.

"Are you sure you don't mind?"

She smiled at him. "Go."

Terrence's eyes lit up at her words, and she thought he might actually giggle when Colton stood to follow him.

"Five minutes," he said over his shoulder as he and Terrence walked away.

Ella decided to go ahead and try on the different hiking boots while she was waiting. One type, she liked pretty well and would probably go with them—midrange in cost but still completely adequate for what she needed. She decided to try on one other brand, but she needed a different size. But when she tried to find the salesclerk to help her, the girl was nowhere to be found.

Actually, *nobody* was around.

It'd definitely been more than five minutes. She texted Colton.

> Need more time?

She got up and looked at some of the other boots as she waited for him to respond, but there was no reply.

> Everything okay?

Once again, no response, and there didn't seem to be any employees around either. Hell, there were hardly any customers around.

Taking the box of boots she'd decided on, she made her way up the escalator to the second floor.

No wonder there hadn't been anybody in the shoe department. They were all here, trying to get pictures with and autographs from Colton. It looked like the whole store was here.

She managed to catch his eye, and although he didn't look panicked, the scene around him was definitely chaotic. He grabbed his phone and held it out toward her. She muscled her way through the crowd so she could grab it from him.

"Text Tony: *Public 9-1-1* and give him this store's address."

She did so immediately. And then sent the text. Tony responded just a few seconds later.

> You okay?

>> This is Ella. I have Colton's phone. He wanted me to text you.

> I'm already on my way. I'm nearby. How bad is it?

She wasn't sure how to define "bad."

>> It's a lot of people, and they all want pictures and autographs.

> Does he need immediate help? Cops? Is he being overrun?

>> No. But it's just a lot of people.

> I'll be there in two minutes.

Two minutes? He hadn't been joking when he said he was nearby. Sure enough, not five minutes later, Tony was there in the middle of the crowd directing traffic. He had two security guards and two store managers with him.

"Okay, people. Listen up! Colton has no problem taking pictures or signing whatever you want, but we're going to have to do this in an orderly fashion. If we can't get everything under control, then he's going to have to leave."

The security guards and managers helped Tony set up a sort of queue that wrapped around the whole winter sports section of the store. A couple of people didn't want to leave Colton's side even though they'd already had their selfie and autograph, so a security guard had to step in. Colton could've easily just let security handle it, but he gave the two young men backslapping hugs and told them he appreciated their enthusiasm.

"Thanks for texting me." Tony came over to stand near Ella where she was in the back. "Colton doesn't usually do big stores, and even when he does, it doesn't usually get this crazy without some sort of social media tip-off."

"I'm just glad you were nearby. Nobody seemed to know exactly how to handle this."

Tony chuckled. "It's both their wet dreams and their worst nightmare." He pointed to where some employees were stacking up merchandise that had been associated with Colton throughout the years—skateboards, snowboards, and some T-shirts and hoodies. Customers were immediately grabbing them, wanting to be able to get something autographed while Colton was there. The store was going to make a killing.

Colton took it all in stride. He was charming, talking with people, smiling and laughing. Taking the photos they wanted. He did it over and over, his smile never faltering. He seemed to be enjoying it, which didn't surprise her.

"Does this happen a lot?"

Tony shook his head with a shrug. "Honestly, it used to happen more. His popularity has been waning in the past few weeks."

She hated the thought of that. "Do you know why?"

"The public can be very fickle."

She watched as Colton got down on one knee so he would be eye to eye with a little girl holding a skateboard nearly as tall as she was. Whatever he said made her squeal with delight then drop the skateboard so she could hug him.

"He's such a natural," Ella whispered.

"Yeah, he really thrives in situations like this. Loves to know he's influencing a new generation of adventurers. I hate that he can't see he's losing that."

"How is he losing it?"

"Out of sight, out of mind, you know? He's taking a lot of time out of the public eye."

"Maybe he needed a break."

Tony shrugged while still watching over what was happening. "Sure. He deserves a break whenever he wants one, and I totally support him taking one. Encouraged it after the accident, even."

"But…" There was very definitely a but in Tony's sentence.

"But the truth is, Colton Harrison is a *brand*. One that's been carefully cultivated for years. And lately, he's been making questionable choices that don't necessarily align with his brand. The people who look up to him have certain expectations. His choices are hurting his image and will eventually end his livelihood if he's not careful."

"Like what choices?"

"Like choosing to…" Tony faded off then glanced over at her. "You know what, never mind. I shouldn't have said anything. Colton will be fine. He always is. I'm going to go make sure he's okay. Again, thanks for contacting me."

She watched him go grab a bottle of water and hand it to Colton, who accepted it with a grateful smile. Tony obviously cared about his boss and knew how to take care of him. Ella should've thought of the fact that Colton might need water, given all the talking and smiling he was doing, but it hadn't crossed her mind.

Colton looked up and gave her a little wave as he finished his water bottle, mouthing *I'm sorry*.

She smiled and waved back. *No problem*.

A couple of women saw the exchange and glared at Ella for a moment before laughing and leaning their heads close together to whisper. Ella couldn't hear, and didn't want to be paranoid, but she could swear they were saying things about her. As they got closer in line, they waved Tony over to ask him something, looking in her direction again. Whatever he responded made them roll their eyes. Tony shrugged and walked away.

Was she being paranoid? Ella had never been one to make everything about her—she preferred to be out of the limelight. Though she couldn't help but feel like these women were talking about her. Although it shouldn't matter. Even if they were, there was nothing she could do about it.

But more concerning had been that discussion with Tony. Arguably, he knew Colton better than anyone else, especially when it came to his career. And she couldn't help but think that when Tony had been talking about the questionable choices Colton had been making recently...

He was talking about *her*.

# CHAPTER
# THIRTY

ELLA SAT up in bed from a sound sleep, trying to figure out what was wrong. Sometimes this happened when she'd forgotten to do something at the bakery and her subconscious realized it. Had she forgotten to turn off an oven? Were there some ingredients she'd forgotten to order that she would need later in the week?

No, that couldn't be it. She's gone shopping yesterday with Colton and—

*Colton.* He wasn't in bed with her. That's what had woken her up.

She glanced toward the bathroom but that door was open, so he wasn't in there. She made her way out of bed and padded into the kitchen. Maybe he'd gotten hungry. But he wasn't there either.

*Had he left?*

They both had gone to bed a little early, the incident at the sporting goods store having taken a lot of Colton's energy. He'd apologized multiple times for it taking so long. Not that an apology was necessary.

She walked over to a front window and peeked out. His truck was still parked out front, so he had to be here somewhere.

"Colton?"

She wasn't sure that searching for him was even the right thing to do. Maybe he needed some time to decompress. Maybe he wanted to be alone.

She didn't call out for him anymore, but she walked around and noticed all the doors were open so he couldn't be here inside. Her house wasn't very big, and unless he was sitting in one of the closets, he wasn't in here.

She rubbed the heels of her hand against tired eyes. Where could he be? She glanced out the window one more time, thinking perhaps he was out walking. But the sidewalks were clear. He couldn't—

Wait, was that a shadow in the cab of his truck? She squinted and watched for a few more seconds. Yes, he was definitely in there. Maybe he'd forgotten something. But he didn't seem to be moving or looking for anything.

Finally, she decided to go out there and see if he needed something. Wrapping herself in her favorite cardigan, she walked out and tapped on the window.

She knew immediately he wasn't okay. He jerked away from the window at the sound, but his eyes were wide and unfocused.

*Shit.* He was in the middle of a panic attack.

She slowly eased the truck door open. "Colton? It's Ella." She wasn't sure how coherent he was during these events.

His breath sawed in and out of his chest at way too rapid a pace for someone as fit as Colton who wasn't doing anything.

Should she touch him? Should she leave him alone?

She couldn't stop herself; she had to try to help him. She slowly moved her hand toward his arm, ready to jump back if he got violent. She touched him as gently as possible, concerned at how clammy his skin was under her fingers. Cold, yet she saw sweat beading on his forehead.

He stared down at her hand, his breath still coming way too fast.

"Colton?" She was careful to keep her voice even. Not betraying any of her own panic at seeing him this way. "Can you come back to me?"

She had no idea if she was saying the right thing.

"It's late. Still dark out. Do you think you might want to come inside? I would like for you to come inside."

He blinked rapidly at her. Maybe she was getting through to him. She kept talking and rubbing his arm gently.

"I woke up and you weren't in bed with me, and I missed you."

More blinks.

"If you want, I can make you something to eat. It won't necessarily involve rainbow sprinkles, but maybe some food would make us both feel better."

His breathing seemed to be slowing just the slightest bit.

"That's right. Come back and talk to me. We've always had a good time talking to each other. Do you remember that time in high school when we all got stuck in the gym during that storm? None of us could get home because the bridge washed out, so they made us stay there till nearly midnight?"

She continued on with the story, talking about how they all ate food from the basketball game concession stand and slept on the gym floor.

After that, she launched into another story from even further back about the time Colton and his brother Tucker had snuck out with Lilah and Scarlett. When the girls' dad, a former Navy SEAL, found out about it, he threatened to kill both thirteen-year-old boys. Only the fact that Gabe Collingwood and Boy Riley were good friends stopped any bloodshed. Ella remembered the story because it had been the weekend her sister had gotten married.

By midway through a third story, Colton's breathing was almost back to normal.

"Hi," she said gently when she could see his eyes were more focused than they had been for the past...however long she been talking. "How about we go inside?"

He nodded, moving slowly as he got out of the truck and walked beside her into the house. Once there, he still seemed a little lost, so she guided him over to the couch before grabbing them both bottled water from the fridge. He took his bottle and drank it down in one huge gulp. Then he just stared at the plastic in his hand.

"I'm sorry," he finally said. "You shouldn't have had to see me like that."

She sat down on the couch but gave him space. He didn't look very receptive to someone being close to him. "We all have low points. There's no need to apologize for that. But how did you end up in your truck, do you remember?"

For a minute, she thought he wasn't going to answer, but finally, he found his voice. "Sometimes I can't sleep. It doesn't seem to matter what bed I'm in. I discovered that somehow my brain relaxes in my truck, so I try to sleep there. I know that's stupid."

"Not at all. It's good that you have somewhere you can get rest when you need it."

He just shrugged.

"It didn't look like you were actually asleep out there."

He rubbed the bridge of his nose with his thumb and forefinger. "No, tonight was bad. I wasn't able to sleep here. I didn't want to disturb you, so I thought maybe I'd go sleep in the truck. But then that didn't work either."

"So, that was a full-blown panic attack?"

He stood up and began pacing. "Yeah. One of the worst I've had in a while. Just when I thought things were finally getting better."

She so badly wanted to go over and wrap her arms around him. "My parents are forever saying that the healing progress isn't always—"

"Linear," they both finished at the same time.

"My parents say that too. And I know it's true. But still…" He ran his fingers through his thick brown hair, causing it to stand on end. "It's been months since the accident. I shouldn't still be having these problems."

"But—"

He held out a hand. "I know. I know. I need to have patience. I need to be gentle with myself. I went through a traumatic event. Trust me, I've heard it all. Mom and Dad asked me to see a therapist, and I did. But it's just not working."

"You need more time. You need—"

"How can someone who does stunts for a fucking living have panic attacks at the thought of danger?" he yelled.

Ella just blinked at him. She couldn't remember him ever yelling in frustration.

He immediately looked contrite. "I'm sorry. I'm not mad at you at all. I'm just frustrated that I can't seem to move past this. I feel like a fraud."

Her heart cracked. "Don't say that. You're not a fraud. There's nothing wrong with struggling after what you went through. You still do stunts, and everyone still loves you. All those people at the sporting goods store were a prime example of that."

"They wouldn't like me if they could have seen me out in my truck a few minutes ago."

"Do you really think that's true?"

"How can it *not* be? I'm a coward." He looked more despondent than she'd ever seen him, shaking his head before picking up his pacing again.

She wanted to be as gentle as possible, but sometimes being too sweet made things worse. Sometimes the kindest thing you could do for someone was speak the truth. "I don't think you're a coward, but I think you might be a liar."

That stopped the pacing. "*What?*"

She held out a hand before he could jump into an argument. "When you say you're a coward, you're making it sound as if doing something brave or adventurous means not having any fear at all. Were you not just telling Marshall that he was still heroic for trying to save Ashley from falling into that river even though he wasn't able to?"

He shook his head. "It's not the same."

"Maybe not directly, but it's similar enough to still be true. What makes you *you* and so appealing to your fans is that you do the things you do *despite* any fear or hardships, not because the fear doesn't exist."

He scrubbed a hand over his face. "Maybe. But I still feel like I should have more control over my reactions than I do."

Ella had always believed in coming at problems as logically as possible. Maybe he couldn't control his reactions, but he could at least try to understand as much as possible about them. "Have you tried to keep track of when you have panic attacks? Attempt to figure out what triggers them?"

"I thought for sure they had something to do with stunts that affect my airway in some way—limited oxygen supply or something like that. That would make sense, right? Or ones having to do with snow and ice, things that remind me directly of the avalanche."

"That would definitely make sense."

"Right. But that doesn't seem to be the case." He threw up both hands. "There doesn't seem to be any rhyme or reason to this panic. All I know is that I can't control it."

"It's interesting that you had an attack tonight, but not last night after the river incident. That would make more sense."

He nodded. "Exactly. For just a second after I jumped into that water after Marshall, the cold stole my breath and I had to regroup."

"But you did. You didn't even hesitate."

"I know. I was proud of that. I just ignored it and kept going. And then last night, I was fine. Hell, all day today, I felt fine until…"

"Was it the people? Signing autographs and the pictures? You looked like you were having a great time, but were you faking it?" Had Tony been wrong about how much Colton loved this?

"No, I liked being with the people. I always do. I was a little concerned that you weren't having much fun, but otherwise, it wasn't stressful. It wasn't till afterward when I was talking to Tony that I started to get stressed."

"What were you and Tony talking about? Was it about the stalker? Has that topic caused the attacks? That would be understandable too."

He finally stopped pacing and came to sit down on the couch next to her. "No, the opposite. The more I'm focused on something dangerous, the less the panic seems to occur, even with the stalker. Like, when we were trying to draw her out? I was completely focused and didn't have one iota of anxiety. But he and I weren't talking about the stalker anyway."

"What were you talking about?"

He shrugged. "I don't know. Nothing dramatic. Plans for the future. How to get my numbers back up. The stuff the PR team is thinking about all the time."

"Were you fighting?"

"No. To be honest, I wasn't interested in it at all. I just don't give a shit about that stuff."

Annoyance was clear on his face, but when she looked down at his hand, it was starting to tremble slightly.

Maybe they'd been thinking about this the completely wrong way.

"What if your panic attacks aren't about the accident at all—or at least, not fear of those types of stunts?"

"What do you mean? I never had any anxiety until the avalanche."

"Or maybe it just never manifested itself until you were so abruptly faced with your own mortality and how short life can be."

"I'm still not sure I understand what you're saying."

"Have you considered that your panic attacks are about you feeling trapped in your own career?"

She half expected him to laugh or scoff, but he didn't. He sat there staring at the space in front of him for a long time.

A really long time.

"Colton?" she finally asked, hoping she hadn't offended him. "Are you okay?"

He looked over at her slowly. "I think you're right. I've been going through my panic attacks in my mind, and yeah, early on, they might have been a little centered around the avalanche—"

"Understandable."

"—but I think they're really about how I was feeling before the accident. That I was done with the constant treadmill of stunts just for the public glory of it. That I'm ready to retire."

"Retire completely?" She hadn't been expecting that.

"I don't know. Maybe not *completely*. But simplifying everything. Getting back to the basics."

There was no tremor in his hands now.

"It sounds like you know what you want to do, you just need to do it."

Again, he stared out in front of him. But instead of looking lost like he had a few minutes ago, he looked determined. In charge. Ready to take on the world.

Like the Colton she'd known and loved almost her whole life.

"You are one hundred percent correct about that." Almost before she saw him move, he'd picked her up and deposited her across his lap. "And right now, I know what I want to do and *definitely* need to do it."

"Oh yeah?"

"You, Butterscotch. I want and need *you*."

He laid her back against the couch and proceeded to prove it to her.

# CHAPTER
# THIRTY-ONE

COLTON COULDN'T REMEMBER the last time he felt this good. He was on his way to Fancy Pants. Ella had offered her office so he could talk to Tony about his retirement idea and they could formulate a plan.

*Retirement.* He'd been thinking about that even before the accident. He wouldn't get totally out of the game—he loved the action too much. But there definitely needed to be a shift.

No more pandering to the public. No more continuous pressure of what would get the most likes or views or potentially go viral. No more planning stunts shot by shot until it was nothing more than a rote exercise.

And maybe not so many stunts by Colton at all. If the last couple of weeks with the campers had taught him anything, it was that he enjoyed teaching and training along with the action. Maybe he could open his own camp and gym for kids here in Oak Creek.

He stopped walking at the thought, struck by how right that felt. A chance for kids like Marshall—or any kids who had a desire for adventure—to come train with him for a little while?

Hell yeah. That felt more right than anything had for the past couple years.

He started walking again, considering what all this meant. He took the jobs of his team seriously. He didn't want to put anyone on the unemployment line. But if he did something like this camp, or a mobile version where Colton traveled around, there could still be jobs for them. Not all of them would want to make the transition to this new vision, but if they did, there would be a place for them.

His phone buzzing in his pocket interrupted his thoughts. It was Callum.

"Hi, Sheriff. What's going on?"

"I wanted to give you an update on Jeremy Ritter. I brought him back in today to re-question him. See if all his facts stayed the same."

"Anything interesting?"

"Not for the most part. No real inconsistencies on anything major."

Colton was waiting for the rest. The older man wasn't calling him to tell him there was no new information. That would be a waste of both their time, and Callum Webb had never been one to waste time.

"However, Jeremy wasn't too trusting that he would actually get paid, so he spied on his mysterious benefactor when the bag was dropped off. He didn't discover anything concrete—Jeremy didn't want to get caught snooping, but there was one interesting detail."

"What's that?"

"The person Jeremy saw was a man."

"He's sure?"

"Yep."

Colton stepped out of the way of a young family. "What does that mean? I was sure the stalker was a woman."

"I agree. The phrasing of the letters—especially before she got aggressive—suggests a female author. So, I don't know. Maybe it's a couple working together? Maybe the stalker is a woman, and she hired a man to deal with Jeremy?"

"Seems complicated."

"Yeah, and generally, the more complicated the theory, the less correct it is. Occam's razor and all that."

*The simplest answer tended to be the correct one.*

"Agreed. What does this mean for us?" Colton stopped outside of Fancy Pants. He didn't want to continue this conversation in Ella's bakery.

"Gives us more to look into. We need to go back through the notes and our sting attempts within the framework of it being more than one person involved. Maybe have Lincoln look through everyone again—especially the men."

"Okay, I'll tell my team. I'm on my way to a meeting right now."

"Good," Callum said. "We'll want to coordinate efforts even after you leave town."

"I'm not leaving town. At least not permanently. Maybe to catch this stalker, but then I'll be coming right back."

"Found something to stick around for, did you?"

Colton didn't even try to stop the grin that spread over his face. "More like found *someone* stick around for."

Callum chuckled. "It didn't take much detective work to see that one coming. Congratulations."

"Believe me, the thrill is all mine. I'll be in touch. If anything else comes up, let me know."

"Roger that."

He hadn't talked to Ella about his plans to stay in town, but that didn't matter. He would take care of this stalker then do whatever was necessary to woo her. Even after last night, he wasn't going to assume she was a sure thing.

They could take it fast, they could take it slow…he didn't care. All he cared about was him and Ella being together when everything was said and done.

And honestly, he was a little pissed at himself that he hadn't realized what an amazing gem he had in his life earlier. How had he managed to live without her all these years? He'd known she was a great friend but had somehow missed that she was so much more.

He could only be thankful that no one else had come along and scooped her up.

Colton ended the call and walked into Fancy Pants, moving straight back to the office Ella had left open for him. Tony was already there, and Colton grimaced when he saw Rick sitting over by Ella's desk.

Tony caught it. "Don't worry, he's going to stay over there and keep his damn mouth shut."

Colton nodded, but honestly, he was in too good of a mood to worry much about the younger man.

"Guys, we need to talk." Colton wanted to handle this delicately. They were both professionals—even if Rick was sometimes an asshole—and Colton appreciated the support they'd always provided.

"Yeah, we do," Tony agreed. "We figured out what happened yesterday at the sporting goods store."

That wasn't a topic Colton was expecting. "What do you mean, *what happened*? We had a crowd, but it ended up being fine."

"Not exactly," Tony explained. "Evidently, someone deliberately released on social media that you were at that store at that time."

He scrubbed a hand down his face. What the actual hell? "How the fuck did that happen when I didn't even know I would be in that store at that time?"

Tony shook his head. "I'm not sure. But here's the account that announced you were there." Tony flipped his electronic tablet around so Colton could see it.

He studied the account on one of the most popular social media sites. "It's called *Colton Harrison Guaranteed Sightings*? Not a very original name. And doesn't even seem to have many followers."

Tony shook his head. "It's brand-new, opened yesterday. Individual accounts don't need many followers now if they know where to post and what hashtags to use—that gets them all the traffic they need. Whoever set up this account definitely knew exactly where to post to start yesterday's frenzy."

"When did they post?"

"Yesterday afternoon at 2:18 p.m."

Colton rubbed the back of his neck. "I'm not sure exactly when we arrived at the store. Probably around then."

"I got the text from Ella on your phone at 2:42 p.m."

What the actual fuck? He worked out the timing in his head... "Then that would mean this got posted when we pulled into the goddamn parking lot. It's not like it was somebody inside the store who saw the crowd and then posted."

"Yeah, I know," Tony said.

"That means somebody was following us yesterday."

Tony shrugged, and Colton looked over at Rick, who was still standing in the corner by Ella's desk. The other man shrugged also but didn't say anything.

"None of us like the thought of that, but I'm afraid that may be the case," Tony said.

Colton walked over to the small couch along the south wall and sat down, trying to wrap his head around all of this. "Allow me to make this even more complicated... Sheriff Webb called me a few minutes ago and told me that Jeremy Ritter admitted to observing a *man* involved with paying him. Didn't get any sort of description, but Jeremy definitely knew the person was male."

"Wait, are we saying your stalker is a guy?" Rick asked, even though he wasn't supposed to be talking.

Colton nodded. "Callum thinks maybe it's a partner of some kind. Regardless, we have to widen the scope of who we're looking for."

Tony leaned up against the wall. "That puts us back at square one a little bit, but it's not like we had much to go on anyway."

It was time to get to the main point. "Stopping this stalker is my number one priority, but there's other stuff we need to talk about too. I'm going to leave Oak Creek."

"It's about time," Rick muttered.

"But only to catch the stalker, and then I'm coming back. Permanently."

Rick threw up his hands in exasperation but didn't say anything.

Good, because nothing was going to change Colton's mind. Rick sat down in Ella's office chair, shaking his head. Colton ignored him.

"There're going to be some big changes for me. I recognize that means there're going to be big changes for you and the team also."

"If we're talking about moving our headquarters here from Denver, I think that's doable for the most part." Tony already had his electronic notebook in his hands and was typing away on it. "Not everyone will be able to relocate, but some of the team is really only utilized when we're traveling for stunts, so—"

"I'm not sure how many stunts I'm going to be doing. I'm talking about a complete shift. I want—"

"Hey, what was the name of that social media site that leaked Colton's whereabouts yesterday?" Rick interrupted.

Colton had had just about enough of this bullshit. The younger man was totally ignoring what he was saying. "Damn it, Rick—"

"It was *Colton Harrison Guaranteed Sightings*, right?" Rick continued.

"Jesus, Rick. Read the room," Tony replied. "But yes, that was the site. Why?"

Rick held up a sticky note. "This says *CH guaranteed sightings. Post at 2:15.*"

*What the hell?* "Where did you get that?"

"It was right here, stuck on the edge of the computer monitor."

"On *Ella's* computer?" Colton shook his head. That didn't make any sense.

Rick shrugged. "I guess so. I mean, this is her computer, right?"

"Why would Ella have a note about that site?" Tony looked as confused as Colton felt.

"I have no idea—"

He was interrupted by the door bursting open and Caroline, one of Ella's young shop workers, rushing in. She stopped short when she saw them.

"Shoot! Ella told me you guys would be in here, but I forgot. I'm so sorry. I just need the checkbook for…" She shuffled to a halt. "Oh my gosh, you're Colton Harrison."

Colton forced a smile on his face, even though right now, all he could think about was that sticky note. "Guilty as charged."

"Oh my gosh, does Ella know you're using her office? I'm so stupid, of course she does. She's the one who told me you guys would be in here. Oh my gosh. Ella is your *biggest* fan."

"She and I have known each other for a long time."

"I mean, I'm a fan too but not nearly as big as she is," Caroline continued without even really listening to what Colton had said. "Really, I guess I became more of a fan after her showing me that digital scrapbook. But, oh my gosh, I can't believe you are here in her office."

"A digital scrapbook?"

If possible, Caroline's eyes got even wider. "Oh yeah. That thing is amazing. Hang on, let me show you."

She rushed over to the computer, shooing Rick out of the way. He moved, just as overwhelmed by the little whirlwind as Tony and Colton were.

Caroline plopped down in the chair that Rick had just vacated. "Password...Colton." She grinned at him over her shoulder, while the unease in Colton's belly grew stronger.

Caroline's fingers flew along the keyboard, and a few moments later, Colton's dread was even worse.

"See! She's basically been collecting every electronic clipping about you she could find for years. Pretty amazing, hmm?" She flipped through page after digital page of articles and clippings about Colton's stunts and his life. Hundreds of images... Maybe thousands. All sorts of articles.

"Holy shit," Tony whispered.

Caroline, very belatedly, became aware of the emotional temperature of the room. "Oh my gosh, should I not have shown you that?"

Colton mustered a smile. "No, it's fine. It's...flattering."

The relief on the girl's face would've been comical if Colton hadn't been about to freak out.

"Okay. Good. I better get back to work. I just wanted you to know how much Ella loves your career." She grabbed the checkbook and breezed out the door as quickly as she had breezed in.

The room sat silent for a long moment.

"Your girlfriend leaked your outing yesterday," Rick whispered. "I mean, between that sticky note and that creepy-as-fuck scrapbook? Hell, are we sure she's not the stalker?"

"She's not the stalker. And we don't know it was her who leaked the outing." Colton rubbed the back of his neck.

Rick shook his head. "Fine, she's probably not the stalker, I'll give you that. But damn, Colton, things definitely point to her having leaked your whereabouts yesterday."

Colton had to agree. "I'm not believing anything until I talk to Ella. And even if it was her, I'm not going to blow it out of proportion."

Rick rolled his eyes. "Whatever. This fucking town has you blind to everything."

Without another word, the younger man walked out the door. Colton watched him go then collapsed back down on the couch, shaking his head. He looked over at Tony, who seemed to be taking this much better than either he or Rick.

"I agree that you need to talk to Ella before we jump to any conclusions. Although it would be understandable if she didn't want to admit to what she's done."

"I don't know why she would do this at all." Colton couldn't even begin to wrap his head around it.

"People do stupid shit all the time for misguided reasons, you know that."

Colton did know that, but for the life of him, he couldn't figure out what would make Ella want to leak that info.

"I was going to bring this up later, but you should probably know that there were a lot of posts about you at that store," Tony said. "And a lot of posts concerning Ella."

Colton scrubbed a hand down his face, all of today's earlier energy completely gone. "Stuff you think she may have posted?"

"No. Normal stuff, but—"

"Then I'm not interested. Regular social media will have to wait."

Because comments didn't matter right now. The only thing that mattered was why Ella would've done something like this and how he'd allowed himself to be so blind to it.

# CHAPTER
# THIRTY-TWO

ELLA SIGHED as she finished putting away the last items that had finished drying from her final class with the campers. Both Ashley and Marshall had stayed to help, but she'd sent them on their way a few minutes ago.

She was going to miss these kids. Heck, she was going to miss the whole experience. She needed to sit down with Bear and find a way that they could make this happen more often. Sure, it wouldn't be this same group of campers, but this entire event had been nothing but worthwhile for everyone involved.

She might have stuck around and hung out with the kids a little longer if it weren't for the fact that she was meeting Colton for dinner. She couldn't wait to see him, had loved how excited he'd been at his breakthrough last night. He kept crediting her with figuring it out, but she had no doubt that he would've gotten there himself very quickly.

Regardless, she wouldn't be ungrateful for how he'd spent most of the night thanking her. She definitely hadn't gotten much sleep. And was sore in places she didn't even know someone could be sore.

A smile lit up her face; she couldn't help it. She was so in love with Colton Harrison. That was nothing new. What was new was the fact that, for the first time, she thought this might actually work out.

She wanted to head home, take a shower, and get herself as dolled up as she could for her dinner date with him. Maybe she was never going to look like some of the models that he'd dated in the past, but Colton hadn't done anything but make her feel beautiful from the moment he'd set foot back in Oak Creek.

It didn't matter what the public thought about them. It only mattered what they thought about each other.

She was folding the last hand towel and getting ready to leave when Lilah stormed in the door.

"Are you okay?" Lilah rushed over to Ella's side and grabbed her hand. "It's going to be okay."

Ella's heart froze. The last time she saw Lilah look like this had been the day of the avalanche.

"What?" she whispered. "What happened?"

Lilah made a strange face. "Nothing. Never mind."

Now, Ella grabbed her hand. "I know it's not nothing. Is someone hurt? Is it Colton?"

"No." But her friend flinched.

"Lilah. Tell me what's going on. You're freaking me out."

The other woman let out a sigh. "You and Colton were at that new big sporting goods place in Reddington City yesterday."

"Yes. It was a madhouse. Colton got swamped by fans, but he handled it beautifully. Why does that have you so upset?"

"There was some...*stuff* about it on social media."

Ella still didn't understand why Lilah was so upset. "I'm not surprised. Like I said, it sort of grew into a frenzy."

"Do you still follow the chats about Colton?"

Ella felt her face heat at the fact that Lilah knew she did that. "No, it just hasn't felt right since he and I got together at the wedding."

"Good." Lilah nodded enthusiastically. "I think that's very healthy."

This was the exact opposite of how she'd looked when she'd

first come in a few minutes ago. It didn't take a genius to put together what was going on.

"What did the social media sites say?"

Lilah shook her head. "Nothing. Never mind. I shouldn't even have brought them up. Ignore me."

It had to be pretty bad if her friend had come storming in here to see if Ella was okay. Ella grabbed her phone so she could open the social media networks herself.

"Elly-Belly, don't. It's not worth it."

"I know I'll eventually look anyway, so I might as well rip the Band-Aid off right here."

Ella wasn't sure what exactly she'd been expecting, but this was much more brutal.

Sure, there were plenty of pictures and captions about people meeting Colton, but there was a particular section, complete with hashtags, that was only about Ella.

She only skimmed through it, but the attack was thorough and savage.

"The Wyoming mountain air may be doing great things for Colton Harrison's health, but evidently not for his eyesight." That was attached to a picture of Ella that had been taken while she was mid-sentence with Tony, but Tony had been cropped out of the picture, so it just looked like Ella was making a weird face.

The comments got uglier from there.

"I didn't know his standards were so low."

"I didn't know they made an outfit in that size. Oh, maybe she's wearing a tent."

It went on and on.

*Plain. Chunky. Ugly.*

"Elly-Belly…"

Ella jerked back from the friend she'd known most of her life. "I've always hated that nickname."

Lilah blinked, then nodded slowly. "I didn't know."

"Yeah, because how could you know that a nickname highlighting my fat stomach would bother me?"

"You don't have a fat stomach. But regardless, I'll never use it again."

Ella felt tears fill her eyes, and she wiped them angrily from her cheeks as they fell. She was yelling at one of her best friends, who had done nothing but come here in an attempt to protect and comfort her.

"I'm so—"

Lilah cut her off. "If you finish that apology, we might have to fight. You have every right to ask us not to call you that. I'm just sorry that we never understood how much it hurt you."

"It doesn't hurt me as much as—"

Lilah reached over and grabbed both of Ella's upper arms. "It does hurt you, and I should have known that. I'm the one who's sorry."

"They said really mean things about me, Li." Her voice quavered, and tears rolled down her cheeks. "I've always tried to be nice to people. Those are strangers who don't even know me, and they said such horrible things."

Lilah yanked Ella into her arms. "Some people are just mean and bitter and have too much time on their hands. That's a reflection of *their* ugliness, not your beauty."

Ella stayed in the comfort of her friend's embrace for a long minute. "This is why I can't be with Colton."

"You can't let some random strangers who take pleasure in saying malicious things from the comfort of anonymity keep you away from the man you love."

She pulled back so she could look at Lilah. "It's not just this. Last week when we were trying to catch the stalker, I was in the bathroom and Samantha from the grocery store came in with another woman. They were basically saying the same things, just not quite as mean or creatively. Everyone who looks at Colton and me is always going to feel like he's slumming it."

"That is utter bullshit." Lilah cracked her knuckles then leaned forward and gripped one of the prep tables. "I know for a fact that man is over the moon about you. What did he say when you told him about the bathroom incident?"

"I didn't tell him. I didn't want to make a big deal about it, and honestly, I guess I was hoping maybe it was a one-time thing. But obviously, it's not."

"Then you need to tell him about that incident and these posts. Colton wants to know, believe me. He does not want you trying to handle this on your own. There are things you guys can do to be proactive about this sort of stuff."

"I'm just afraid it's going to make me feel pathetic." Mortified was more like it. "The thought of him reading these posts makes me feel sick."

Lilah stroked her hair gently. "Because you think it's going to make him think of you in a different way? You know it's not. And hell, if it did, then you'd want to be rid of him as quickly as possible anyway."

"I'm embarrassed, Lilah. Having people say publicly the worst things you've ever thought about yourself? It's horrible."

"The only people who should be embarrassed are those bitches who wrote that. They are petty and jealous and a waste of space." Lilah cracked her knuckles once again, violence in her brown eyes. "You say the word, and Lincoln will figure out who they are and where they live, and I will pay them a visit and show them what ugly *really* looks like."

She would do it, too. And Lincoln would make sure she never got caught.

"You're a good friend, Lilah. Thank you. But let's be the bigger people."

Lilah rolled her eyes. "I don't have much interest in being the bigger person, but I will because you have always been the bigger person. You've always been kind and patient and beautiful to everyone around you. But promise me that you're going to talk to Colton about this. These petty biddies are trying to break you up—don't you dare give them the satisfaction."

Her friend was right. "I'll talk to him. I promise."

*"Today."*

Ella really didn't want to ruin their dinner and was about to make the argument that the discussion could wait until tomorrow when a text came through from Colton.

> Do you mind meeting me at your office? I need to talk to you.

Good. That would work better all the way around. She could explain how much she was struggling with this, they could come up with a plan, and it wouldn't have to ruin their first *actual* official date.

The first of many.

---

Fancy Pants had closed for the day by the time Ella got there thirty minutes later. She waved to the closing staff and walked straight back to her office. She found Colton sitting on the small couch.

She wanted nothing more than to walk over and hurl herself into his arms, but he didn't stand up.

As a matter of fact, his face was pinched and his hair looked like he'd run his hand through it multiple times—exactly how he tended to look when a panic attack had happened.

"Are you okay?" She meant what she'd said when she told him that progress wasn't linear. Just because he had another panic attack today didn't mean that the breakthrough he'd had yesterday was invalid.

He let out a sigh. "I need to talk to you about yesterday's events at the sporting goods store."

That wasn't what she was expecting him to say, but she was glad they were on the same page. "I agree. I'm glad you want to talk about it too."

Colton wasn't one to read social media about himself, so she was a little surprised he'd already heard what had happened.

Maybe somebody from his team had told him. The important thing was, they could get it out in the open.

Still, she wished he would stand up so she could press herself up against him as they talked about this. She needed to be close to him but wasn't exactly sure how to ask for it, especially when he already looked so stressed.

She let out a shaky laugh instead. "Okay, so this is definitely a huge elephant in the room. How do we talk about it?"

He still made no move to come anywhere near her. "Why did you do it?"

That caught her off guard. "Why did I do what?"

"Yesterday, Ella. Why? I mean, it ended up being fine, but it could've gotten out of hand."

Ella rubbed her eyes. She couldn't figure out what he was talking about. "I don't know what you mean."

He slid forward to the edge of the couch and looked up at her. "Look, I've given it a lot of thought, and I'm not mad. But you can't do stuff like that."

"Like what?" Now, she was getting frustrated. "What are you talking about?"

"We've never been dishonest with each other, Ella. Don't start now. Caroline showed us your digital scrapbook. So, I know just how much of a fan you are."

Oh shit. That damn scrapbook that everyone had contributed to for years. Ella rarely thought about it, but taken as a whole and out of context, it would have to seem a little overwhelming to Colton.

She could feel her face burning. This was beyond *patheticity*. And it was going to make talking about the social media comments so much harder.

"That thing is a little hard to explain. It's embarrassing. It's sort of a joke that all our friends constantly play on me." She'd stopped adding to it a while ago, but the gang still contributed to the group file all the time. She should've deleted it.

"Are you saying that's not your digital scrapbook? It had your name on it."

Oh hell. "I mean, yeah, technically, it is mine. I started it years ago, and then it just grew into a sort of community project from there. People in town like to keep your clippings. You're a celebrity. It's exciting."

She wasn't explaining this well. Couldn't quite come up with the words that would explain how Lilah and Becky and Bear and even Lincoln had gone out of their way to collect information on Colton for her digital book.

Partially because they knew how much she cared about him, partially their way of gently teasing her about it.

She let out a laugh that she meant to be light but instead came out tinged with hysteria. "I'm not your stalker, I promise."

He didn't laugh. And that's when it occurred to her that he'd already had that thought.

"Jesus, Colton. Is that what you think?"

He ran a hand through his hair again. "No, of course not. I…"

Now, he stood up, but the desire to hug him was long gone. Instead, she wrapped her arms around her own middle.

"I'm just trying to fathom this situation, Ella. Do you want attention? Is that what this is about?"

She shook her head. "No. The opposite, actually. As a matter of fact, I came here to talk to you about what we could do to help mitigate the stuff happening on social media."

"If you want to mitigate it, then announcing where we're going to be in order to draw a crowd is not the way to do that."

"Of course it's not. What are you talking about?"

He pulled out his phone and showed her a social media post that had been made yesterday announcing he was at the sporting goods store. "Why did you do this?"

"Do *what*?"

"Make this post, Ella!"

She felt like the entire universe was slowing around her. "You think *I* posted that?"

"We found a note next to your computer that had this account's name on it. I might not have thought anything about that until your employee came in and showed us the four-million-page scrapbook you had of me."

And the slowing universe stopped completely.

Lead filled her gut as she realized he truly believed she had announced where they would be on social media. Not only that, but he thought she'd done it because she wanted attention for herself.

The irony that she'd come here wanting help dealing with people's online cruelty, only to be accused of wanting online attention for herself, was not lost on her.

There was no way she could talk to him about that at all now even if she wanted to. But she didn't want to because all this proved was that Colton didn't know her at all.

She stood there and shook her head. She couldn't even formulate words. She had never expected to have to defend herself from something like this.

"Look," he continued. "You said it yourself. Lincoln spilled the beans at the wedding when he told me you had a crush on me. I didn't really think much of it at the time. I mean, we've known each other forever. I didn't think you thought of me that way. That you were such a...*fan*."

Ella was afraid she might vomit right here in her office. What could she say to any of this?

"Don't look at me like that, please, Butterscotch."

The endearment just made it all so much worse.

"I do want us to find a way to work this out. You grew up with a famous father, so I sort of expected you to understand more how it all works. The need for privacy. Not drawing unnecessary attention."

He reached for her, but she slid back and closed her eyes. If he touched her now, she might shatter into a million pieces.

"I just want to understand why you did it and make you understand that you can't do stuff like this, okay? It's not good for either of us."

She opened her eyes and found him looking at her with such

sincerity that it made the situation unbearable. He truly did just want to understand.

Ella understood something, too, but not what he thought.

She understood that this could never work.

"How about if we just agree to this, Colton: You don't ever have to worry about me doing something like that ever again. Lock the door behind you when you leave."

Without another word, she turned and left.

# CHAPTER
# THIRTY-THREE

LATE AFTERNOON THE NEXT DAY, Colton sat in the far back booth of the Eagle's Nest, nursing a drink. His face was grim enough that nobody had approached him, not that there were many people here.

He'd gotten up before dawn and gone rock climbing. The activity never failed to help clear his head.

Except today, it hadn't helped. All he could do was see Ella's face as he tried to talk to her last night. He'd run the conversation over and over again in his mind. Trying to figure out exactly where it had broken down. They'd both seemed to be on the same page when she'd first shown up—wanting to talk about the social media post concerning the sporting goods store.

Yeah, she'd been embarrassed about that scrapbook, and maybe he could've been a little gentler in how he'd brought that up. Coaxed her into explaining more about that.

Because...that look on her face. He hadn't been able to sleep at all last night, but if he had, that look would've haunted his nightmares.

He couldn't wrap his head around it. He thought he was doing the right thing by giving her a chance to explain. Yeah, they would need to establish some ground rules moving forward, but the important thing was he still definitely wanted to move forward.

Nothing in the way she'd left her office last night had suggested she wanted the same.

The thought of that did way more than send him into a panic attack—it sent his whole world crashing down. He had to find Ella and figure out a way to make things right. Figure out a way to make her understand that one indiscretion was completely forgivable. The fame elements of his life could get overwhelming and out of control.

Yeah, he'd expected her to understand a little better, given her family, but they could still work this out.

He should have gone after her last night as soon as she left the office. Should've dragged her back and fought it out and then cleared the air. That's how it had always been between his parents. Tempers could burn hot, but then after the fight, the anger dissipated and the air between them was fresh. That was what he'd been expecting from Ella—for her to push back with some anger of her own to match his.

But the more he thought about it today, the more he realized that wasn't sweet, gentle Ella's style. She was a peacemaker, through and through. Fighting was not in her nature.

He sat up straighter in the booth. Neither was drawing undue attention to herself.

*Fuck.*

She hadn't done it. She hadn't been the one to leak the info about the sporting goods store. Of course she hadn't been. He couldn't believe he'd been stupid enough to even consider it. He didn't give a shit what it had said on that sticky note.

*She. Hadn't. Done. This.*

He needed to find her now more than ever. He'd stopped by her house last night, but she hadn't been there. He should've gone by again this morning—hell, camped out in front of her front door—but he'd thought he'd been in the right and had gone rock climbing to try to take care of his own mental needs instead.

Putting himself first. Goddamn it, Ella constantly put others' needs in front of her own. They all took for granted the fact that she never let them down.

And then he'd gone and accused her of the unthinkable.

He had to find her and make this right. If he *could* make this right. He was sliding out of the booth as Tony slid in across from him.

Colton shook his head. "Whatever it is, it's going to have to wait."

"It's about Ella and what happened on social media."

"She didn't do it, Tony. I know it looks like she's the one who leaked our location, but I promise you she's not the one who did it."

The other man looked surprised. "I know that. But how do *you* know that?"

"I just know." Tony's other words registered, and Colton tilted his head at him. "Wait, how do *you* know?"

"I know you don't want to talk, so I'll make this brief." He flipped around the tablet that was always in his hand so a signature page was facing Colton. "This is an employment termination notice for Rick. I found out he was the one who released the information about you being at the store. He must've been following you. He's the one who opened that social media account and knew exactly where to post it. Then he tried to blame it on Ella by pretending to find that sticky note."

Colton wanted to put his fist through the wall. But he was just as pissed at himself as he was Rick. Rick may have been the one who started the problem for whatever dumbass reason, but Colton should've been the one to shut it down before it ever went anywhere.

"We can talk about the details of everything later," Tony continued. "Just sign, and hand me your phone so I can finalize everything."

Colton did what the other man asked almost in a daze. The true ramifications of what he'd done—what he'd accused Ella of—were finally starting to hit him. Fear was a fist in his throat at the knowledge that he'd broken something so precious.

He signed and slid the tablet back to Tony and took his phone back from the other man. "Okay, done. Rick Wynnsworth is no longer in the employ of your team, and I've notified him that there will be an official inquiry into everything. You can probably sue him for what he did."

"Money isn't going to help." Colton scrubbed a hand down his face. "I have plenty of money. It's not going to change the fact that I accused Ella of something unforgivable."

Tony let out a sigh. "I don't know. She seems like the forgiving sort to me. Maybe you just need to give it a little time. A little distance."

"What if I've lost her over this?"

"You went rock climbing this morning, right?"

Colton nodded. He wasn't sure how Tony knew that, but then again, it was Tony's job to know pretty much everywhere Colton went.

"How did you feel up there? Better? Worse?"

"Better, I guess. It always helps me clear my head." But then again, he hadn't had all the information when he'd been out there.

Tony gripped the edge of the table and leaned forward intently. "Colton, I've been with you day in and day out for over a year now. I know things are in a state of flux with you, but I'm telling the truth when I say I think you might ought to give this a little bit of time and distance. Let's just get back to work. You want to simplify for a while? No problem. No social media. No television. But let's get you back out there doing what you love. It's what you need. Then, when the time is right—six months, a year—you can come back here and see if you still feel the same way about…everything."

Colton stared at the other man. Maybe Tony was right. Maybe he'd jumped the gun when he'd decided to retire. Maybe staying here in Oak Creek was the wrong plan, even with Ella.

His hands started shaking, jerking him out of those thoughts.

No. Damn it, *no*.

"No. I'm not going back into stunts full time. Even if Ella won't take me back, I'm still done with that part of my life." Immediately, his hands stopped shaking. Because he was making the right decision. Because he wasn't going to allow himself to be talked into a life he didn't want any longer.

"Colton, I really think you should reconsider—"

"Have we switched to day drinking?" Bear didn't even wait for an invitation, just slid into the booth beside Colton, forcing him to scoot over.

Tony shook his head. "I've got to go take care of some things. Think about what I said, Colton. I'll catch you later."

"I'm not going to change my mind, Tony."

Tony didn't say anything, just slid out of the booth.

Bear moved over to the other side to replace him. "He doesn't seem too happy."

"Tony is the least of my concerns right now."

Bear nodded. "Is this about that social media snafu?"

*Jesus.* Word had gotten around fast even for a town as small as Oak Creek. "How'd you know? It wasn't Ella."

"What wasn't Ella? Lilah was pretty sure that shit was targeted at her."

"Targeted at her? What do you mean?"

"All that *mean girl* shit. I'm not one to condone violence toward women, but I would not mind watching those bitches get a taste of their own medicine."

Colton shook his head at his friend. "Dude, I don't know what you're talking about."

Bear pulled out his phone and showed Colton one of the most popular social media websites and what had been said during and after the sporting goods store incident.

If Colton had felt awful before, it was nothing compared to how he felt seeing this.

And furious. So very fucking furious. At the posters of these malicious remarks. At Rick for having planted the seed of doubt that had kept him away from Ella.

But mostly at himself.

"I'm sorry, man, I thought you already knew. Ella was upset—rightfully so—when she saw this."

"Who wouldn't be? Basically being called fat and ugly by a number of strangers when she hadn't done anything but stand over to the side and mind her own business?" Rage was eating through Colton's system.

"Lilah told her to talk to you about it last night. I guess this isn't the first incident."

Colton pushed Bear's phone back over toward him, unable to handle reading any more. "It's not?"

Bear shrugged. "Yeah, the night she was helping with the sting operation, she overheard a couple of people talking some shit about her in the bathroom."

Goddamn it. He'd known something had been wrong that night and even the next day when they left for the wilderness survival camping trip. Ella wasn't one to complain, but he should've pushed. Should've made her talk about it. Should've figured out how he could help.

But he hadn't, and now he'd made it all so much worse.

"You're looking a little green around the gills there, brother."

"I've fucked up worse than anything I've done in my entire life."

Bear raised an eyebrow. "I've been around when you've done some pretty stupid shit. Are you sure about that?"

Colton explained everything that had happened in the past twenty-four hours.

"Goddamn, you did fuck things up," Bear said when Colton was done.

"In my defense, somebody showed me this scrapbook thing Ella had collected over the years, and it sort of freaked me out."

"That thing?" Bear looked sheepish. "Not to make you feel any worse, but that scrapbook is not even Ella's. Or at least, not *just* Ella's."

"But it was on her computer."

"On a shared file we all use. A few years ago, somebody came across some articles she had collected about you. You know all of us, we are such assholes, we all started collecting every digital clipping about you we could find and sending them to her in a group file. That thing has to be huge at this point. It's a running joke between us all."

And there was strike three against him. "I am the biggest asshole on the planet."

"Today, I'm afraid you don't get much argument from me."

Colton couldn't blame his friend.

"I need to talk to her. I went by her house last night, but she wasn't there. And today, like the self-obsessed jerk I am, I went rock climbing rather than figure out that I should be groveling at her feet. I wonder where she is right now."

"She's not at Fancy Pants. I went by there an hour or so ago. Lilah said she wasn't at home either. Maybe she just needs a minute to cool off."

"I need to see her. To explain how stupid I was."

"I think it's gonna take a lot more than that. Better prepare to grovel."

Colton scrubbed a hand down his face again. "I'll do whatever it takes. No matter what."

"Holy shit," Bear laughed. "You're in love with her."

"Hell yes, I'm in love with her. There's not even one piece of me that's ashamed to admit that."

Bear leaned back against the booth seat, looking smug. "Maybe telling her that is the first step in getting back into her good graces. And here's the good thing about Ella O'Conner…the woman is as softhearted and kind as they come. Wouldn't know how to carry a grudge if someone put it in a backpack and tried to slip it on her shoulders. She will forgive you."

"She has to, Bear. I can't live without her."

"Then that's the line I would start with."

# CHAPTER
# THIRTY-FOUR

It was almost dark when Colton pulled up to his cabin at Linear Tactical. He sat in his truck, staring blankly ahead. Ever since leaving the Eagle's Nest a few hours ago, he'd been driving around everywhere trying to find Ella.

Evidently Ella didn't want to be found.

He'd gone everywhere. Her house multiple times. Fancy Pants Bakery multiple times. Even to each of her friends' houses.

He'd started with Eva here on the Linear Tactical property. She'd answered the door, Theo standing protectively just behind her. They both still had that newly married glow to their faces.

They'd invited him in, but he hadn't wanted to lose any time in his search for Ella. Eva had heard about the cruel social media posts against Ella, but Ella hadn't told her what Colton had done.

Because Ella was good and kind. Because she knew it would hurt her friends to know he'd done something like that. Because for whatever reason, she was still nice even after he'd been an asshole.

Colton did not provide himself the same consideration Ella had afforded him. He spelled out exactly what he'd done and why he was looking for her.

Eva had been mad and told him he better make it up to Ella. When he'd gone over to Becky and Derek's house next and repeated his transgressions to them, Becky had pretty much responded the same way Eva had. They wanted him to make it up to their sweet friend.

He planned to.

When he got to Lilah's cabin and told her what he'd done, she'd been much more direct than Ella's other girlfriends.

"You will make this right, jackass. And I'll see you in the ring tomorrow."

With that, she slammed the door in his face. Knowing Lilah, she probably shut the door to keep from drop-kicking him right then and there.

He had no doubt the woman could do it. In some ways, he wished she would have. He deserved it.

He looked down at his phone when it buzzed. A text from Bear.

> Any luck?

> Can't find her anywhere. Checked work, house, friends. Texted five dozen times.

> Don't worry. She'll definitely show back up for tomorrow's goodbye lunch for the campers. She wouldn't miss that, no matter how pissed at you she is.

That was true. She would definitely want to be able to say goodbye to Ashley and Marshall and the other kids.

But damn it, Colton didn't want to go another night without being able to tell her how sorry he was. Even if she didn't forgive him—which he wouldn't blame her at all for—he wanted to try.

He swiped a hand down his face and got out of the truck. What *he* wanted didn't matter. If Ella needed time on her own, he would give it to her. Not that he had any choice at this point anyway.

He was so lost in his own stupidity that he was completely unaware of the attack until he was being tackled on the ground.

The wind was knocked out of him as he hit the dirt, but Colton had spent all of his career reacting to unexpected circumstances that changed in a split second. He caught a punch on the jaw, but he was able to roll over to his side and then kip back up onto his feet.

For a second, he wondered if Lilah had decided not to wait for the sparring ring after all, but almost immediately, he realized that the person who tackled him was too big to be Lilah. She was strong and fast, but she was tiny.

"You son of a bitch!"

Colton blinked twice when he realized it was Rick standing in front of him like some sort of bull in front of a red flag.

"Rick? What the fuck are you doing?"

Not only was he here, he was wearing a black hoodie.

"Why would you fire me?" He flew at Colton again, but this time, Colton was ready and he sidestepped, letting the younger man fly through the empty space.

Rick stumbled but caught himself without falling. He spun back around, glaring at Colton. "You ignore my calls? And you don't even have the guts to fire me to my face, especially after what I did for you?"

"What you *did* for me? I fucking fired you because you made it look like Ella was the one who posted that social media message."

"All I did was mention the damned sticky note! And yeah, it did look suspicious. But then I figured out that she wasn't the one who'd posted it, yet you *still* fired me."

"Nice try."

Rick threw his hands up in the air. "You little prick. You were just looking for a reason to get rid of me, weren't you? Just because I don't like your precious town."

"Go home, Rick. You're fired. There, now I've said it to your face."

Colton just wanted to go inside, but there was no way he was going to turn his back on Rick. And damn, if the man had a weapon, this might get ugly quickly. Colton had a concealed carry permit and kept a Glock in his truck. He casually started easing in that direction, hoping he wouldn't need it.

"You're so damn ungrateful. Always thinking about yourself."

Colton shrugged. "Actually, on that, we agree. Although I'm hoping to change."

Rick continued to glare at him. "I knew I'd been a dick about this town and about your precious Ella. That's why I started digging deeper into who posted that announcement on social media. I was the one who discovered it wasn't her."

"Why should I believe you?"

Rick rolled his eyes. "Why would I make something like that up?"

"To get your job back?"

He threw up his hands. "I told Tony all this before you fired me. Because, yeah, I knew I'd been an asshole and deserved to be fired. But I thought discovering this would make a difference."

Something wasn't making sense here. "Wait. What? You told Tony?"

"Yeah. I told Tony, and I thought everything would be good. But then a couple hours later, he shows back up to say you'd fired me and you'd gotten a restraining order against me."

What the hell was going on? "Rick, that's not even how restraining orders work. I can't just order one and have it ready thirty minutes later. And especially not without some sort of probable cause. Plus, why would I get a restraining order against you? They don't give them out for people being an asshole. You must've misunderstood what Tony was saying."

Rick reached into his pocket, and suddenly, getting the gun out of his truck wasn't an option. Colton had no idea if Rick was going for a weapon, so he did a flying tackle of his own. Once they were on the ground, Colton didn't waste any time getting Rick flipped over and pulling one arm up behind his back.

"Ow!"

"If I jerk this much farther, it's going to break your arm. What were you going for in your pocket? Gun? Knife?"

"No, man, my phone. I just wanted to show you what Tony showed me."

Colton patted down Rick's front pockets. Sure enough, the only thing he had on him was a phone. He let the man go, and they both rolled over to sit on the grass. Rick got the phone then a second later stuck it in Colton's face.

"See?"

Colton had to admit, it looked like an electronic copy of some sort of restraining order. And it was signed by Colton.

Colton hadn't signed anything of the sort.

"This isn't right. Yes, I signed the paperwork to fire you, but that was because Tony said you'd had a plan to blame Ella from the beginning."

"It wasn't me. I'm telling you, it wasn't me."

Colton had a sick feeling in the pit of his stomach. "Why didn't you call me and tell me what happened?"

"I've been trying to call you all day. But my calls were blocked."

"I didn't block your calls." Colton took his phone out of his pocket and looked up Rick's contact info. Sure enough, the contact was blocked.

Colton knew for a fact that he hadn't been the one who'd done that.

He also knew that Tony had taken his phone for a minute at the Eagle's Nest today. Colton had been so caught up in his guilt over Ella that he hadn't thought much about it.

Until now.

"I think something really bad is going on, Rick."

He dialed Tony's number, but it immediately went to voice mail. He sent a text.

> Need to talk to you. STAT.

No response. In the year that Tony had worked for him, he had never once not responded to a text within just a minute or two.

Something definitely wasn't right.

"Yes, I did fire you, but I thought it was because you'd set Ella up. But it sounds like somebody might be setting *you* up."

"What do you mean?"

They both got to their feet.

"Is that your hoodie, Rick? I've never seen you wear it." Colton definitely would've remembered if he had.

Rick looked down at the piece of clothing. "No, actually, I found this in my car. Somebody must've left it there, but it was cold tonight so I thought I would wear it." He shrugged sheepishly. "Also, because it meant it would be harder for you to see me as you got home."

The guy was a good cameraman, but he wasn't the sharpest tool in the shed.

"You know that Ella saw the stalker in a black hoodie at her shop, right? And you remember how we were talking the other day about there being a man involved in all this, maybe as the stalker's partner?"

"Whoa. That's not me. I have nothing to do with the stalker."

No. *Tony* did.

"I'm pretty sure that Tony was setting you up to make it look like it was you." And Rick just happily got his DNA all over a piece of clothing that no doubt would become a big factor in making him look guilty.

Colton froze as he thought this through. *Shit*. If Tony was behind all this and was setting Rick up as his patsy, the only way he could be successful was if Rick was out of the way *permanently*.

Otherwise, Rick would defend himself. Maybe no one would believe him, but he'd still plant seeds of doubt about his guilt.

Tony had probably thought Rick would drive back to Denver after being fired. And since he didn't have direct access to Colton, since his calls were blocked and Tony filtered through all of Colton's emails, Rick wouldn't have any way of getting in touch with Colton.

Tony hadn't counted on Rick's idiotic temper driving his actions and that he would come here to confront Colton tonight. The man had probably saved his own life by doing so.

Colton hoped he was wrong about all this and Tony wouldn't go to such extremes just to keep Colton in the game. Because it wouldn't. Colton wanted to be wherever Ella was.

*Shit*. Dread pooled in his stomach. Tony had to know that too. Which meant…Tony had to plan to do something to Ella too.

Where the hell was she?

Colton rushed toward his cabin. "Get on your phone and call Sheriff Webb. Tell him that Tony is our stalker and that we don't know where Ella is and that everything has gone to shit."

"What are you going to do?"

"I'm calling in the people I trust most."

———

All his friends came through exactly the way Colton knew they would. Within thirty minutes of Rick tackling him, Theo and Lilah had arranged a house-to-house search in Oak Creek. The search would be guised as friendly visits and touching base, but the true purpose would be to make sure Ella wasn't there. Callum Webb was checking businesses.

The fact that everyone in Oak Creek was so friendly and open—and cared so much about helping find Ella—reaffirmed to Colton that this was where he belonged.

Rick had actually provided some useful information—reminding Colton that he'd given Tony permission to put a tracker on Colton's truck right after the avalanche since he'd been spending a lot of time alone in the wilderness. Colton had forgotten about it, and they'd never removed it.

No wonder Tony was always able to find Colton so easily.

But he and Ella hadn't been driving Colton's truck the day they'd gone shopping at the sporting goods store. Yet, if Tony had released that social media announcement, he'd been following him. So maybe he'd put a tracking device on Ella's car too.

Colton had already put a call in to Lincoln, asking him if he could reverse-engineer the info from his truck's tracking device and maybe gather some details if Ella's vehicle had one placed on it too.

If anyone could do it, it was Lincoln.

Colton kept trying to call Tony also. Finding him before he made his move was just as important. Colton had to pretend like everything was still business as usual until they caught him.

Colton froze when Tony answered on his fourth time calling him.

"Hey, boss, what's going on? Sorry I missed your other calls. Battery died."

Colton forced himself to stay cool. He could not give away that he knew what was happening. "Just wanted to talk over some possible plans with you. You got time to meet? I'm sure the Eagle's Nest is still open. We could grab a bite."

"Actually, I decided to go back to Reddington City. I wanted to talk to the manager of that store again. Get all the details I can so we can move forward."

Reddington City. Shit. If he had Ella, they couldn't do any door-to-door search there.

"Okay, I hear you. But I'd really like to talk about this tonight, if we can. I'm wondering if you're right and we need to just get back to work."

This was a delicate balance. Colton wanted to disarm Tony by seeming compliant to the other man's ideas, but he didn't want to change his tune so much that it made him suspicious.

"Really?"

A text came through from Lincoln.

> I was able to locate Ella's car. Coordinates 40.8056°N 106.9442°W

Colton rolled his eyes. How the hell was he supposed to know where that was off the top of his head?

"Honestly, I don't know," he continued with Tony. "I just want to talk options, you know? Pick your brain." He needed to keep this conversation going with Tony while he texted Lincoln back.

> Is it near Reddington City?

No. Montana. Closest town seems to be some place called Garnet Bend.

She'd gone to the cabin. Relief flooded Colton's gut. Tony didn't have her.

"Okay," Tony said. "I'm happy to talk plans out with you. Let me handle this at the store, and we can touch base maybe tomorrow morning? I know it's been a long day for you."

"Sure, tomorrow morning sounds good. Let's plan on breakfast. I'll call you."

But he wouldn't be meeting Tony for breakfast. He disconnected the call and immediately called Callum Webb. The sheriff agreed to go to Reddington City and bring Tony in for questioning. Theo and Lilah were going with him in case Tony decided to make a run for it.

Colton trusted his friends to get the bad guy.

He was going to get the girl.

# CHAPTER
# THIRTY-FIVE

ELLA DIDN'T KNOW why she had come back to this cabin near Garnet Bend. She'd just known she couldn't stay in Oak Creek. She loved her hometown, but sometimes having everyone know everything wasn't beneficial to her mental health.

She'd needed to be alone. Hadn't wanted to talk to friends or family. Although she knew they loved her, this was something she needed to work out for herself. The relationship between her and Colton only had to do with her and Colton.

She'd already decided that she wasn't going to tell anybody what he'd accused her of. Not because he had any justification in doing so, but because she needed to fight her own battles. Not just let her protective friends fight them for her.

She could only imagine what Lilah would say—and do—if she found out. Probably beat Colton to a pulp. So, Ella would keep it to herself.

Some would probably argue that she was protecting him and she shouldn't do that. Yet she wasn't. But she also didn't want Lilah to fight her battles for her.

It was time for her to stand up for herself when it came to Colton Harrison.

She let herself inside the cabin using the hidden switch to unlock the door that he'd shown her. She was immediately surrounded by the memories that permeated this place. She could almost feel his lips on her skin and couldn't even glance over at the hot spring without blushing after what they'd done there.

She loved him. She'd loved him most of her adult life. That was true, and nearly everyone knew it.

But she'd also faced a hard truth coming up here.

*If Colton Harrison couldn't appreciate her, then he didn't get the privilege of being with her.*

Because she was enough for any man—even Colton—just as she was. Yeah, she was a few pounds overweight and was probably on the plain side. She didn't wear makeup, didn't care about fashion, had better things to do with her time than spend an hour doing her hair each day. But she was smart, industrious, hardworking, and kind.

And she wasn't going to be a doormat, not for anyone.

Just because she'd loved Colton first didn't mean she was less worthy of his love. And if he couldn't give her that, and the respect and consideration that went along with it, then they had no future at all.

The relief she felt at having finalized this in her mind was immense. She could live without Colton Harrison. She didn't want to, especially not after seeing how good they were for each other, but she could do it.

And while loving him had been an important part of her life for a long time, loving herself was always going to be the most important thing.

So yeah, she and Colton were going to have a showdown. He owed her an apology, and she owed him an explanation about that damn scrapbook.

But she wasn't just going to give up on their relationship and run away crying. She was going to stand her ground. And see if Colton was willing to fight for their relationship too. If he wasn't, she would walk away with her head held high.

She slipped off her shoes and dipped her feet in the hot spring, pulling out her phone as she did so. There were a number of messages from Colton, but she didn't want to look at those yet. She had another set of demons she needed to face first.

The people who had posted all those mean things about her on social media. Because like it or not, even if Colton decided he was changing directions in his career, he would still be in the public eye.

And there would always be petty people who posted petty things.

The comments were just as ugly as when she'd glanced at them with Lilah, and Ella couldn't help but shed a couple of tears.

But those were the last. She wouldn't be shedding any more tears based on strangers' comments about her.

People were jerks sometimes; you just had to accept that and move on. She wasn't going to live her life based on their opinions. She deleted the app from her phone. That wouldn't stop them from saying their ugly things, but she didn't have to subject herself to it.

Then she moved to Colton's messages. She had to admit, it did quite a bit for both her heart and self-esteem to see so many. Probably fifty texts and at least two dozen missed phone calls.

Apologies. Requests for forgiveness. Self-flagellation.

If she had any doubt that he wanted her back, these communications put it to rest. She listened to the first few messages, then deleted the rest.

She would go back, they would fight it out, but she wouldn't continue to drag out his pain. That wasn't in her nature. Yes, they were going to restart their relationship on more equal footing, but she wasn't going to make him suffer needlessly.

"You know, you've made my life so much easier by being out here and leaving the door ajar."

Ella let out a little shriek at the sound of a voice behind her. She spun, hand at her heart. She relaxed a little when she saw who it was.

"Tony. What are you doing here? Is Colton okay?"

"He will be. After today."

She didn't understand. "Did something happen? Another accident?"

Tony shook his head slowly. "No, no accident. At least, not involving Colton."

Something wasn't right here. How had Tony found her in the first place?

"I don't understand."

"I know you don't. I know you have questions. How could you not have questions?" He walked farther inside the cabin, and she froze when she saw the gun in his hand.

"What's going on, Tony? How did you know I was here?"

"The same way I knew you went to that sporting goods store and leaked the information online—I put a tracking device on your car."

"*You* leaked the information about Colton at that store?"

He stretched his neck as if it was sore. "Yeah. I was hoping it would scare you off, but it didn't. Then I had the brilliant idea of blaming you for it, hoping that would scare Colton straight out of Oak Creek, but that didn't work either."

"I don't understand."

"Trust me, I tried to get Colton back into the headspace he needs to be in by reasoning with him. I spent weeks doing that, but it didn't seem to have any effect."

"What headspace?"

"The one where he's most productive. Where he's the best version of himself. And when talking it out with him didn't work and reasoning with him didn't work and giving him time didn't work, I had to resort to more drastic measures."

"Like what?"

"Like pretending to be a fucking stalker."

Ella felt sick. "You're the stalker?"

"It didn't start that way. There was a real stalker, but she'd already been phasing herself out. Hell, I even know who she is. She was never going to hurt Colton or even make contact with him. She just got a little overzealous after the accident and sent him a few letters. Normally, I would consider that to be a pain in the ass, but it actually helped Colton focus. Got him to forget about his little panic attacks."

"You know about those?"

Tony began pacing back and forth. "I know *everything* about Colton. I researched him for over a year before I ever started working for him. That little scrapbook of yours is nothing compared to the information I collected about him."

Sweat broke out on Ella's forehead. This went way beyond merely being a good employee. Tony was obsessed with Colton.

"I don't understand what you want."

She flinched as Tony waved the gun around. "I want him to focus. What I said at that store was true. He could be so much more famous than he is now. Like, household-name famous. If he would just *focus*."

He stopped waving the gun around, but it was so much worse because he came and crouched right next to where she sat at the heated pool.

"You unfocus him." His voice was calm, friendly even. But his eyes were cold and hard.

"I don't mean to unfocus him." She couldn't stop the tremor in her voice.

She flinched as he stroked the back of her hair. "I know. That's the hardest thing. I believe you legitimately care about him. But you're still too much of a distraction."

He stood back up. "I recognized you as a problem a long time ago. I tried to keep him from you, even after the avalanche, by making it so you couldn't get in at the hospital." He began pacing, lost in his words, almost not even paying attention to her. "The last thing he needed was a little Florence Nightingale helping him heal. That sort of coddling doesn't encourage growth."

Ella's phone buzzed underneath her hand where it rested next to her on the rock ledge. She glanced over and saw another text from Colton.

> I know you're at the cabin in Garnet Bend. I'm coming to you, Butterscotch. I'm almost there. You have every right to be mad, but I hope you'll at least hear me out.

Oh no. Colton was coming here. He had no idea about Tony—and especially not about Tony's gun. She had to find some way to warn him.

"But then he ended up in Oak Creek anyway," Tony continued. "When I couldn't keep him away from you, I tried to make you irrelevant. An enemy, even."

She had to think of something. She pulled her legs out of the water so that she could move quickly if an opportunity presented itself. While Tony was turned partially away in his pacing, she pressed the text message on her phone so she could respond.

> No

It was all she could get out without Tony noticing. Colton would probably think she was mad, but as long as it kept him from walking in on this nightmare, she would take it.

"I couldn't keep him away from you and I couldn't make you irrelevant, so now I'm having to resort to much uglier measures. I have to get rid of you. Rick too, unfortunately. He's collateral damage. It's a shame because he sees the bigger picture. Sees what Colton could truly be."

"What do you mean, *get rid of?*"

He stopped his pacing and nodded solemnly. "I think you know exactly what I mean by that, Ella."

"Tony, this is insane. You're talking about killing two people." She didn't know how Rick fit into this, but she didn't want him to die either. "There's no need to do any of this. Let's just sit down and talk to Colton about your plans. I can help make him understand."

Her phone buzzed again under her hand, but she didn't dare

look at it. If Tony got a hold of it, he would know Colton was coming.

"Talking is a waste of time. What I'm going to do is make Colton one of the greatest athletes ever. I will create an empire for him. Something people will talk about for generations."

Tony was crazy. She had no idea how he'd fooled them all, but he was completely obsessed and unstable.

"Colton will be sad when you die, of course. And all those social media assholes will change their tune and say how much they loved you and how they regret that they were so mean. They'll be sad that they drove you to suicide. I was thinking I would do it with the gun, but now, I'm thinking drowning in that hot spring will work even better. Maybe an accident, maybe suicide—adds to the mystery."

She scooted back from the water. "You don't have to do this, Tony."

"His ratings will go through the roof. The avalanche proved that—people love a tragedy." He was so lost in his own thoughts, she wasn't even sure he was registering what she was saying at all.

But one thing was clear: Tony felt completely righteous in whatever he was about to do here. That did not bode well for Ella. She had no idea what to do.

The phone rang in her hand. That shocked Tony back to reality, and he lifted his gun and pointed it right at her.

"Don't answer."

"It's Colton. If I don't answer, he's going to know something's wrong."

If Tony would just let her answer, she could yell that he was here.

"Fine. But if you warn him or mention my name, the next place I'm going is to visit your pregnant sister." She let out a gasp as he continued. "That's right, I did my homework about you too. You say anything to Colton now, and that baby will never be born."

She held back a sob. "Okay."

"Put it on speaker." He pressed the muzzle of the gun against the back of her head as she answered the phone.

"H-hello."

"I know you're mad, but I have to talk to you."

"Colton, you need to leave me alone."

"Don't say that, Butterscotch. I'm almost—"

"I have one thing I want to say to you." She cut him off before he could finish the sentence and reveal to Tony how close by he was. "I want you to listen for once."

She knew she was coming across as harsh, but there was no way around it.

"Okay. Say what you need to say."

This was so tricky. She didn't want to be so sharp that he turned around and went home. Then all she would've done was sign her own death warrant. But she was also convinced that Tony was completely unstable.

He was talking like he would do anything for Colton, but the truth was, he was after his own glory. If Colton came in here and spoiled his plan, then he wouldn't hesitate to take Colton out also. He might monologue about it for a long time, but he'd eventually kill Colton along with Ella.

"Just leave me alone. I need time. I am out here in nature trying to figure out what I want."

"I know that, but—"

A painting of a field of flowers on the wall gave her an idea. "I just want to be out here with the larkspurs, Colton. We talked about that. How they are my favorite flowers and they bring me peace. I picked some, and having them nearby is helping me think through some stuff. Right now, I just need time with these beautiful flowers and nothing else."

She was rambling, not making much sense. She could only hope Colton would pick up what she was throwing down.

There was silence for a few seconds. "You want a chance to be with your larkspurs alone. That's understandable. I can respect that. But I hope we can talk when you're ready."

She had no idea if he understood or not based on that response. But there was nothing else she could do.

"Goodbye, Colton." She disconnected the call.

"Very nicely done. I honestly expected you to start yelling your head off. It wouldn't have saved you, but it definitely would've made my life harder."

"Don't do this, Tony. We can find another way. Sit Colton down and explain your plan to him. He may want it too. We can—"

"No. The time for talking has passed. It's time to say goodbye, Ella."

# CHAPTER
# THIRTY-SIX

COLTON WAS DIALING Callum Webb as soon as Ella disconnected the call. He turned off his flashlight as he walked through the dark woods. He couldn't take a chance that Tony might see him out here.

Because Tony was very definitely with Ella. Colton had no doubt she'd been trying to warn him with her talk about larkspurs.

"Colton, we still don't have any word on Tony. He did not come to the sporting goods—"

"I know. He's at the cabin with Ella near Garnet Bend, Montana."

"Shit. Are you sure?"

"Sure enough that I'm trying to figure out if I should go back and get my gun from my truck or if I should continue the hike to the cabin."

"Does he know you're coming?"

"I don't think so. Ella was trying to get me a message in code."

"I was going to tell you this later, but the deeper we dug into Tony, the worse this whole thing looks. Lincoln found some pretty scary shit. The guy is obsessed with you and clearly unstable."

And now he had Ella.

"I'm going in. I'm not leaving her alone with him one second longer than I have to."

"We're too far to be of any help, but I'm on my way. I'll call Lucas Everett with the Resting Warrior Ranch, and get him out there. His team are former military and security also."

Plus, the Resting Warrior guys knew this area like the back of their hand. "Yeah, I know some of them. I'll take all the help I can get, but I'm not—"

He didn't finish his sentence because a gunshot rang out.

The entire world stopped for Colton, and he bolted toward the cabin. Damn it, he was still too far, and he didn't know if shouting her name would do harm or good.

He ran faster than he had in his entire life, ignoring the branches that scraped his skin and slapped him in the face. He knew he was in danger of an injury since he couldn't see where he was going at all without a light, but he pushed forward at top speed anyway.

An injury wouldn't fucking matter if Ella was dead.

The cabin came into view, and relief flooded his system as the door burst open and Ella rushed out. But his relief was short-lived as Tony's frame filled the doorway, gun lifted and pointed toward Ella.

"You'll be dying for something more important than either of us, Ella!" Tony yelled. "I'm truly sorry it had to be this way."

"Not as sorry as you're going to be!" Colton yelled the words as he ran the last few yards toward the door. He caught a glimpse of Tony's surprised face as he dove through the air and tackled the man.

The gun went off again right before Colton made contact. "No!"

Oh fuck, had the bullet gotten her? Colton had no way of knowing, and all he could hear was his own enraged growl and the sound of his fists hitting Tony over and over.

He didn't stop, not when the other man fell unconscious and not when burning pain started eating through his system.

He couldn't stop. He had to protect Ella.

Ella was the only thing that mattered. If Ella didn't make it out of this, his life wouldn't be worth living anyway.

Ella.

*Ella.*

"Colton, stop."

A soft hand touched his shoulder, but he couldn't stop. He had to protect her.

He grabbed Tony by the shirt collar and pulled his unconscious form off the ground, vaguely surprised by how heavy he was.

He hit him again. Colton's vision was getting blurry, but he hit him again.

"Colton, it's Ella. Look at me."

Ella.

*Ella.*

Ella was here. She was alive. "Ella?"

She cupped his jaw with her hands. "He's down. Tony is completely out. You stopped him. Let's move away from him."

She kicked the gun away from Tony's motionless hand. Colton stayed where he was. Nothing felt right at all.

"I didn't know if you would understand my message. I'm so glad you did." She turned and smiled at him, that angelic smile he wanted to see every day for the rest of his life.

But right now, something was very wrong.

"Butterscotch." The word came out slow, slurred. "I think I might be having another panic attack."

All the color drained from her face as she looked over at him then ran to catch him as he toppled over.

"My other panic attacks didn't feel like this."

He felt pressure against his midsection.

"It's not a panic attack. You've been shot."

---

"Colton! Stay with me, Colton!" Ella grabbed Colton as he fell over. He was already out cold. She continued putting pressure on the bullet wound in his side.

He had dived in front of the bullet that Tony had meant for her.

She glanced over at Tony, wondering if she needed to restrain him, but after the beating Colton had given him, he wouldn't be waking up for quite a while.

And if he did wake up, she would shoot him herself. Right now, all that mattered was Colton. She needed to get him to medical attention now.

He groaned, regaining some consciousness, and she grabbed his hand and pushed it hard against his side.

"Pressure. Do you hear me, Colton? Press hard."

He groaned unintelligibly, but his hand stayed there when she moved hers away. She rushed into the cabin's small kitchen and started opening cabinets.

"First aid kit. Where are you?"

She found it in the third cabinet she opened then rushed back to Colton's side. The wound didn't seem to be near any vital organs, but she wasn't a doctor. Plus, you didn't need a medical degree to know that he was bleeding a lot, and that was going to become a problem.

She had to get him back to her car. But that was at least a mile away, and there was no way she could carry him.

She wrapped up the wound as best she could with the medical supplies, which should at least help slow the bleeding. But he was going to have to help her get him moved. She slapped his cheeks gently.

"Colton. We've got to go. We need to get you to the car."

"Nap."

"You can nap when you get to the car."

Colton's phone rang, and she saw it was Callum Webb.

"Callum, Colton's been shot." She could hear the hysteria in her own voice.

The older man muttered a curse. "How bad?"

"Not critical, I don't think, but he's bleeding. A lot. I need to get him to the car."

"What about Tony?"

"He's unconscious. Colton beat him pretty bad."

"Good. Can Colton walk?"

"He's going to have to. The only way I'm going to be able to move him is if he helps."

"Okay. Restrain Tony and then start moving Colton toward the car. You've got help headed in your direction."

She glanced over at Colton. "He doesn't look good, Callum."

"He's strong. You just get him moving. There is a bad storm coming in that direction."

Great. The last thing she needed.

She disconnected with Callum and found zip ties to restrain Tony's wrists and ankles, not that she thought he would be going anywhere anyway. Then she walked back over and tapped Colton's cheeks again.

"Okay, buddy, naptime is over. We've got to get moving."

"Tired."

She moved his shirt and looked down at his wound. Blood was starting to seep through the bandage. *Shit.*

"We've got to go, Harrison."

She slid his arm around her shoulders and slipped her arm around his waist, careful of his wound, hooking her fingers into his belt loop. "On three we get up, okay? One, two, three."

It took all of her strength to get him to standing, and even then, most of his weight was on her. They started taking a few shuffling steps out into the darkness, and she prayed she'd be able to find the car.

It was slow going. Colton could only take a few steps at a time and fell more than once. She was running out of energy herself, but there was no way she was going to stop. Especially once the rain started.

The storms here in Montana were just as quick and violent as the ones they sometimes got in Wyoming. Less than a minute after it started sprinkling, it was pouring. Every inch of her was soaked. She didn't know how they were going to make it.

She found a small overhang by a group of rocks and pulled him under it.

She just needed to rest for a few minutes. But she knew they couldn't stay there; water was already starting to pool around them. Flash flooding was probably a concern around here.

"Go back to the cabin." Colton's voice was frighteningly weak.

"We're closer to the car than the cabin. I can't get you all the way back to the cabin."

"No. You."

"Fuck that shit." It wasn't language she normally used, but it was definitely appropriate for this situation.

He chuckled just slightly. "Butterscotch. Love you."

His voice was getting weaker.

"Damn it, don't you start professing love now. Let's get you to the hospital, and this time, Tony won't be there to keep me out."

He grunted again but didn't argue when she shifted them out from under the overhang. The wind and rain had really picked up even more in the few minutes they'd been out of it.

She managed to haul Colton up to his feet one more time, but that was using the last of her strength. If they didn't make it to the car soon, she didn't think they would make it at all.

And he was definitely slowing. Finally, he stopped moving altogether.

"Come on, Colton. We can do this. We can do anything together." He couldn't stop now. Lightning crackled overhead, dangerously close.

"Promise. Promise me."

She turned so she could look him in the eye. "I'll promise you anything you want in this world as long as it's not about leaving you here alone and saving myself."

His lips tilted up in the tiniest of half smiles. "Anything?"

"Anything, as long as you keep walking."

He did. He was slow, he was unsteady, but he kept moving. One foot in front of the other, even as the storm crashed around them.

They were about a hundred yards from the car when she spotted it. The length of almost a football field. But it might as well have been a hundred miles. There was no way for her to bring the car any closer with all the trees around them.

They weren't going to make it. This close, and they weren't going to make it.

She wasn't going to leave him. Not even to save herself. She had no idea how he was still on his feet. Only out of sheer willpower. But obviously, even his impressive willpower wasn't going to get him the rest of the way. He was drooping over more every second.

"I think it's time for that nap, Colton."

He immediately collapsed onto the ground, completely unconscious. She curled up next to him.

She didn't know if they would survive this storm or not. But if this was the way she had to go, then she was glad it would be next to Colton.

She closed her eyes.

"Miss? Hello?" She felt a hand at her throat and batted it away. Then she realized it had been someone trying to take her pulse.

Ella had no idea how long she'd been lying there. She blinked her eyes open and saw five men standing around them.

"My name is Lucas Everett. These are some of my team. We're part of the Resting Warrior Ranch. We're going to get you out of here."

She wanted to make a joke about being rescued by a bunch of handsome military guys, but everything faded to black before she could do it.

# CHAPTER
# THIRTY-SEVEN

When Colton woke up in the hospital this time, Ella was next to him.

Getting shot was no joke. He'd lost count of the number of times the medical staff had used the word *fortunate*.

Fortunate the bullet hadn't hit any vital organs.

Fortunate Ella had the presence of mind to dress the wound as best she could then get him nearly out to the car.

Fortunate the Resting Warrior team had found them when they had.

One inch. If the bullet had hit anywhere else in his midsection by one inch, he probably wouldn't be here right now. Colton did stunts all the time where an inch made the difference between success and failure. But this was the first time it had made the difference between life and death.

They'd removed the piece of metal from his body in surgery not long after he'd arrived two days ago, and he'd been getting stronger minute by minute since.

Yes, he would have to take it easy for a while. Easy was fine with him as long as Ella would be by his side.

"Hey, you." His voice was still a little hoarse, but stronger than yesterday. The doctors planned to release him tomorrow.

Ella sat up in the recliner that was positioned by his bed. "Hi. Your parents were just here but didn't want to wake you. Let me go get them."

"No, that's okay." He'd already seen and talked to his parents multiple times since they'd arrived yesterday.

Half of his friends from Oak Creek had come by too. Bear couldn't because he'd been in the middle of the farewell lunch for the campers. Rick had been the one to volunteer to drive to the hospital so Colton and Ella could be part of the event via video.

So, between the visitors, the videos, and the fact that Colton's body needed as much sleep as it could get, he hadn't had a chance to talk to Ella alone yet.

He still owed her an apology.

"I like being here with just you," he continued.

"I like that you're here at all, Harrison. No more jumping in front of bullets."

"Then you better stay away from people with guns. Because I will jump in front of every bullet aimed at you for the rest of my life." He raised an eyebrow at her, daring her to argue.

She didn't. "We need to talk."

Those words had him warding off a panic attack, even though they were nothing but the truth. "Yes, we do. Starting with my apology."

"Colton…"

"What I accused you of is unforgivable. More than that, it was preposterous. As soon as I thought it through, I knew you weren't the one who leaked that info. That's not who you are."

"You're right—it's not."

"I know you want to say some things to me, and I want to give you all the freedom to do that. Anything. You have every right to"—God, it was hard to say these words, but he was going to say them anyway— "never speak to me again and tell me to fuck off."

He wasn't going to tell her that, if she did, he planned to use every trick he'd ever known to get her back. Clean tricks, dirty tricks, groveling tricks—whatever it took to get her to let him back into her life.

"But," he continued, "I'd like to say a few things before you say what you need to say. If that's okay with you."

She nodded slowly. "I do have things I need to say, but go ahead."

"I truly am sorry. It never should've crossed my mind that you'd done something like that, and I can promise you that it never will again."

"Thank you."

"But that reaction made me realize that I need to get my damned priorities straight. That being with you is a privilege, and if I can't appreciate that, then I don't deserve you."

She simply looked at him, surprised. "I was actually thinking the same thing over the past couple days. Almost exactly."

"Good. Because it's the truth, and both of us need to embrace it. I want you just the way you are, Butterscotch. I am so sorry about those cruel things people posted and said, but that is not how I feel in any way. I consider it such an honor to be with you. To be the man at your side. To be the man taking you home."

She smiled. That gentle, kind smile that was uniquely Ella and lit up her whole face. "I forgive you, Colton. We all make mistakes."

It was all he wanted to hear, and for the first time, he felt like he could breathe again. He hadn't screwed up the best thing he ever had. He and Ella were going to make it through this, and he was never going to be this stupid ever again.

And God, he loved this woman. Loved her tenderness and kindness, her feistiness and intelligence, her beauty and her curves. He had to believe that if Lincoln hadn't spilled the beans, they would've still found their way to each other eventually.

She was one of his best friends who had become the love of his life without his even being aware it was happening.

He was the luckiest bastard on the planet.

But still…

"I don't accept your forgiveness."

Her big green eyes blinked at him. "Uh...what?"

He grabbed her hand and threaded their fingers together, bringing the back of her palm up to his lips. "I'm eternally grateful for your forgiveness, but I don't accept it. Not yet."

"I don't understand."

He kissed her hand again. "You're kind and gentle and amazing, Ella O'Conner. It's not in your nature to make anybody grovel, but this time, you don't get a choice."

---

Ella received a bouquet of flowers every single day for the next month. Roses. Lilies. Tulips. Orchids.

Colton said he couldn't send larkspurs, but that it was flowers—and her quick thinking—that had kept them both alive, so the blooms had double the sentimental value to him now. It was only after her house had started to resemble a florist that he'd finally agreed to stop sending them every day.

Not that the switch to every *other* day was so much better.

And then there were the dates. Every night, Colton had taken her somewhere. Sometimes to the Eagle's Nest or one of the small restaurants in town. Sometimes to Reddington City. Once even involved whisking her off to New York City for a weekend to the opening of a new restaurant there.

Colton was attentive, charming, and persistent as hell.

Tony was out of their life—the man was awaiting trial on multiple charges, including attempted murder. There was no more danger, no more stalker. Colton had been using the shake-up as an opportunity to begin implementing the changes he wanted to make in his career.

Ella loved to see him so passionate and focused. He'd still had a couple of nightmares about the avalanche but none of the full-on panic attacks that had plagued him.

Because his mind knew he was moving in the right direction.

Including shutting down his social media accounts, which he'd done this morning.

Ella hadn't asked him to do that. She'd made her peace with the fact that people could be cruel. There would always be someone who'd post negative things just because they could. She wasn't going to live her life worrying what strangers thought of her or her appearance or her weight.

For her, getting rid of her social media accounts had been easy: just delete them.

For Colton, with his millions of followers, it had been a little more complicated. He'd issued a statement rather than merely deleting the accounts.

*Adventure.*

*For as long as I can remember, it has been my focus, my passion, my muse.*

*Nothing was ever more important to me than reaching the next level. Than pushing myself to do more. Than transcending limits.*

*Thank you for coming on those adventures with me.*

*But now, I leave you to take my next adventure—my greatest adventure—privately.*

*And I am the luckiest man in the world.*

Ella couldn't tear her eyes away from the picture accompanying the statement. One of Colton staring at her, with nothing short of awe on his face.

It was from their first actual real date a month ago. No sting operation, no pretending.

Just them.

She didn't know who snapped the picture, but she couldn't deny the look of love on Colton's face. Love for *her*.

Which was why she closed Fancy Pants early today and sent everyone home. She had some baking to do.

It took her a few times to get the treat correct—combining both butterscotch and rainbow sprinkles into something delicious wasn't particularly easy. But she knew the combination would work, given enough tweaking.

Just like she knew she and Colton would work in the same way.

A mini butterscotch choux au craquelin—with a light dusting of rainbow sprinkles on the top—made it into the final treat box a few hours later. The cream-puff-type French pastry was delicious, if she said so herself. It would definitely become a regular in her shop.

Colton had been busy today and had texted her to ask if they could meet at the Eagle's Nest for dinner. Looking at the clock now, she would have to hurry to make it on time.

She loved that she didn't have to worry about what she looked like—didn't have to rush home to change or primp. Colton didn't mind her hair in the messy bun or her in jeans and a sweater.

Although, when she got to the Eagle's Nest and saw that nearly everybody in town had decided to hang out there that evening, she wished she had at least made sure she'd gotten all the flour off her face.

Colton waved to her from the booth he was standing near, talking to Bear and Lincoln. Becky and Lilah were in another booth, so Ella stopped by there on her way over to Colton.

"Do I look okay?" she asked. "Colton and I are having dinner. But I didn't expect the entire town to be here on a Wednesday night, for crying out loud."

She knew this was her deep-rooted insecurities talking, but she also knew that it was going to take longer than a mere month to move past them.

"You're glowing, Ella-Bella," Lilah said. They all liked the new nickname her friend had come up with much better, since Bella meant *beauty*.

Becky smiled gently. "She's right. You're gorgeous."

"What's that?" Lilah pointed to the treat box in Ella's hand.

"I made something sweet especially for Colton."

Lilah and Becky shot each other a look.

"What?" Ella asked.

Becky reached over and tucked a stray strand of hair behind Ella's ear. "Nothing. I'm sure he'll love it. Get over there and say hello before Colton storms over like a Neanderthal and throws you over his shoulder."

She glanced up to find his gaze pinned on her. Everything in her body heated and melted at his look.

She couldn't tear her eyes away from him. "Did you guys see what he posted this morning on social media?"

"Oh, we did. Believe me," Lilah said. "We all did."

Ella barely heard her. She gave her friends a wave as she walked toward Colton—unable to resist him any more than she'd be able to resist gravity.

"Hey, you." She reached up onto her tiptoes to kiss him.

"Finally." He wrapped both arms around her hips and lifted her so they were eye to eye. "I missed you."

"We'll see you guys around," Bear said, he and Lincoln walking away. Once again, Ella was only barely listening. She couldn't do anything else when she was this close to Colton.

He kissed her, both of them very aware they wanted more, but then set her back down on her feet. He slid his arms from around her but didn't let go of her hand as they both slid into the booth across from each other.

"The guys didn't have to leave. Do they want to eat with us?"

Colton didn't so much as look over at them. "Nah. They have plans."

"Okay, that's probably good anyway. Because I have something for you." She pulled out the small white box containing her new creation and set it on the table.

Colton just stared at it, saying nothing.

"It's a new treat I came up with. I wanted you to be the first official person to try it." He was still staring at the box. "What's wrong?"

He shrugged then brought up an identical box from beside him and set it on the table. "I also have something."

"What's that?"

"I baked you something too."

She laughed. "You did? Why didn't you come do that with me? We could've done it together."

He still looked a little shell-shocked. "I wanted to surprise you."

She reached over and squeezed his hand. "I wanted to surprise you too. Whose should we try first?"

"Yours!" The word was surprisingly adamant.

She blinked then laughed. "Okay. Go for it."

He opened the box slowly, almost reverently, folding the sections of it down so it became a flat cardboard plate. "Rainbow sprinkles."

"Yes, just for you. It's called a choux au craquelin. It has butterscotch-flavored pastry cream on the inside."

He looked up at her then back down at the treat. "Rainbow sprinkles and butterscotch."

"For us," she said. "Try it."

He did, popping the whole mini-pastry into his mouth and closing his eyes in bliss. "That is the most amazing thing I've ever tasted."

"Good. Because I want it to be a symbol between us. It's time for you to accept my forgiveness. You don't need to keep doing all the things you're doing for me, Colton. I truly do forgive you."

He stared at her for a long moment before finally pushing his box toward her. "I baked this for sort of the same reason. Like yours, I also want this to be a symbol between us."

She couldn't believe they'd done the same thing on the same day, but she loved that they were so in sync with each other.

"Can I try it?"

He nodded, and she folded down the box like he had until it was flat.

It was the ugliest looking mini-cupcake maybe in the history of the world. It looked like someone had spilled an entire bottle of rainbow sprinkles on this poor creation, and the mound of frosting had begun toppling to the side with the weight.

But Ella was a professional baker. She knew that sometimes things could look pretty bad but taste amazing.

"You made this yourself?" It was the most neutral thing she could think to say.

"Yes. Rainbow sprinkles on a butterscotch cupcake with butterscotch icing."

"For us."

He smiled. "For us. Try it."

Like him, she picked up the mini-treat and popped the whole thing in her mouth.

And immediately wished she hadn't. It was *awful*.

There was nothing to temper the sweetness, so it was just sugar on sugar on sugar. She tried to keep her face completely expressionless as she chewed.

And chewed and chewed. Was this thing growing?

Finally, she was able to swallow it. "Wow," she managed.

She didn't want to say anything negative. The important thing was that Colton had tried to do something special for her. There was no way in hell she was going to make him feel bad for it.

"What do you think?"

"I think the fact that you made this for me makes me love you even more than I already did."

To her surprise, Colton burst out laughing. And then so did most of the bar. Everyone had been watching her eat that thing.

"You guys!" But Ella laughed too. "You got me. That thing was awful."

"We know!" Bear yelled. "We had to try them earlier when he was making them."

She laughed over at Colton and went to push the box back toward him when something shiny in it caught her eye. She hadn't seen it at first because it had been under the cupcake.

A ring.

She blinked up at him. "Colton?"

He dropped to one knee right there in front of the booth.

"I know traditional wisdom says it's too soon, but I've known you most of my life, Butterscotch. Please tell me you'll marry me and that you'll do it as soon as possible."

She looked around and realized that all her friends were staring at them with smiles on their faces. They had known this was coming.

"I wanted them all to be here to witness this. Wanted them all to know that I can't live without you and I don't even want to try. Wanted them to see me beg if you say no, and then call in that promise you made."

"What promise?" But she already knew.

"I may have gotten shot, but don't think I don't remember that you promised me anything as long as I kept walking that day. I'm using it right here and now to make sure you agree to marry me."

"You don't have to use it. I'll marry you, Colton."

Cheers rang out all over the bar as he slipped the ring on her finger, then stood up and pulled her in for a kiss.

Everyone was hugging and laughing, so Colton pulled her close to make sure she could hear him. "Thank you for forgiving me, but I'm never going to stop doing all the things I've been doing for you. You deserve them."

She kissed him. "I love you. I always have."

He cupped her face. "I love you. And I always will."

THE END

# ALSO BY JANIE CROUCH

All books: https://www.janiecrouch.com/books

HEROES OF OAK CREEK

Hero Unbound

Hero's Flight

Hero's Prize

Hero's Heart

Hero Mine

GILDED EMPIRE (as MJ Crouch)

Broken Crown

Damaged Kingdom

Fierce Monarch

Vicious Throne

ZODIAC TACTICAL

Code Name: ARIES

Code Name: VIRGO

Code Name: LIBRA

Code Name: PISCES
Code Name: OUTLAW
Code Name: GEMINI

NEVER TOO LATE FOR LOVE (with Regan Black)

Heartbreak Key Collection

Ellington Cove Collection

Wyoming Cowboys Collection

Holiday Heroes Collection

RESTING WARRIOR RANCH (with Josie Jade)

Montana Sanctuary

Montana Danger

Montana Desire

Montana Mystery

Montana Storm

Montana Freedom

Montana Silence

Montana Rain

Montana Heat

Montana Memory

LINEAR TACTICAL (series complete)

Cyclone

Eagle

Shamrock

Angel

Ghost

Shadow

Echo

Phoenix

Baby

Storm

Redwood

Scout

Blaze

Hero Forever

INSTINCT SERIES (series complete)

Primal Instinct

Critical Instinct

Survival Instinct

THE RISK SERIES (series complete)

Calculated Risk

Security Risk

Constant Risk

Risk Everything

OMEGA SECTOR (series complete)

Stealth

Covert

Conceal

Secret

OMEGA SECTOR: CRITICAL RESPONSE & UNDER SIEGE (series complete)

Savior

Protect

Rescue

Pursuit

Revenge

Stalked

Daddy Defender

Protector's Instinct

Cease Fire

Major Crimes

Armed Response

In the Lawman's Protection

SAN ANTONIO SECURITY (series complete)

Critical Strike (Luke)

Edge of Danger (Brax)

Two Steps Ahead (Weston)

Last Resort (Chance)

# ABOUT THE AUTHOR

"Passion that leaps right off the page." - Romantic Times Book Reviews

USA Today and Publishers Weekly bestselling author Janie Crouch writes what she loves to read: passionate romantic suspense featuring protective heroes. Her books have won multiple awards, including the Romance Writers of America's coveted Vivian® Award, the National Readers Choice Award, and the Booksellers' Best.

After a lifetime on the East Coast, and a six-year stint in Germany due to her husband's job as support for the U.S. Military, Janie has settled into her dream home in Front Range of the Colorado Rockies.

When she's not listening to the voices in her head—and even when she is—she enjoys engaging in all sorts of crazy adventures (200-mile relay races; Ironman Triathlons, treks to Mt. Everest Base Camp...), traveling, and hanging out with her four kids.

Her favorite quote: "Life is a daring adventure or nothing." ~ Helen Keller.

- facebook.com/janiecrouch
- amazon.com/author/janiecrouch
- instagram.com/janiecrouch
- bookbub.com/authors/janie-crouch

www.ingramcontent.com/pod-product-compliance
Ingram Content Group UK Ltd.
Pitfield, Milton Keynes, MK11 3LW, UK
UKHW020732050525
5762UKWH00034B/512